# Courting Choices

Colby County Series, Volume 2

Diana Rock

Published by Diana Rock, 2022.

## COURTING CHOICES

Copyright © 2022 by Denise M. Long
All Rights reserved.

No part of this book may be used or reproduced in any manner whatsoever including audio recording without written permission of the author and Copyright holder.

This author supports the right to free expression and values copyright protection. The scanning, uploading, and distribution of this book in any manner or medium without permission of the copyright holder is theft of the property. Thank you for supporting this author's creative work with your purchase.

<u>FIRST EDITION</u>
Print ISBN: 9798986757117
Digital ISBN: 9798986757100
Editor: Lynne Pearson, AllthatEditing.com

This is a work of fiction. Names, characters, places, and incidents either are the product of the author's imagination or are used fictitiously. Any resemblance to actual persons (living or dead), business establishments, organizations, events, locale, or weather events are entirely coincidental.

# DEDICATION

This book is dedicated to
Firefighters

# CHAPTER ONE

She smelled like a cow barn. That was to say, cow poop. She sniffed at a length of brunette hair. *Is that a hint of blood?* A glance at her clothes revealed a small reddish splotch near the hem of her sleeveless T-shirt, damp and clinging to her torso. Her yoga pants were the same. The cow's labor had been long, exhausting, and messy. But now mother and calf were doing fine. And Cortland, who had been away from her job at Colby County Veterinary Clinic for the entire six-hour labor, was tired. And hungry. She steered her Acura MDX SUV, a graduation gift from her father, to the nearest place she knew for a quick meal.

The call had come in just after five. Being on large animal duty this week, she had to leave the warmth of her bed on a rainy May morning to help the mother, who was having difficulty birthing her first calf. On the way out her apartment door, she grabbed a stale bagel and ate it while driving to the Sunflower Dairy Farm on the far side of Colby. It was even too early for the local fast-food restaurants to be open.

Her stomach ached and rumbled as she parked her car alongside the road near the truck stop where food trucks set up every morning. From as early as six in the morning until midnight, hungry truckers and anyone else could get a quick, cheap, and delicious takeout meal. There wasn't an eating area per order of the town health department though some diners gathered in groups, all standing while eating and trading insults. Most vehicles came and left quickly along the widened shoulder areas on both sides of the road.

Being nearly noon, the place was packed with luncheon traffic. That day, five trucks sat in a row beside the usual hot dog cart. She sat in the car, gazing at the options: barbecue, Middle Eastern, fried seafood, Mexican, and Greek. *One of everything, please!* As she recalled, the last time she'd been here, she'd had the fish and chips and later suffered acid reflux so severe she'd had to chug some Gaviscon. Barbecue was too messy, as was the falafel though being a non-animal protein, it would be better for her health. Tacos? Nope. That was another spicy, greasy, messy meal her stomach couldn't handle. "I guess it's Greek today." Her stomach rumbled again in consensus.

She stepped up to the line, waiting her turn to order. When her nose caught a whiff of the grilled chicken and kebabs, her stomach growled so loud the man in front of her turned around and stared with eyes wide open.

"I guess you're hungry, little lady." He doffed his baseball cap and invited her to step before him with a cavalier wave.

Her face burning, Cortland held up her palm. "No, that's quite all right. I can wait."

He nodded and replaced his hat. "Suit yourself." Before turning around, the man sniffed once, twice, three times. "Is that you?" he asked, his face scrunched up in disgust as his eyes looked her up and down.

Her body tensed, drawing itself into a tighter, more compact form than her five feet as if that might stop or mitigate the vile odor coming from her clothes and person. With a sigh, she promised herself to complain to Barbra that the disposable Tyvek coveralls for just such a purpose were completely useless. They might keep most of the yuck from soiling her clothing, but the smell seeped right through it. "I'm sorry, yes. I spent the morning in a cow barn. I apologize for the smell."

He doffed his hat again to scratch his forehead. "Cow barn? What were you doing there? Milking?"

Not wanting to go into too much detail about her morning, Cortland shook her head and only said, "Helping a calf come into the world."

"Yikes, no wonder you stink." He turned back around and abruptly stepped forward as the line moved up.

Rolling her eyes, she repositioned her own hat and pulled out her cell phone to call the clinic. It was about time she let them know where she was and when she would be back in the building. As the phone rang, Cortland thought about how she didn't mind smelling like cow dung. It reminded her of her summers in Alaska, some of the best times of her life.

The receptionist, Alissa Granger, answered. "Colby County Veterinary Clinic, how may I help you?"

"Hey, It's me, Cortland. I'll be there in about twenty minutes. I'm just grabbing a bite to eat. I'm starving."

"No problem, Dr. Stewart. Your next client isn't until one o'clock."

Cortland felt her anxiety level drop several notches. "Great. What is it?"

"A guinea pig. Not acting normal."

"The great diagnostic dilemma. Why does everyone say 'not acting normal'?"

"Because they have no clue what could be wrong?" Alissa offered, her tone distracted by the sound of rustling papers in the background.

"No rest for this wicked woman." Cortland heard another phone at the receptionist's desk ringing.

"You and me both," Alissa said and ended the call.

Waiting to order, she scanned the chalkboard menu looking for her favorite.

When a gruff voice yelled "next," she stepped up to the food truck window, calling out, "Hey Nick, How are you today?"

"Better than you from the looks of it." He picked up his pencil and scrawled on an order pad. "Whatcha having, love?"

"Chicken souvlaki, no fries. Please. And a diet Dr Pepper."

"You got it."

She paid for the meal, accepting her can of soda from Nick before stepping aside to wait in the cluster of people at the pickup window. The smells from the window made her mouth water and her stomach growl all the louder, much to the amusement of the people standing nearby. Their laughter and guffaws continued as her stomach rumbled and complained.

# DIANA ROCK

"Goodness, for a little lady, you sure have one hungry stomach." Another elderly gentleman called out, causing the waiting crowd to break into fresh laughter. Behind her, someone said, "Maybe she'll grow to adult size with some food." Another round of boisterous laughter. Cortland could feel her ear tips getting hot. Thankfully they were well hidden underneath her hair and baseball cap. George, Nick's brother, called out "chicken souvlaki."

Without thinking, Cortland stepped forward, reaching for the Styrofoam takeout container. Grasping the left side of the container, she was surprised to find the right side gripped by a large, dirty, masculine hand. As she pulled her lunch toward herself, the container was yanked away.

Dumbfounded, she looked at the hand's owner. Tall, dark, and probably handsome. His face was rugged beneath black soot and grime, and his scruffy chin squared off. But his light blue eyes blazed under thick eyebrows.

"That's mine." His dimpled jaw hardened as she would not let go of the container.

"I think it's mine. I ordered the chicken souvlaki." The breeze shifted, and she caught a whiff of him. Smoke. He stank of smoke. Glancing down his length, she saw his light brown T-shirt stained with large sweat areas. Black edged the short sleeves and hem. He wore a serious-looking pair of heavy-duty knee-high boots.

"So did I. I called ahead ten minutes ago," He continued, his tight grip on the Styrofoam starting to crush the container. "I'm in a hurry."

"You stink worse than me." She pulled the Styrofoam again, but he resisted. "I have a client to meet in an hour. And I have to shower and change beforehand." Really, the last thing she wanted was a tug-of-war with a man over her lunch. Even a hot one like this guy.

"I have to get back ASAP." Turning toward the order window, he called out, "Hey Nick, is this one mine or hers?"

## COURTING CHOICES

Nick looked at the two locked in battle over a lunch container. "It's hers." He called before turning back to the next customer. "Dawson, yours is coming up next."

Frowning, he abruptly released his grip on the takeout box. "Sorry." Without another word, he stepped back into the waiting crowd.

Cortland fumbled, nearly dropping the box; his action had been so sudden. *Well, so much for an apology.* As she adjusted her hold on the box, a siren started so close by she jumped in reflex like everyone else on the sidewalk. Turning around, she noticed the large fire engine double-parked in the street. The siren cut off quickly, replaced by the squawk of the PA. "Cap, another call. Let's go."

As she watched, her mouth hanging open, the man named Dawson called to Nick. "I got to go! I'll try to get back for my lunch."

It all clicked. The smoke smell, the disheveled and sooty appearance. This Dawson character was a firefighter. Without thinking, she grabbed his muscular arm as he turned to jog to the fire truck. Shoving the box at him, she said, "Here, take mine."

His eyes widened at her offer, though he grabbed the container. "Thanks, I owe you."

"No, you don't. I'm going to take yours when it comes out." She bobbed her head to the side, indicating the food truck.

Dawson nodded too. "Whatever. Thanks."

She watched his lean, muscular form jog off to the fire truck.

Behind her, the crowd broke out into clapping. Were they clapping for him, the first responder and hero? Or for her, the compassionate little miss giving up her lunch for the hungry firefighter? Whatever the applause was for, her chest warmed at her quick thinking. Hopefully, he'd get a bite or two before they arrived at their next location. Full lights and siren blaring, the truck sped through the closest intersection and disappeared down a side street.

"Honey. Nick's calling you." A man bent over to tap her shoulder, bringing her back to the present.

She turned toward the food truck to find Nick holding out a Styrofoam container. As she neared the window, he said, "Here's Dawson's lunch. You take it. That was really nice what you did for him."

"It was just courtesy." The heat in her cheeks returned.

"Whatever. You come back again, I'll give you a chicken souvlaki on the house."

Clutching the box, she nodded. "Thanks."

In the back of her mind, she questioned why she had done it. Was it just a kind gesture toward a hard-working civil servant? Or was it those eyes and his muscles that motivated her to somehow make up to that gorgeous, if smelly, guy? *At least I know where he works if I ever want to run into him again.*

· · · ·

It was several hours later before Dawson Michaels got to finish the food. He'd had a few bites of it on the way to the dumpster fire. But it wasn't until they'd returned to the station that he had a chance to sit peacefully at a table and chow down. He thought of the brunette with the big light green eyes who had given him the lunch container. She was pretty, even if she smelled awful and looked bedraggled. Her yoga pants accentuated every inch of her slim hips and legs. A damp tight-fitting sleeveless T-shirt clung to her torso, emphasizing the curve of her breasts and her flat belly. More than his curiosity was aroused. She'd said she had a client to meet. Had she been to a yoga class and needed to get to work? She wasn't wearing any jewelry, specifically any rings on her left hand.

He pondered the thought in the quiet firehouse kitchen. All seven shift crew members were off doing their duties. *Or they should be*, he thought. The firehouse sat square to the curb of the busiest street on this side of town. The two-bay area held the engine and a tanker truck. Behind the bays were storage rooms for equipment, a small room the senior officer on duty used as an office, the old hose tower, and an air pack tank storage and refilling unit. Beside the bay area, separated by a swinging door, was the kitchen.

Large at nearly thirty by twenty, the kitchen also functioned as a training area when needed. Along the back and one side wall were inexpensive pressed-board wood kitchen cabinets filled with toilet paper, paper towels, dish and laundry detergents. The only appliances besides the fridge, stove, and dishwasher were the toaster, coffee maker, and a Crockpot. Over the sinks was the only window looking out into the back parking lot holding the crews' vehicles, a basketball hoop, and a gas grill. After every meal, the double-basin sink was polished to a shine, and the countertops were scrubbed and disinfected. They each took turns doing the dishes and washing up after meals. Everyone except Lucas Campbell.

Lucas Campbell, the firehouse chef, walked up behind him and messed his hair. "Hey, Cap. I heard you worked for Captain Enrico yesterday. You're on your second twenty-four-hour shift?"

"Yup," Dawson said between chews. "What's for supper?"

Lucas's voice got animated. "Nice juicy pot roast with all the fixins. It'll be ready in two hours. Don't fill up on whatever you're eating." Like most paid fire departments, each station had a designated cook for the day. Usually, the men and women took turns. But Lucas had volunteered to do it for each shift he worked. Having been a short-order cook before joining the Town of Colby Fire Department, he was welcome to take the job. Since he also had to answer fire calls, he either created a Crockpot meal or a fast but delicious feast to sustain his fellow firefighters' energy levels during their twenty-four-hour shifts.

Lucas was the rookie of the team. Barely on the job for the last eight months, he was thin as a golf club and only 5'8" inches tall. He worked out daily to increase his strength in the station fitness room upstairs. The muscles in his chest, arms, back, and legs proved it.

Walking over to the Crockpot, he took the lid off and sniffed. His face lit up, obviously happy with the smell. He dipped a spoon inside to extract a little taste of the sauce. His head bobbed, a look of delight on his face. A lock of his light brown hair flopped over his forehead as he nodded. He flicked his head sideways, knocking the lock back into place. Dawson made a mental note to talk to him about it. In an emergency, a shift in his hair like that could obstruct his vision at the wrong moment.

The swinging door banged open. "Don't worry about the bottomless pit here. He'll eat anything, anytime," David Korth said, sauntering into the kitchen. Lucas took one look at the lieutenant, dropped his spoon on the counter and escaped up the stairs to the upper rooms.

Dawson felt the lieutenant's pencil-thin and lanky figure standing behind him and tensed. The image of a snake came to his mind, as it did whenever he saw Korth.

"I hear a little old lady gave you that lunch box."

He was used to Korth's behavior though it grated his nerves. Usually, he ignored the jeers and borderline insults. Today, he wanted to set the record straight. "She was little but definitely not old." The slight woman had looked just as bedraggled as he had felt, her limp dark hair pulled into a messy bun on the back of her head, loose tendrils swirling around her tired heart-shaped face. It was a beautiful face with smooth skin, a sprinkling of freckles around her adorable nose, a wide mouth with crimson lips and pink cheeks. "The top of her head barely reached my shoulder."

Korth sat at the table across from Dawson, who groaned inwardly, wishing he'd gone elsewhere. Upstairs to the TV room, bunk room, the fitness room, or even the bathroom, rather than sit and harass him. "I heard she was real pretty," he said with a sarcastic smirk. His thin lips crooked into a sneer while his small, close-set eyes narrowed.

"She was." Her eyes had struck him as poignant and deep. Her flash of anger over the tug-of-war intrigued him. In his experience, a feisty woman was a great bed partner.

## COURTING CHOICES

"What's her name?" Korth smirked again, tapping the tabletop with his left middle finger as though demanding an answer. And flipping him the bird at the same time.

Momentarily distracted by the possible signal, he didn't hear the question. "What?"

Korth repeated it.

Startled by the idea, he wished he had gotten her name or knew how to reach her. "I don't know. Before I could ask, I had to bug out on that dumpster call." He considered her outfit. If she hadn't been exercising, what had she been doing? She might have already put in a hard day's work by noon. Yoga instructor? A third shift worker? Probably not. Most third shifters went straight home after their shifts and went to sleep. She had smelled funny, though it was tough to tell with his own smoke-infused clothing. He didn't have any clues as to her identity. Maybe if he returned to the truck stop, he'd run into her again. His heart lifted with the idea of discovering more about this mysterious woman. *You can't hang around a truck stop waiting for a woman.* He shook his head and gulped down the last of the food.

Finished with his lunch, or her lunch, as he thought of it, he crumpled up his napkin and threw it into the empty Styrofoam container. He stood and tossed it like a Frisbee in the trash barrel beside the door. "Did you change out the air tanks on the SCBA used in our last house call, Lieutenant?"

Korth's teasing smirk dropped. "I haven't had a chance yet."

Dawson glared at him. "You have time to yak, you have time to check. Chores come first."

The lieutenant gave a tired sigh then got up.

Dawson watched Korth's backside disappear behind the apparatus room door with foreboding. The man might have some smarts, but he was lazy as shit and a brown-noser to boot. David Korth wanted the title of lieutenant but didn't like doing the work it involved. Dawson was tired of having to question him like a seven-year-old procrastinating over homework. If they had gone out on another call with half-empty air pack tanks, the wearer could land in serious trouble. Perhaps even life-threatening trouble. *I should write the lazy bastard up. Teach him a lesson.* But Dawson knew he would shrug it off and continue his lackadaisical attention to his duties. He'd had a chip on his shoulder as large as Plymouth Rock since Dawson beat him out of the captain's position several years ago. As time passed, Korth's attitude toward him had changed to near outright hostility. *One of these days, he's going to get himself fired.*

# CHAPTER TWO

The appointment with the guinea pig had gone quick enough. Dispensing shots was easy work for even the tiredest of vets. With her energy renewed slightly from scarfing down the firefighter's souvlaki and the curly fries that came with it, she got through all sixteen afternoon appointments. She sighed grateful nearly all were routine exams—nothing serious had been on the docket today. Her boss and coworker, Doctor Hannah Woodbridge, had covered the urgent and emergency appointments. And Hannah had been able to handle the Zoom job interview for the part-time position when Cortland got held up with questions by a first-time dog owner.

Walking into the conference room, she spied Hannah already closing her laptop. "Hey, is the candidate online yet?" Cortland asked, setting her own laptop down on the large conference table that served as the break and lunch room. She liked this room. It had bright yellow walls, cheerful pictures of serene landscapes, and a bulletin board filled with jokes and shift change requests. In the far corner stood a refrigerator and a counter with enough room for a small sink, a Keurig, and a toaster oven.

"We just finished," Hannah said, shaking out her long dark brown hair and refastening it with a barrette. "Not five minutes into the interview, the applicant decided every weekend and holiday wasn't for her."

She'd told Cortland she didn't feel good about this candidate. According to her Curriculum Vitae, she'd had five jobs over the last six years. None of the four previous candidates had impressed them either. All clearly didn't read the job posting well, disappointed that the shift was part-time, weekends and holidays only.

"What are we going to do?" Hannah asked her work associate and best friend. They sat in companionable silence before Hannah added, "Know what I really wish?"

Cortland opened the refrigerator door. "No, what?" she said, her head inside the fridge, looking for her lunch bag.

"I wish Tulsi was free to join us. Wouldn't that be great?"

Her head popped out of the fridge as her chest ached, thinking of their mutual friend from vet school, Tulsi Anthony. After vet school, she interned in the reptile room at the Woodland Park Zoo in Seattle before getting a job at a vet hospital in Louisiana. It occurred to her they had not had any word from her in over a month.

"Sure would." She shrugged. "I can continue my Wednesday through Sunday schedule until we find someone." Having spotted her lunch bag, she opened it and removed a can of diet soda.

Rapping her hand on the table, Hannah frowned. "I could really use you Monday and Tuesday. You know how Mondays are."

She swigged some soda before nodding. "I know. Mondays are the worst. Everyone held off over the weekend with their concerns and issues, and it's now urgent they be seen on Monday morning." She shrugged again. "Not that I don't have enough to do on weekends, but they seem to have gone from one extreme to another since your newsletter article."

Having been fed up with the non-emergency emergencies that happened every weekend, Hannah had written about appropriate reasons to call for an emergency and the inappropriate reasons that should wait until Monday morning. "I think my words have backfired on us."

"Well, at least the weekend hours are better, the staff seems relieved, and the clients are better informed." Cortland was silent a few minutes. "You know, I could change my hours to Thursday through Monday. At least until we hire someone." Deep in her stomach, she hoped Hannah wouldn't take her up on the offer.

"That's actually a great idea." Hannah's face brightened despite her exhaustion with the situation. "Would you mind terribly?"

"As long as we both agree it's temporary."

## COURTING CHOICES

Hannah picked up the phone and called Barbra, the practice manager. In minutes, Barbra entered the conference room and glanced around.

*Probably looking for space to put some of her plants.* Barbra's office was like a jungle. Every horizontal surface held a plant except for a twelve-inch square section of her desk for her computer. Plants even hung from hooks in the ceiling in front of the double-hung window.

"Cortland and I were discussing the workload problems on Mondays. She's agreed to temporarily change her hours to Thursday through Monday." Hannah said, swiveling in her chair. "How difficult is that going to be? Can we shift her Wednesday appointments to other time slots?"

The middle-aged woman crossed her arms over her chest, saying, "We're scheduled four weeks out on Cortland's Wednesday appointments. Rescheduling them would be a nightmare. Doable but still not client friendly."

Barbra continued, "My suggestion is that Cortland covers Wednesday through Monday for the next four weeks. In the meantime, the office staff can try to reschedule some. And they won't make any additional appointments for her on Wednesdays."

"What do you think? Can you do it?" Hannah cast a hopeful gaze her way.

Crap, Cortland thought. A six-day work week for the next four weeks? *Not what I wanted to have happen with my offer. Me and my big mouth.*

• • • •

The behemoth of a fire engine inched toward him as he directed it. Backing a half-million-dollar engine-pumper truck into the firehouse was not an easy task. Most newer firehouses had drive-through parking bays. But Colby's Engine Two was housed in a brick, two-story firehouse built back in 1933. As department policy, every vehicle had to be spotted as it backed into the station. Dawson waved and directed the truck's driver as she backed the rig into the far left of two bays. Dawson, the shift captain, liked doing it. He'd been doing it for the entire twelve years of his tenure with Colby Fire Department. Besides, if the apparatus was damaged, he'd have a shitload of paperwork to fill out. He considered it self-preservation.

Finished, Dawson didn't leave until the engine turned off. Walking from the bay into the kitchen, he was surprised to see his mentor, Jackson Huntington sitting at the table, an empty coffee cup before him. His surprise fizzled as his gut seized up. When Jackson refused to meet his eyes, his head sank to his chest.

"Let's go outside," Jackson said, standing and heading for the bay door.

Dawson followed him back into the apparatus bay and then through the open massive overhead doors. He stopped on the public sidewalk and waited for Dawson to join his side.

Dawson barely heard him over the roar of traffic speeding by the fire station. A dump truck loaded with dirt rumbled by spewing diesel fumes over the sidewalk.

"I got news," Jackson said plainly and without emotion, though his expression said it all. His face looked grim. It was always very angular and taut. The skin seemed to stretch to its limit over his cheekbones, merging at his boney chin. Even his eyes were hardened with age, and what Dawson knew would be bad news.

It was so matter-of-fact he opened and closed his fists, trying to work out the desire to punch something. Like his future was of no consequence. "Let me guess. The answer was a resounding no. Again."

Jackson's eyes found his. "I'm sorry."

He chuckled heartily at that one. "Sorry? Sorry I missed out on the promotion or sorry as in, 'that's the way it goes'?"

"Sorry you didn't get what you wanted."

# COURTING CHOICES

Dawson cursed under his breath. "What reason did they give this time?"

"Same as last time. You're too inexperienced."

He spit on the grass strip between the sidewalk and the road, trying to control the hammering in his head and chest. "Again? Why is it I've been called the wonder boy since I joined at eighteen and made it to captain eight years later. But now I don't have the experience? Two years as captain isn't enough?" Dawson started to pace the concrete. "You know as well as I do, it has nothing to do with experience. And everything to do with hierarchy."

"Can't argue that. Especially since the guy who beat you to the district chief's job has been here for over twenty years."

"Mansada?"

"Yup." He kicked a rock on the edge of the sidewalk, as Jackson explained. "Look, your fast rise to captain was as much due to your history as a former firefighter's son as to the mass exodus when the golden handshake was offered to all the guys with twenty-five years or more, including me."

Feeling his mentor's hand squeezing his shoulder, Dawson stopped pacing. "My father didn't have anything to do with my hiring or climb to captain. How can a dead man cause that?"

"Firefighters look out for their own. When your dad died during that basement fire, you, your sister, and your mom became wards of the fire department. We've looked after you since you were eleven. I looked after you, trying like hell to keep you out of trouble and keep your head pointed in the right direction. Your father was my best friend in this brotherhood. We had a pact."

"I know, I know. If something happened to you, my dad would look after your wife and sister. And if something happened—" Dawson had to stop. The thickness in his throat wouldn't allow him to finish his sentence. *Damn it, why did it still hurt so bad? Why couldn't he keep his emotions in check?* He turned away so Jackson wouldn't see his eyes filling with tears. Jackson's hand squeezed his shoulders again. Roughly this time. The man knew about loss too. His wife had died not long after his retirement.

After a few moments, he regained control. "So, the buck stops at captain?" His eyes connected with Jackson's. "Is this as far as I'm ever going to get in this department? Does the upper echelon consider the duty to my father's memory well paid, and now they're willing to leave me in this post for the rest of my career?"

"I don't know for sure. But such a thing has happened in the department's history."

At Dawson's quizzical look, he continued, "About fifteen years ago, before you started here, another firefighter, the son of a man who died in the line of duty, had the same thing happen to him. He never made it past lieutenant."

Searching his brain for more information, only one name met that description. "Was that Lieutenant Miller?"

Jackson nodded.

"He left a couple years ago. I always wondered why he never tried for a promotion."

"Oh, he tried all right. Like you, he was stalled on the back burner." Rubbing his jaw, Jackson smiled wryly. "Course, he wasn't as bright or as talented as you. Which is why he remained a lieutenant and why you made it to captain."

The two men were silent for a few minutes, each lost in their thoughts as they watched the cars pass the firehouse.

Dawson looked his friend and mentor in the eye. "So, you're telling me that I'm never going to ascend any higher in this department."

"Not saying that. But if you look at history ..." Jackson wrapped his arm around Dawson's shoulder, giving it a squeeze. He hadn't lost any strength despite being retired. "If you're looking to climb the ladder, you have a better chance elsewhere. Besides, I hear you met a lady." Jackson's grin split wide across his face.

## COURTING CHOICES

Dawson felt the blush rising up his neck. He couldn't get the petite woman out of his mind.

"Did I hit a nerve?" Jackson smirked and slid his arm up around Dawson's neck playfully, in the same manner he had when Dawson was a kid.

Using the maneuver as a change of topic away from the woman, Dawson struggled against his friend's arm. The two men tussled on the sidewalk, finally breaking it up with a spell of laughter. Suddenly Jackson jerked up, his hand pressing into his back.

"What's wrong?" Dawson bent down eye to eye with his mentor.

Stiffly and slowly, Jackson straightened up. "Oh, I think I pulled a back muscle or something. It's been pestering me for a couple weeks."

The alarm box sounded, five long rings, two short and three more long ones. They paused, almost frozen in place, listening to the dispatcher's words blaring from the overhead speakers. Car fire on the interstate.

Both men jogged into the bay, Jackson's hand clenching his back. A flurry of activity met them. Three firefighters donned their gear: stepping into boots, pulling up protective bunker pants, and settling suspenders over their shoulders. The Nomex neck protector and turnout gear coat came next, covering their torsos from the neck to nearly their knees. Dawson did the same while Jackson watched.

"Want to come with us?" Dawson called out as the radio continued to give details over the speakers at a volume that reverberated inside his head.

Shaking his head, Jackson declined. "My days in the rig are over."

"Suit yourself."

"Thanks for the offer, Captain." Jackson stood back against the cinder block walls of the room and threw a salute.

"Get that back looked at, will ya?" Dawson tipped his helmet just before the apparatus left the firehouse.

# CHAPTER THREE

Anne Faith Watson's name popped up on the screen as Cortland's phone started ringing. It was after work hours, but she was still at the clinic, checking on a few inpatients before going home. Excusing herself, she headed for her office, answering the phone on the way. "Aunt Faith?"

"Cortland, is now a good time to chat?" a wispy voice inquired over the phone. "I can call back later if you'd like."

"No, now is fine. I'm on my way to my office." Her nerves felt a little unsettled. They usually spoke every other Monday morning. It was a Friday night. "What's wrong?"

"Oh, nothing. Can't I call my niece and goddaughter any time I want?"

Evasive as usual, Faith was exceedingly private and eccentric, with a heart full of love for her brother and the family she'd left behind. Cortland couldn't understand it. "Any time is fine. I'll always make time for your calls. You know that." Still, she wondered what was happening that precipitated this out-of-the-ordinary contact.

"Good. I was thinking about you and pulled out all my old photo albums of your visits."

Cortland could picture her sitting at the kitchen table slipping through those tattered albums, her gray hair well past her shoulders, the blue-green eyes wide, her smile rising and ebbing on her delicate features. Last time she'd seen her aunt, she'd lost a lot of weight. Her skin was loose over her prominent hand bones, the blue-purple veins traceable under the thin translucent skin. She was the eldest of eight, sixteen years older than her youngest sibling, Cortland's father, Kirk. *Which makes her seventy-four since Dad is fifty-eight. Damn. How time marches.*

# COURTING CHOICES

She smiled into the phone, blinking rapidly. A sudden feeling of homesickness overwhelmed her so much she couldn't speak. Memories came flooding back to her mind.

As a little girl, her father would fly up to Alaska with her, taking her to spend the summer with her Aunt Faith, as she preferred to be called. For eight summers, Cortland had gone to Aunt Faith and Uncle Mayer Watson's homestead outside Hope, Alaska, a tiny rustic hamlet on the Kenai Peninsula. Thinking of the blueberry pie, she frequently devoured at the Discovery Café, her mouth watered. Located on the south shore of Turnagain Arm, part of Cook Inlet, the summers had bustled with salmon fishermen and tourists who went out of their way to visit the quaint community.

"I have a picture of you with blueberry pie smeared all over your face." Faith laughed heartily. "I think you were about twelve."

"Funny you should mention that pie. I was just thinking about it." Cortland smiled. Her aunt had an infectious belly laugh that came deep from her gut. "How are the animals?"

"Oh, you know. They're still here though I've cut back a little."

"How so?"

"Let's see, there are a dozen or so cats, four dogs, three donkeys, two horses, five cows, a six-pack each of pigs, sheep, and goats." Faith quickly added, "I've lost count on the number of chickens, ducks, and turkeys. Pegasus is still here. I think he's waiting to see you again. Like me."

"Aww, Pegasus! Give him a hug and kiss for me. I do miss seeing him and you." Cortland was shocked. Faith and Mayer's homestead used to have twice as much of everything. They were a self-sufficient couple, living off the grid on wind, wood, and solar power. "Wow. What caused the reduction?"

"Oh, you know. I don't need so much now that your Uncle Mayer's gone."

Cortland remembered working with Uncle Mayer to take care of the animals. It was the beginning of her love of animals. Her desire to be a veterinarian had grown out of all those summers caring for and getting to know the homestead's critters. "Are you having some difficulty taking care of so many?"

"Nah, it's fine, dear. The numbers are slowly whittling down on their own. I'm doing fine."

"Maybe I should come out to see you?" She had a feeling the homestead might be getting to be too much for Aunt Faith.

"No need, Cortland. Everything is fine. I'm just a silly old woman who wanted to hear your voice after a morning reminiscing." She chuckled. "I'll let you go and talk to you again on Monday."

"No, wait. Can we make it Tuesday? My hours have changed at work. Is that okay?"

"Yes, of course."

A dip in her aunt's tone filled her heart with longing. "Love you, Auntie Faith." Cortland's heart ached for one of Aunt Faith's crushing hugs.

"Love you too, apple pie." And the connection broke.

Apple pie. God, she hadn't heard that phrase or been called that in so long it made her teary-eyed as she closed the cell phone. As a small child, she'd thought the phrase "apple of my eye" was really "apple pie." Her father and Uncle Mayer used to say that about her, shortening it to "apple pie" after learning this fact. And the nickname stuck.

This time she couldn't stop the tears welling in her eyes. Tired, hungry again, and homesick for those she loved, she let go. Sobbing out her heartache on her desk, she eventually cried herself out of tears.

After a little while, her stomach was growling again, as it had this morning. The face of the firefighter, Dawson, sprang to mind. She was very glad she had given him her lunch before he ran off on another emergency call.

## COURTING CHOICES

Dawson. The fire truck driver had called him Cap over the truck's PA. Did that mean he was Captain Dawson? She chuckled as the image of him with an eye patch and dressed like Captain Jack Sparrow came to mind. He certainly was dirty enough for the part.

She wondered which firehouse he worked out of. Clearly, he was from the Town of Colby, as that was what the lettering on the truck had said. There were three firehouses in Colby. Her curiosity piqued. Could he be stationed at the one down the street from the clinic? It was also the one closest to the lunch truck stop. Maybe if she drove by, she might see him and reimburse him for the curly fries he'd purchased, but she ended up eating. It was worth a shot.

Gathering her belongings, she would check on the patients one last time before riding by the firehouse. Her feet froze a few seconds. *What am I going to do if he's there? If I do see him? Am I really going to hand him a five-dollar bill for fries?*

Cortland slowed her vehicle as she approached the area where the firehouse was located. At half-past seven, it was getting dark, and the lights inside the upper floor were lit. As she got closer, she discerned there weren't any windows on the lower level except a window in the door on the side of the building. The lower-level front of the building consisted of two large, red-painted garage-style doors. Big enough for a fire truck to pass through. Probably barely, from the looks of the worn tire path on the asphalt pavement leading to the street.

An urge to stop and watch for a minute overcame her. She pulled over. Keeping her eyes on the front of the building, she waited, chewing her lip. She wanted to see him. Was he even there? A shiver ran through her body as she pondered the options. If he was there, what would she say? She shook her head to clear it of the idea and considered the other scenario. What if he wasn't there? How foolish would she look?

A sudden movement snatched her attention. One of the red doors was going up. When it was completely open, the fire truck started to exit, emergency lights flashing and the siren wailing. Cortland could tell several firefighters were inside the front cab, one being the driver. And there were several more in a back cab. As it went by, she tried to make out the man's profile, the front cab passenger. Whoever it was, had a radio microphone in hand and was speaking. But he turned to glance her way as the truck accelerated.

It looked like Dawson. It was hard to be sure considering the lack of light, though a street light was on over her car.

Funny thing, she could have sworn the firefighter had also recognized her.

• • • •

The incessant ringing of her phone woke her up. Groaning loudly, she rolled over and answered the call. All the while hating that she was on emergency vet duty this week.

The answering service announced itself, advising of an emergency halfway across town, near the vet clinic. The clinic had the contract to supply veterinary services to the Town of Colby as needed, and this was one of those calls. Her boss's fiancé, Andrew Kelly, the Town of Colby Animal Control Officer, requested her presence. Kittens stuck in a wall.

*A wall of kittens?* Her brain was a little foggy as she got off the phone and started dressing. Within ten minutes, she was in her car, on the way to the emergency scene. Her mind switched to thinking of the injuries the little tykes might have incurred. *How the hell do kittens get into a wall anyway?*

As she neared the location, she saw flashing red, white, and blue lights. Slowing before the house, she noted with curiosity that the fire department was there. The fire department from down the street, at station number two. Parking her car a few yards away, she grabbed her medical bag and approached the animal control van. But Andrew was nowhere to be found.

## COURTING CHOICES

The house's front door was propped wide open, allowing the emergency crews to enter and exit unimpeded. Approaching the door, she saw Andrew across the room. Noticing her arrival, he met her at the door. His rugged face burst into a smile when he saw her, a twinkle igniting his dark brown eyes.

"Hey. Thanks for coming. The fire department is just trying to assess the location of the kittens. They're not all in the same spot."

Cortland peered around the corner of the living room into the hallway, which probably led to bedrooms. The backs of three firefighters in turnout pants but no coats stood staring at the wall. Only one wore a helmet. "I have my stethoscope with me. It might help."

"I think they're trying to use a heat sensor, but kittens don't seem to give off a lot of heat. I'll let them know what you have available." He walked off to the tallest firefighter, who turned around.

Her breath caught in her throat. *Dawson*. She couldn't hear exactly what Andrew said from where she stood, but Dawson looked up, and his eyes penetrated hers as a look of recognition filled them. He crooked his index finger at her, beckoning her to approach. "You."

"Yes, it's me. Doctor Stewart. Veterinarian."

Andrew stood between the two of them, his face registering surprise. "You two know each other?" He glanced back and forth between them.

"Sort of, but not really," Cortland replied.

At her response, Dawson cocked his head and smiled. "We had a little disagreement over lunch."

Clearly dumbfounded by the look on his face, Andrew stepped back, clearing the air between the two of them while not clearing the air between them. "Let me know if there's anything I can do."

"You could officially introduce us," Dawson suggested his hands on his hips.

Andrew, reluctant to step back into the line of fire, waved his hand. "Captain Dawson Michaels, this is Doctor Cortland Stewart from the

Colby County Veterinary Clinic. Doctor Stewart, this is Colby Fire Department Captain Dawson Michaels. He's in charge here."

Captain Michaels smirked. "Nice to meet you."

Trying not to look like a jerk, Cortland responded, "Nice to meet you too. I have a stethoscope. It might be easier to hear the kittens than see them through a wall."

Andrew's trim body stepped in again. "They were just lamenting that the thermal sensor can't actually visualize them behind the wallboard. But as their body temperature warms the wall, we get an image of where they are. The increased infrared heat energy on the wallboard shows as little blobs on the wall."

Her eyebrows scrunched together. It wasn't that she didn't hear him. She was too busy checking out Dawson and listening to the thundering in her chest. "Huh?"

Shoving Andrew aside, Captain Dawson got closer. Holding the thermal camera so Cortland could view it, he described what the picture showed. "The brighter colors, the orange and yellows, indicate warmer temperatures on the wall's surface. The darker colors, the cooler temps." He gestures with his free hand at the screen. "So, this spot here," he touched the wall where the spot showed orange and yellow on the screen, "may be where there's a kitten on the other side of the wallboard." He moved the camera upward about three feet from the ceiling. "There's another spot here." He shifted the camera over to the right about two feet. "And another here."

"Hmm." Cortland stared at the camera image. "So, three kittens might be behind the wall in three separate areas."

"Actually, the owner says there are a total of five kittens missing. Two or more could be bunched together," He motioned toward the spot near the ceiling. "Probably here since this spot is considerably larger than the others and more orange-colored on the imaging screen."

Cortland pulled her stethoscope out of her coat pocket. "Let me have a listen."

## COURTING CHOICES

While Captain Dawson held the camera, Cortland found the first, lower spot, set the head of the stethoscope on the wall where the orange blob showed, and listened. "I can distinctly hear a light scratching noise and kitten vocalizations."

"Kitten sounds?" Dawson asked. "Like meows?"

"Yes, sort of. Some kittens don't meow like adult cats." She poked at the wall spot. "This one is making noise."

"So, it's still alive?"

"Yes, definitely."

Digging into his pocket, he pulled out a marker and made an X on the wall where that orange blob was located. "Try the one up there." He motioned toward the larger spot near the ceiling.

Cortland repositioned herself and stretched as far as her arm would go, but she still couldn't reach the spot near the top of the ten-foot ceiling. Two large hands gripped her waist and lifted her off the ground.

"Hey! Put me down!" Cortland tried to turn, but the grip on her waist prevented it.

"Just check with the scope first, would you?" Dawson said, his teeth clenched as he held her up to the spot.

Reaching out, she set the stethoscope diaphragm on the spot.

"Over to the left another five inches," Andrew said, holding the thermal camera.

The heat from Dawson's chest warmed her back through her light coat. Held effortlessly in his hands, she seemed to defy gravity. Her feet dangled in the air as she reached over to the spot Andrew indicated. She held her finger to her lips to silence the others in the hallway. "Yup, there's probably a couple in there. I can hear two distinct voices. Do you want me to mark the spot?"

Someone thrust a marker at her, and she added a second X to the wall.

Gently, she was set down on her feet, and the strong, masculine hands about her waist disappeared.

"And the third?" Dawson asked.

Andrew aimed at the yellow spot on the wall. "Try here," he pointed to the region of the wall.

Once again, Cortland set her stethoscope on the wall and listened while the hallway fell silent. "Yup, I can hear some scratching, but no vocalizations here."

Andrew and Dawson looked at each other. Andrew gave the nod, and Cortland added another X mark.

Dawson called out, "Okay, let's try it."

The other two firefighters, silently hanging back, stepped forward with cutting tools in hand.

Cortland felt her heart jump into her throat. "Wait! What are you going to do?"

Dawson put his hand on her arm to steer her away down the hallway. "They're going to open the wall about half a foot beneath each spot."

Her heart raced as her body tensed. "But what if they hit the kitten?"

Dawson pushed his helmet back from his forehead. "That's what you're here for."

Behind her, Andrew put his hand on her shoulder and pulled her back. "It'll be okay. Don't worry."

She turned and looked at Andrew, who patted her shoulder. "Are you sure?"

He raised his voice over the noise of the saws. "This isn't their first animal stuck in a wall. They've extricated squirrels, opossums, and raccoons before."

"Raccoons? Aren't they kind of big and nasty?"

"Yeah, that was a harrowing call. As I remember, one firefighter got bit."

# COURTING CHOICES

Looking back at the activity, she saw the first kitten being pulled through the opening in the wall. Stepping forward, she took the cat handed to her by the firefighter.

Crying incessantly, the kitten looked dusty and scared but otherwise uninjured from its ordeal. Andrew held up a cat carrier, and she placed the feline inside.

It took another ten minutes, but the ceiling hole provided three kittens while the one off to the side gave them one. Cortland briefly wondered what the homeowners would think about the mess before turning to her new patients. A quick assessment revealed none of the kittens were severely injured. The five felines clustered together inside the towel-lined carrier.

"Great job, guys," Andrew called out to the firefighters as they picked up their tools and headed out of the house. Following them, he put the carrier in the animal control van. "I'll bring them over to the clinic. Will you be meeting me there?"

"Yes," Cortland nodded. "I'll check them out in the office." She watched Andrew get in the van and drive off. The overnight person would assist them on their arrival.

"Thanks for your help."

The deep voice from behind her nearly scared her out of her wits. She turned around to face him. "Dawson."

He looked at her, his head tilted and helmet askew. "Were you stalking me tonight? Was that you I saw in an SUV in front of the firehouse earlier this evening?"

Cortland's face ignited in flame. "Um, it might have been me. But I wasn't *stalking* you."

He smiled. "Are you sure?" The smile played on his lips as if threatening to explode into an ear-to-ear grin.

Her shoulders stiffened. "Of course, I'm sure." She crossed her arms over her chest.

"Then why were you there?"

She looked down at her sneakered feet. "I thought I should pay you back for the curly fries."

His eyebrow rose. "Curly fries?"

Her left foot started digging a hole in the grass. "Yeah. You know. The fries in your lunch."

Dawson stood there a few seconds, then his eyes lit up. "You mean the fries in my lunch order?"

"Yeah. Them."

He started to laugh. Well, not laugh, really. It was closer to a guffaw or a robust burst of hilarity. "Why?"

Miffed now that he was laughing at her intention, her spine straightened, and her arms dropped stiffly to her sides. "Because you paid for them with your order, right? But you didn't get them. You ended up with my lunch without curly fries. So, I thought you deserved to be paid back for the fries you never got to eat."

The explanation made Dawson laugh harder. Doubled over for a few seconds, he finally caught his breath just as she spun and marched away. He latched onto her upper arm. "Wait. I'm sorry I laughed." He chuckled again before reining in his amusement.

She frowned as she felt the heat of a blush spreading across her face. "Never mind. I'm sorry you didn't get your fries, and I'm sorry if you felt I was stalking you."

"You can stalk me anytime, Ma'am." He turned around to look at the fire truck. The men were waiting patiently inside it. "I've got to get them back to the station." He brushed his index finger across her left cheek. "Thanks for your help tonight." He walked off to the truck, got in, and left as Cortland stood on the sidewalk, speechless, her insides quivering.

# CHAPTER FOUR

Dirt flying when the wheels locked up after slamming on the brake pedal, the SUV screeched to a halt beside Andrew's vehicle. Belatedly, Dawson hoped his all-terrain bike in the back hadn't slammed around too much. His nerves were on fire as he got out of the vehicle. He saw Andrew, his bike waiting beside his truck, geared up and ready to roll. "Sorry, I'm late. There was a call right at shift change."

"I heard it on my radio. I figured you might be late," Andrew said, affixing his riding gloves on his hands. "It sounded like a cluster-you-know-what."

He growled and shook his head while pulling his bike out of the SUV. "It was. Half the on-coming crew was late. Either my crew took the call, or we mixed the crew." He set the bike down, applied the kickstand, and reached for his pile of gear. "Since I would be senior officer, I took my crew back out."

Andrew reached for his helmet resting on the top of his truck. "I'll bet they were real happy about that." His words dripped with sarcasm.

"You got it." After clipping his helmet on, he reached for his riding gloves. "It wouldn't be so bad if it didn't happen so often. That shift is perpetually late."

Nodding his head toward the trailhead, Andrew said, "Let's go get rid of your anger."

Dawson looked around at the other vehicles in the parking lot. "Wait, where's Bryan? Isn't he coming?"

"He got called home to help with the kids."

He grunted. Bryan might be Andrew's brother-in-law, but Dawson thought he was a dick for how he'd treated Hannah and wouldn't miss his company.

The two men mounted their bikes and started on the trail. They rode for nearly twenty minutes before stopping. Both men, breathing hard from the full-out exertion, reached for their water bottles.

There was a nagging in the back of Dawson's head. After a long drink, he gathered up some gumption and asked Andrew the question that had been irritating him for four days. "So, tell me more about Dr. Stewart."

Andrew's eyebrows shot up. "Cortland? What do you want to know?"

Rolling his eyes, Dawson muttered, "The usual."

"Great vet, Hannah's best friend in vet school. I gather they shared a small apartment." Andrew announced between sips of water.

"And …?"

Andrew looked at him with a blank expression. "And what?"

Swearing under his breath, Dawson planted his hands on his hips. "You know what I'm asking."

Breaking into an ear-to-ear grin, he chuckled. "I'm so glad you asked, my friend. Single, no relationships." Andrew started laughing.

"You can wipe that shit-eating grin off your face." Dawson mounted his bike again. "And stop laughing."

"This is way too much fun to stop." Andrew mounted his bike with another mischievous grin but said nothing further. In seconds they were back on the trail.

Concentrating on his predicament rather than watching the trail, Dawson hit a large rock that sent him flying into the thick brush along the trail. Riding in front of him, Andrew hadn't noticed and kept going. Dawson brushed himself off, annoyed and limping slightly. He hoped to work it out on the ride back down the mountain. But first, he needed to catch up with Andrew. Righting his helmet, he picked up his bike and started again.

Starting again. Funny he should have that phrase stuck in his craw. The thoughts that had caused his inattention had been related to starting again. Since he'd been passed over by the fire commission for the last two district chief jobs, maybe it was time to move on. But he didn't want to start over, per se. He wanted to find that next step up, whatever it might be, elsewhere. He was young yet. Too young to be pigeonholed into a job. The more he thought about it, it seemed like the only recourse.

Pounding furiously on the pedals, he caught up with Andrew just as he was getting off his bike on the plateau. With trembling knees, he decided to run his thoughts past Andrew to see what he thought. "I've been thinking I have to move."

His friend's face snapped around. "Move? To the other side of town or just out of your fire district?"

Unclasping his helmet, Dawson tried to explain. "No, I mean move out of town. Maybe far away." At Andrew's quizzical look, he continued. "I got a pass on the district chief's job for the second time. And it was even my district."

"Whoa. Are you searching for another job?" Andrew also removed his helmet and sat down on the nearest rock. His rugged face upturned toward the sun, his wide generous mouth grinning.

"Not yet. But it makes sense, doesn't it? Or am I being too picky about losing the promotion again?"

"Well, what are the pros and cons?"

Sitting down on an opposite rock from Andrew, he started counting on his fingers. "The pros: one, I get the advance I feel capable of doing. Two, more money and a more secure future. Three, another pension opportunity. I'm already vested here in Colby. But another pension elsewhere would be good."

"And the opposite?" Andrew said, stripping off his riding gloves and exercising his hand and fingers, yet his dark brown eyes never left Dawson's face.

His eyebrows bunched together. "The cons are, one, I know this city like I know my own dick. Two, my family is here, and my dad served in this department until his untimely death. Three, I—"

Andrew smirked. "You'd like to check out that veterinarian, Doctor Stewart."

Feeling the tips of his ears go hot, Dawson nodded. "Yeah, I can't say I'm not interested. There're possibilities there." He smirked back. "Did I tell you she was stalking me?"

Chuckling, Andrew replied, "Really?" His face broke out in that wide smile again. "Hmmm, this gets better and better."

A sudden warming in his chest distracted him for a second. "Um, yeah." He went on to give Andrew the explanation she had given him.

"Sounds serious, man."

"Nah, not that serious. But I thought it was kind of telling." He smirked again. "I think she likes me."

Andrew glanced at his watch and then stood. "So, what are you going to do about that?" He began putting on his gloves and helmet again, signaling it was time to head back before they lost the daylight.

"I'll have to think of something. We don't associate in the same sphere."

"I could invite the two of you over to our house for a backyard barbecue or something like that. We should do that anyway to fill you both in on a project we're considering."

Putting his gear back on, Dawson mounted his bike. "No thanks. I'll try it my way, whatever that might be." He turned toward the trail, then back to Andrew. "Say, any of those kittens we pulled from the wall up for adoption?"

• • • •

It was Wednesday evening. Cortland had finished another grueling day on service.

Sitting in her office making notes about today's cases on her computer, she was relieved. Despite her day, she was glad she wasn't on large animal service. It was Hannah's turn, and she had been called out to a horse farm for a possible laminitis case. If that were true, Hannah would have a worse day since laminitis was considered crippling and usually ended by euthanizing the animal.

## COURTING CHOICES

Her thoughts turned again to the handsome hunk of firefighter she's met officially four nights earlier. A knock on her door jamb interrupted her admiring the image of Captain Dawson seared into her mind. "Come on in."

A haggard Hannah stumbled in and flopped down in the rocker Cortland liked to keep in her office.

"I won't ask," Cortland said, giving her friend her full attention.

"Good," Hannah mumbled as her hands scrubbed her face. "God, I hate that." She set the chair in motion, the pace fast and furious.

"I know. I do too." She got up and poured Hannah a couple ounces of wine in a paper cup. "Here. You look like you could use this."

Taking the cup, Hannah shot it back and handed the empty back to Cortland. "No more," she said when Cortland gestured to fill the cup again. "It just sucks because there's nothing you can do that will cure them."

"Not entirely anyway." Cortland placed the bottle back in the mini-fridge and sat at her desk again. "Maybe he would have gotten better for a little while, but he would likely have relapsed."

"Yup." Hannah looked at Cortland. "What were you doing when I came in?"

Cortland's face flamed.

"Oh my, this should be good." Hannah sat up in her chair.

Waving a hand at Hannah, Cortland answered, "I was thinking of the other night when Andrew called me in about the kittens stuck in the wall."

Hannah's eyes narrowed. "Hmm, Andrew said something about introducing you to the fire officer in charge. You said you had previously met. He started cross-examining me."

"Well, sort of," Cortland explained how she and Dawson met at the food truck, fighting over a Styrofoam container.

"I would have loved to see that!" Hannah smiled, her face brightening.

"Yeah, well. He's not bad to look at." Cortland grinned.

Breaking into a chuckle, Hannah continued rocking furiously in her rocker. "Ha! That he is not."

"You know him?" Cortland couldn't help the curiosity in her voice.

"He and Andrew go mountain biking with Bryan once a week." She leaned forward. "He's single."

Her face flared again. "Okay. Maybe I'm not interested."

Smirking, Hannah said, "Yeah, right. I can see you're very interested." She wagged her index finger at Cortland. "Don't forget I know you. We're practically sisters."

"Okay, so I enjoyed looking at him. He's big and brawny and rugged-looking."

"Just the way you like your men." Hannah scratched her chin. "Maybe I should invite you two over for dinner on the same night."

"Please don't play matchmaker." But a part of her really wanted Hannah to do it. How else were the two of them to get together again?

Clapping her hands together, Hannah pouted playfully. "But it could be so much fun." She grinned. "And you never know ..."

The following afternoon, Cortland picked up a file. Scanning the documents, she saw her next patient was a kitten. Recently adopted from the Colby animal control shelter. Her mind jogged back to the kitten rescue five nights ago. Could it be one of those kittens? Perhaps. There was no notation on the adoption papers.

Tucking the file under her arm, she bustled into the room with her laptop computer. Then abruptly stopped. "You?"

Standing beside a small gray kitten at the exam table was Dawson Michaels. "Yeah. Me. I adopted one of the kittens we rescued. What's wrong with that?"

"First off, you should always get at least two. They play together." She set down the file and laptop on the counter and approached the cat. It purred loudly, if irregularly, as she stroked its back.

"Less mischief?"

## COURTING CHOICES

"Not always. Sometimes more so." Cortland tried to prevent the smirk threatening to overtake her face. And then she caught a glimpse of his eyes.

"What's the second?"

"What second?" She blinked back at him. Mesmerized by his light blue eyes, she hadn't heard him. *With eyes like that, I might follow you anywhere, buster.*

"You started by saying, 'First off' ... so I assume there's a second reason to get two kittens instead of one." He stared back at her, a smile beginning on his face.

She had to turn away before she started drooling. "There are lots of kittens out there that need adoption."

Dawson leaned against the stainless-steel examination table. "So, should I get another kitten from the same litter? Or completely different?" He scrubbed his stubbly chin as he asked. "And should I get the same sex, or is opposite better?"

"My personal feeling is the same litter and same sex. If you're going to have them fixed, and I highly recommend that, two different sexes would be okay." She pulled out her stethoscope and listened to the kitten's lungs and heart.

"Is it okay? You seem to be listening rather intently." He stood straighter, his forehead crinkling and his eyes not leaving her face.

"She's purring pretty loud. I wanted to make sure I wasn't missing anything." She set the instrument aside and continued the exam. "Have you decided on a name?" She quickly added, "I'll need a name for the file."

Dawson cocked his head and looked at the cat. "I think Smokey will do nicely. Don't you?"

Cortland smiled. "It's a lovely name for a pretty little kitty." She bent over and checked the feline's eyes and ears. "Everything seems to be in working order. Do you need any instructions?"

He raised his eyebrow. "Like what?"

"Feedings, bedding, behavior, grooming, et cetera." She crossed her arms over her chest.

"Tell me more about bedding." He grinned like a Cheshire cat.

Rolling her eyes, Cortland replied, "Cats will pick whatever spot they prefer. You could buy a cat bed, but chances are pretty good the cat will ignore it. They're highly independent."

"That's not the bedding information I was looking for, but thanks. Skip the cat bed."

"Perhaps it's my presumption, but I got the impression you're a first-time cat owner."

"I am. Does it show?"

"A little." She smiled back and gestured for him to grab the carrier. He picked up the kitten and deposited her inside. "Do you have any questions?"

"Just one." He set the carrier on the floor and returned his gaze to her. "Would you have dinner with me Sunday night?"

"I'm on duty. I could get an emergency call."

"So, are you saying yes, with a stipulation?"

She thought a minute, during which Dawson folded his arms over his chest in mock patience. "I guess that's what I'm saying. We'll need to stay in town."

Dawson stood up, dropping his hands to his pockets. "We can do that."

"Then it's a date." She gathered her materials, including the laptop, and started for the door, giving him one last head-to-toe look over. Her insides trembled with delight. *Oh, boy!*

Noontime was always the most challenging time each day. While the staff had their lunch breaks, patients still needed to be seen. So the vets continued working, with any extra pair of hands available. Today, adding to the chaos was the arrival of Andrew, with a litter of puppies and their mother.

## COURTING CHOICES

"Bring them in," Cortland said, stepping aside to hold the door open for him. Somehow, he had stuffed all six puppies into one large crate.

He set the crate down. "I'll go get mom and the runt." And he headed out the door again. While she waited, she set up for marking and recording the entire litter.

By the time Andrew had arrived, Cortland had already started. "Looks like four girls and two boys."

"And mom with the third boy." Andrew offered, setting down the last crate.

Methodically, the two of them examined each puppy, including weighing them. Each was given a collar with a temporary name to keep them all straight. Today, they were reindeer names: Dasher, Dancer, Prancer, Blitzen, Comet, and Donner. The mother was named Vixen, and the runt was named Cupid.

After each was examined, it was taken by the available veterinary tech to a holding area.

They were just finishing when Hannah joined them. "Hey, I hear you have your hands full of puppies."

Andrew leaned over to kiss his fiancée. "Yup, I thought since I had them in the van, I'd bring them over rather than having one of you come all the way to the shelter."

"Thanks. It's a big help, especially on a day as busy as today," Hannah answered. "What's their story?"

"The tenant moved out of the house a couple days ago. Neighbors heard the mother and puppies whining and barking. They knew the previous tenant had a pregnant dog, so they put two and two together. No food or water." He shifted the runt back into the mother's cage and removed her for evaluation. "The puppies don't seem worse for the episode, but the mother looks dehydrated, don't you think?"

"Definitely," Hannah said, eyeing the mother. "Some water and food will help considerably. Should we start here, or do you want to take them back to the shelter?"

"Here, then I'll take them back to the shelter. They should fit nicely in a kennel all together. I'll make sure there's plenty of water and an endless supply of food for mom."

Hannah pet the mother. "She doesn't look too bad. Cortland, what do you think?"

Setting aside her stethoscope, Cortland studied the animal. "I think she'll be fine with nourishment and knowing her pups are safe."

After the mother went back with the rest of the puppies for something to eat, Andrew turned toward Cortland. "I hear you made quite the impression with Dawson."

Hannah gave the impression that she was hearing about this for the first time. "What? Dawson, as in your biking buddy, Dawson?"

"Same one," Andrew replied.

The two of them stared at Cortland, who felt sweat starting to dampen her underarms. "It's just a friendly thing."

"Hmm." Andrew rubbed his chin. "I hear you two have a date."

She felt her face go totally hot. "Yeah, so? What's it to you?" She stuffed her stethoscope in her white coat pocket. Ignoring the smirks, she added, "He adopted one of the kittens from the other night."

"Yup. Do you want the others?" He leaned back against the exam table, the expression on his face highlighting that he was thoroughly enjoying the conversation about Cortland's love life.

Hannah asked, "How many are left?"

He glanced her way. "Dawson took another kitten. Someone else adopted one, so there are only two left. You interested?"

Cortland stopped to consider. "Yeah." She nodded. "Harris could use some company at home."

"Great!" he said, clapping his hands together. "If you and Dawson move in together, the kitten family can be reunited. In fact, I think—"

## COURTING CHOICES

Hannah placed a hand on her future husband's shoulder before he could continue. "I think you should leave Cort alone." She leaned over to whisper in his ear, "Don't worry, I'll beat it out of her before the day is finished." Then she winked at Cortland.

"I heard that!" Cortland protested, shaking her head before gathering her materials and leaving the room.

# CHAPTER FIVE

She had Sunday off. Hannah felt bad that Cortland had been covering six days a week at the clinic. Which was a good thing because Cortland hadn't slept well the night before.

She had fallen asleep at about ten o'clock on the sofa at home. The kittens had startled her awake, climbing into her lap. Dozing off again, she slipped into a dream. It seemed real, but it was a dream. Of that, she was sure. Cortland could hear the phone ringing, but she couldn't get to it.

As dreams usually do, this one didn't make sense, though it had remnants of many of her previous nightmares. She could hear her phone's ring tone, but she sat in the front passenger seat of her family's old Jeep Grand Cherokee. And her older sister, Jessica, was driving. They were speeding. In the back seat, her brother, Greg, egged Jess to go faster to get to the phone. Somehow, they all knew it was Auntie Faith calling. The faster sixteen-year-old Jessica drove the louder the phone rang, as though they were getting closer. Suddenly, Cortland was standing alone on the side of the road, the Jeep overturned, her brother and sister gone. The cell phone was clutched in her hand. It had stopped ringing.

Cortland woke trembling and tearful. She bolted from the couch, knowing she'd be awake the rest of the night. Reliving the accident as part of a dream was not unusual but always uncanny. Why the ringing phone before the accident? That wasn't how it happened. Why had Jess been in her dream about Aunt Faith? Had her aunt really called? Or had it been some psychic connection telling her something was wrong? It being four-sixteen in the morning, she was not going to call her godmother, even if it was just after midnight in Alaska.

If Aunt Faith had called, it must have been an emergency. Her mind skittered across a good dozen ideas. Was she ill? Did someone break into the house? Was one of the animals sick? Did she need

## COURTING CHOICES

Cortland? Pacing the apartment didn't help, nor did a glass of warm milk.

Snatching up the phone, she toggled through its recent call history. There wasn't any listing of anyone calling after eight o'clock that night when Hannah had called about a patient. So, the entire thing was a dream?

She went outside, taking her boxer-cross mutt Harris with her on his leash. They walked their usual path through the woods surrounding her small apartment complex. A well-worn path all the dog-owning tenants used for relief purposes. While he stopped and sniffed along the trail, her mind kept jumping back to the dream. It felt too real to not be, yet Jessica was there. Was it the mingling of her recurring nightmare with an imaginary phone call?

Hannah? Was Hannah having second thoughts about giving her the day off? Had something come up. But the cell phone's call history had been blank for the last nine hours. Clearly, no one had called her.

Shaking her head vehemently, she stuffed the phone back in her pocket as Harris pulled at his leash, wanting to sniff yet another tree along the path. Tugging Harris along, she had a long list of things to do in preparation for tonight's date with Dawson. The arrangements had been made, and they would meet at The Irish Harp.

After agreeing to the date with Dawson, she booked herself into the Calypso Day Spa. Preparations for her dinner with him began at nine in the morning. Part of the local casino complex, the spa had everything from a sauna, an indoor and outdoor swimming pool, a whirlpool, and a long list of body treatments. Her agenda for the day included hitting the sauna and whirlpool to ease her muscles, an ayurvedic whole body herbal and oil exfoliating scrub, followed by a massage, a facial, mani and pedi. She would receive a spa salad lunch at noon on the patio. She added a cosmetic consult in the last hour of her stay.

# DIANA ROCK

By six o'clock, she waited impatiently in the restaurant. When she left the house, her spirit should have been light and adventurous. Instead, she didn't feel right. The makeup felt heavy and foreign on her skin though the esthetician had applied it very lightly, going for a natural look. She wasn't dissatisfied with the results, but she wasn't used to having a coating on her face. Or mascara that made her eyelids feel heavy and droopy. Add to all that the new clothes she had bought specifically for her date. The blouse was uncomfortably more revealing than her work scrubs. But here now, waiting for him in a booth, a tremor ran through her, and her stomach ached. *This is stupid. You already know this man. It's just a friendly dinner together.* She clicked her tongue. *And you still owe him curly fries.*

• • • •

Glancing out the window onto the street, she spotted him. Half of her wanted to flee. The other half wanted to shuck his clothes. His form-fitting jeans clung like a second skin to his hips and thighs and probably his ass though she couldn't see them and could only speculate. He was freshly shaved, with his hair cut to perfection. A light blue button-down shirt fit close to his broad chest and disappeared behind a belt on his pants. She wondered how he'd look naked. Anger flared in her chest for even thinking such a thing. Forcing herself to stay, she watched him saunter toward her booth.

He stopped directly before her and paused as if trying to decide whether he wanted to leave or sit down. He flashed her a tense smile and sat down.

Cortland gave him a weak smile. "Hey. You came."

He shrugged. "Did you think I wouldn't? He paused before adding, "I asked *you* to dinner. Remember?"

She stared at him. "Why do you have to be so prickly?" Fingering her virgin margarita glass, she twirled it around and around.

# COURTING CHOICES

"Me! What about your tone? Don't you think you're being a little combative?"

After spending the day at the spa, she really should be more relaxed. Breaking eye contact with him, she muttered, "Perhaps. If that's the case, I'm sorry."

Dawson dipped his chin in acknowledgment, relaxing back into the booth.

The waitress arrived, her pen poised. "What'll it be?"

Cortland snatched up the menu and skimmed it. The last thing she wanted was to add to her discomfort level with gastric upset.

"Corned beef Reuben only a little sauerkraut, no fries, no dressing, and no pickle." She quickly added, "and another virgin margarita." That should be bland enough.

Dawson raised an eyebrow. "Same for me, except I want all the sauerkraut and dressing. I'd like curly fries and add her pickle to my plate. And a Guinness."

As the waitress walked away, Cortland tapped her index finger on the tabletop. "What is it with you and curly fries?" She sat back in the booth. "And how is it you get to have my pickle?"

"What's wrong with curly fries?" His eyebrows rose. "As far as the pickle is concerned, I like them. Why not eat yours?"

"Curly fries are thin and limp. I prefer mine thick and firm."

A slow smile spread over Dawson's face, one eyebrow raised. "Thick and firm, huh?"

Realizing what she'd said, Cortland's face went burning hot.

Wiping a hand over his mouth, Dawson struggled to hold back his laughter. "And the pickle, well, you didn't want it—"

"Maybe I've changed my mind. Maybe I want a pickle now." Honestly, she didn't understand why she was getting so snippy. *Why did I even accept this date? Because he's just your type: handsome, brawny, and with a glint of flirtation and mischief in his eyes.*

Dawson leered at her, still trying to control a grin. "You can have my pickle." He brushed his hand over his mouth again, trying to hide his mirth.

*Oh my God.* Cortland squeezed her eyes shut. "Now you're being suggestive."

Feigning surprise, Dawson reared back in his seat. "Me? You're the one who wants a—"

"Never mind." Feeling her cheeks and ear tips flaming hot, she shook her head gently and stared at the wall. She was feeling too weary for this banter. It might be fun and flirtatious on another night, but she wasn't feeling it tonight. *I should have taken a nap. Or canceled the date entirely.*

Their drinks arrived, breaking the silence.

"Tell me about your job. If I recall correctly, Andrew called you Captain."

Having taken a sip of his stout, his tongue ran over his lips, swiping at the foam left behind.

Cortland's insides trembled watching his tongue. *Thank God I'm sitting down, or I wouldn't be feigning a swoon.*

"I'm a captain at Station Two." He set the glass down. "But you knew that already."

She rolled her eyes. "Yes, I guess I did figure out which station you worked out of."

"To pay me back for my curly fries. *If* I recall correctly." He added and grinned broadly again.

"Hmph, well, yes." *Man, it's getting hot in this little pub.* She wanted to remove her lightweight sweater but was afraid of the comment he might make.

He grasped her hand from the tabletop. "I have an idea. Why don't I get to eat your pickle, and we can call it even." His lecherous leer returned.

## COURTING CHOICES

Cortland buried her face in her hands. "Enough with the pickle already," she said, a note of irritation in her voice.

At that moment, their food arrived; two pickle spears sat on Dawson's plate. "Deal," Cortland said before she sipped her drink.

"Tell me something I don't know about you," Dawson said before digging into his meal.

She thought a half a minute. "You know I have two of those kittens we rescued. But you probably don't know about Harris, my dog."

He tilted his head with what seemed to be interest. "What kind?"

"He's a rescue, and it's hard to tell. A little boxer, a little lab, maybe. His time came up at the shelter, and I adopted him. He's a good boy even if he has a few quirky habits."

"Like what?"

She finished chewing her last bite. "He has this habit of greeting me at the door when I come home. In itself, it's nice, but he always has to carry something in his mouth when he's greeting me: a toy, a bone, or a shoe." She giggled. "When I first brought the kittens home, he met me at the door with one in his mouth. He was very gentle, didn't hurt it, but it scratched his nose. Even so, he wouldn't put it down until I told him to do so."

Dawson stared at her. "You're kidding, right?"

"No! I'm telling you the truth. It's his weirdest quirky thing." Cortland took another bite of her sandwich. "Do you have a dog?"

"No. I'd love to have one again. I had one as a kid, a dalmatian, of course. But my work schedule is not optimal for having a dog. It's one full twenty-four-hour shift on, then two days off. I'd have to find someone to watch the dog while I'm at work."

"I can understand. I hate that I'm away at work for so much of the day. Luckily, my neighbor also has a dog and the two dogs are best buddies. She watches Harris during the day for me. For a price, but it's not much. I'm happy to have him."

They ate in silence for a few minutes.

"What about you? Where did you go to school?" Dawson asked before biting into his Reuben.

"My undergrad degree is from Syracuse University. Then I went to Cornell University Veterinary College. Hannah and I were in the same classes. "

Dawson said, wagging a curly fry at her, "Right, I remember. Andrew told me about that. Weren't you two roommates or something like that?"

Cortland's face heated up again at the sight of the limp fry he was flipping around in his fingers. She caught the glint of laughter in his eyes but chose to ignore his provocation. "We, um, had an off-campus apartment with our other friend, Tulsi Anthony. It was great fun. I miss having those two around." Her sandwich half eaten already, she stretched back in her seat from the uncomfortable feeling in her stomach. "What about you? Where did you learn firefighting?"

"I went to the fire academy and trained for some things on the job."

"What made you become a firefighter?"

Dawson chewed a bite of his sandwich and looked as though he were deciding what to say. "My dad was a firefighter. I guess you could say it's the family business."

"That explains the dalmatian," she quipped with a wide smile. "Did your dad retire?"

"Uh, no." His tone became abrupt, and he looked away. "He died in the line of duty when I was a kid."

Frozen in horror at his admission, she could only stutter, "I-I'm so sorry."

Giving his head a little shake, Dawson replied, "Thanks. It was a long time ago." He took a long gulp of his beer. "How did you get into veterinary medicine?"

Cortland pushed her plate away, the food only half eaten. "As a kid, I spent most of my summers with my aunt and uncle in Alaska. They had a large working farm with all kinds of animals. I was required to help out, and I loved it. Going there every summer was the best time of my year. Taking care of the animals, getting to know them. It was awesome." Her eyes felt wide. She hoped he would understand how in love she was with the place. "Except, in the fall, after I left, sometimes they would cull the herd for the winter months." She frowned slightly, remembering the feeling of hearing who had "left the farm" from Uncle Mayer. "They lived a very self-sufficient life. As much as they could."

Dawson looked rapt, his eyes glued directly to hers. "Wow. That's kind of impressive. Why do you think your parents sent you up there?"

Cortland's insides chilled. "I—" she stopped and started again. "We had a family problem when I was ten. Despite being the first-born, my elder sister was a wild child. Totally unruly. I think my parents thought getting me out of the situation would prevent me from learning her bad attitude."

Dawson was silent. "Do you still go? To Alaska, I mean."

"I did every summer for a long time. Sometimes during Christmas and Thanksgiving breaks at school. But not nearly so much when I hit high school. I went for a visit just after graduation from vet school. It was just before Uncle Mayer died. It was terribly sudden, a heart attack right out of the blue. I went to his funeral, of course. I offered to stay with Aunt Faith for a little while. I didn't have the job here yet, so I had plenty of time. But she said no. She wanted to get used to being alone."

The waitress suddenly appeared beside the table. "I'll wrap the leftovers. Can I get you any dessert or coffee?"

"Great. Nothing else for me, thanks." Cortland said, unable to keep the sadness out of her voice.

"Just the check, please," Dawson said to the waitress, his eyes still riveted to Cortland. "Hey, let's talk about something cheerful." He reached out to take her hand.

She stared at his hand on hers. The sight made her belly quiver wanting more of his touch. At the same time, it made her knees tremble. It was time to end the evening before it progressed to something she wasn't ready for. Giving her head a quick shake, Cortland cocked it. "I really hate to do this to you. But I've had a not-so-great week, I'm on emergencies tonight, and I'm back on duty tomorrow. Would you mind terribly if we call it a night?"

His face closed, and he withdrew his hand. "Not a problem."

The difference between his words and his body language made it clear he was disappointed she was bailing on him so soon. She kicked herself mentally for not calling Aunt Faith earlier. Having to choose between a long evening with Dawson or settling her fears about her aunt wasn't difficult. Her aunt's status was nagging on her conscience strongly. Stronger than any attraction she felt for Dawson tonight.

They rose from the booth and walked outside onto the sidewalk, where they stopped. Cortland looked up into the night sky. It was still dusk. Only a few stars were visible yet. She swayed, suddenly dizzy from looking up.

He grasped her elbow to steady her. "Whoa. Are you okay? What are you looking for?" Dawson followed her eyes upward.

Cortland looked at his hand on her arm as a tingle ran up her arm into her spine. "Stars. Constellations actually. But it's not dark enough yet." Cortland brought her eyes back to his face.

"You're into that kind of stuff?"

"Yeah, have been since I was a kid." She smiled. "Dinner was nice. Thank you. I'm sorry I'm not—not being very—" she tried to let him know she had a lot of things on her mind. Discussing Aunt Faith had brought up a boiling pit in her gut. She didn't know what to do about that situation, and with all the bustle at the spa where they frowned on cell phone use, she hadn't called Alaska to see if everything was okay.

"Look, it's okay. I enjoyed talking with you." He waited a few seconds. "I'd like to get to know you better. If you're interested in doing that."

"Yeah, I'd like that." She scuffed the sidewalk with her shoe. "I apologize about tonight. I've thought of something important I needed to do today but didn't." She shrugged slightly. "I'll feel better once I do it."

Dawson's features showed some sympathy for her predicament. He smiled slowly. "Can I call in a few days?"

"Sure," Cortland said before planting a quick kiss on his cheek. "Thanks, Dawson." *I'll make it up to him another time.*

She itched to dial Aunt Faith's telephone number all the way home. She was tempted to pull over and call, but the call might be long and emotional. It was best to wait until she got home.

Harris met her at the door with her favorite sneaker in his mouth. "Harris. Give." The dog immediately obeyed, smiling as though he'd done something special for her. She petted him and kissed his nose. "You're a good boy, Harris."

Cortland settled onto the sofa, the kittens playing hide-and-seek together while she dialed. A fumbling of the phone sounded as someone answered. Aunt Faith's weak, almost feeble voice saying hello.

Sitting on the edge of her seat, Cortland called, "Aunt Faith, is that you?"

"Cortland?"

"Yes. It's me. Are you all right?" She could hear the tremor in her voice. Trying to rein in the surging feeling of unease, she started pacing the living room. "What's happened?"

"It's nothing. I'm fine."

She didn't sound fine. Cortland had never heard her aunt sound so feeble. And it wasn't a bad connection. "What's nothing? Are you hurt?"

Aunt Faith sighed, "I was trying to wrestle Billygoat into the barn for the night, and he kicked me in the side of my leg. Don't worry, I've been to the hospital. My fibula is broken. They put my leg in a cast. It's going to be fine. It just needs time to mend."

"How are you getting along with the farm? Should I come?" She stood in front of her calendar, eyeing her work schedule.

"Wally, from down the street, is taking care of the critters, and his wife is helping me with food and laundry. If you can come, I'd like that, but it's not necessary dear heart."

"I want to make sure you're okay. Broken bones take longer to heal in the elderly."

"That's what the doctor said. But my fracture isn't too extensive. I just have to be patient for a couple of weeks or so."

As her mind swiftly sifted through what she knew of long bone fractures in animals, she conceded, "It's not a weight-bearing bone in the lower leg, but it supports a lot of muscles, tendons, and ligaments, so it's important in ankle stability. Still, keeping it immobile isn't going to be easy for you, is it?" Cortland knew her aunt well enough to know she would push herself to get back on her feet again as quickly as possible.

A heavy sigh threaded through the cell phone to her ear. "That's true. You know me. Not much can keep me down." The line was silent for a few seconds before she called, "Cortland? Honey? I hate to ask, but maybe you should come for a short visit? There are some things I need to talk to you about."

Walking back to the calendar, she said, "I have a free weekend coming up next weekend. Will that do? Do you need me there faster than that?"

Aunt Faith groaned, "Heaven's no, that should be fine. Hopefully, I'll be in better shape by then."

"I'll call you with my travel plans." She hung up the phone, the anxiety of the situation making her sick to her stomach.

• • • •

Stupidly, he'd failed to get her phone number. If he wanted to reach her, and he did want to reach out to her, he'd have to call the vet clinic answering service. Even though she had mentioned she was on-call that night, the last thing he wanted to do was phone her through work.

# COURTING CHOICES

Calling an hour after they had left each other on the sidewalk outside The Irish Harp might give her the wrong impression, and he recognized she wasn't having a good night. She needed some space, and he should probably leave her alone, but the sadness in her eyes when she discussed her family haunted him.

He shoved his phone into his back pocket and turned off the television. It was dark outside, and he could clearly see a bunch of stars in the sky through the window. *Funny how she's been into stars and such since she was a kid.* He didn't know what to make of that. Most kids don't even look up. Not kids today, anyway.

Collapsing on the worn couch, he lay on his stomach, his head buried in the throw pillow that came with the sofa. Replaying the night, his eyes closed with a groan. He hadn't been in his best form either. He'd been tired and anxious, having worked a partial shift for Captain Enrico earlier that day. Leaving later than he wanted due to paperwork, he'd arrived later than he intended. He wanted to impress her but came off feeling like an ass. His tongue tied up until all he could do was blurt out suggestive comments about their food.

He chuckled softly at the innuendos they'd bantered about the curly fries and pickle. Cortland's face, bright pink cheeks, her eyes flaring, perhaps with anger, perhaps with embarrassment. She looked different than last he'd seen her at the vet clinic: with her hair loose and soft around her made-up face. At several points, the deep cleavage of her pale pink blouse had dipped, revealing the pink lacy edge of her bra, especially when she leaned forward to sip her drink. Just thinking about it, that erotic glimpse made *his* pickle stir. He pressed into the couch cushion, attempting to stifle its response.

As good as she looked, he sensed she was uncomfortable. All during dinner, she tugged and poked at her blouse, frowning often while doing so. She was most definitely intriguing in more ways than one. Enough for him to want to get to know her better, more personally, more intimately. He wanted a second chance.

The reason for her being sent to Alaska was boggling. A family situation big enough to want to send your kid four thousand miles away for several months? Try as he might, he couldn't guess what it could have been. Was there an illness so devastating that they didn't want their daughter around to see it? Or was she starting to act up, perhaps copying her elder sister's antics? Maybe the trip to Alaska was meant to break her bad habits? Andrew might know. He'd have to ask next time the opportunity arose.

Her reaction to his confession about his father had been a surprise. He hadn't expected her to be so empathetic about his fatherless upbringing. Thinking about it, he wondered if she, too knew loss. The expression on her face was of pain, horror, and something else he couldn't define. Making a mental note to talk with Andrew again, he rose from the couch and stumbled off to bed, where he found the kittens lying nose to nose across the center of the bed.

Raising his eyes to heaven and shaking his head, he returned to the couch, kicked off his shoes, and buried his head in the pillow again.

# CHAPTER SIX

Sobbing uncontrollably, Cortland buried her face in her hands to muffle the sound. She didn't want anyone outside her office door to hear her meltdown. The front part of the fifty-plus-year-old Cape housing the clinic didn't have much in the way of sound diminishing insulation. A crushing feeling of loss had her bent over at the waist in her desk chair.

"OH!" She bolted upright as she felt the weight of a hand on the back of her head. Turning, she found Hannah kneeling beside her chair. "I didn't hear you come in."

"I'm sorry." Hannah sat back on her heels at Cortland's feet. "You did everything right. It just wasn't meant to be."

Cortland's vision blurred as she looked at her best friend, a moist tissue pressed to her cheeks, sopping up the tears. "I—I can't believe he died. Everything was looking good. His vital signs were stable, and then …"

"I know. It's the biggest suck this job entails." Hannah reached out again and grasped Cortland's hand. "It was gutsy of you to even try to save him. Most vets would have given up as soon as he arrived." Squeezing her hand, Hannah reiterated, "At least you tried."

Fresh tears welled in Cortland's eyes again. "It didn't work."

"But you tried." Rising on her knees, Hannah turned the chair to face her. "You are not God. You and I and any other veterinarians out there are not miracle workers. We're all perfectionists, but it's out of our hands." She rubbed Cortland's back. "Our patients are our passion. Caring for them gives us meaning and satisfaction. And losing them bruises our hearts."

"Bruise?" Cortland sniffled. "This one was a kick in the teeth and the chest."

"Cort, our compassion and our skill have incredible value. We save and help so many. We all have to focus on the incredible good we do."

"I understand that. It doesn't make it any easier, though. Especially when a good owner turns on you."

Hannah sat back on her heels again. "I heard everything you said to the owner. You never promised her you'd cure her cat. She got her hopes up too high. She wasn't listening to your words of caution."

Cortland sighed heavily. "I know. She jumped to the conclusion I'd save him no matter what." She was quiet for a few seconds. "Do you ever consider quitting?"

Looking up at her wide eyed, Hannah shook her head vigorously. "No, not now. I did during my first internship. I lost the most adorable golden retriever puppy I've ever seen. He ingested an entire bag of chocolate Easter candy. By the time he was brought in, he was seizing. I'd just seen him two days before for his first physical. I cried my heart out for days afterward."

Cortland's hand grasped Hannah's. "That must have been awful." She looked away, breaking eye contact with her. "Do you ever feel like you're on a conveyor belt with an endless supply of patients?" She ran her trembling hand through her hair. "Like you don't own your time anymore?"

"Oh boy, did I ever. When I first got here only to find out Doc Cambria had that stroke, his wife told me I had to cover the clinic and the town vet position without anyone's help. But then, I enticed someone to join me. My best friend," she cocked her head to the side and smiled, "who I must admit is a great veterinarian."

Remembering the call she received about the job, Cortland grinned. "I was so happy for so many reasons." The grin dropped from her features. "But I didn't expect it to be so much like a roller coaster."

"Hmm, you've been working six to seven days a week." Hannah hugged her knees to her chest.

"My schedule will be lightening up soon." Having two days off in a row couldn't come soon enough.

"Even so, tell me, what do you do when you get home?"

## COURTING CHOICES

Her eyes widened. "I usually crash. Most nights, I don't get home until after nine."

"You need to spend less time at the clinic. I don't want you staying after six p.m. unless there's an emergency and you're on-call. The veterinary techs are good here. They know when to call you in and when they can handle something simple. That's an order from your boss. You need a better work-life balance."

Cortland chuckled. "What life?"

"My point exactly. You need either a hobby or a man."

Feeling the blush overtaking her face, Cortland looked away. "I'm working on a man."

Hannah's eyes widened. "Dawson?"

She nodded. "We had dinner last night."

Her friend wiggled her eyebrows saucily. "And?"

"It was nice." She shrugged and looked away.

Hannah recoiled, her eyes narrowing. "Uh oh. *Nice*? I would have hoped it was better than nice."

A flicker of warmth sprouted in Cortland's belly as she thought of Dawson's tongue licking his lips free of Guinness foam. "We discussed our careers. And bantered a little." The skeptical look on Hannah's face forced her to admit the truth. "Okay, so we bantered more than a little. About curly fries and the pickle I didn't want with my dinner. The innuendo feels funny now, but in my frame of mind at the time, I didn't want to hear it."

"Why? It was flirtatious, wasn't it?"

"Yes." Shrugging, she answered, "I was uncomfortable in make-up, heels, and new clothes that were more risqué than my work scrubs."

Shaking her head and raising her eyebrows with a look of surprise, Hannah remained silent.

"Then I mentioned my Aunt Faith, and I got nervous because I hadn't heard from her. I had a dream the other night that she was calling me. In the dream, I couldn't get to the phone. It kind of freaked me out and brought the evening to an early close."

"Did you ever hear from her?"

"I called after the date. She broke her fibula. It's casted, and she's home. But she sounded awful. Her voice was weak. I need to go see her. She wouldn't say why but she wants me to fly out to see her. I was thinking of next weekend. You're covering that weekend, and I can be back by Monday morning on the red-eye flight."

Hannah bit her lip a few seconds before replying. "Sounds okay. If you have any appointments, have Alissa reschedule them."

Cortland stared into space, her mind ticking through all the possible reasons Aunt Faith wanted her to go to Alaska. The conversation left her feeling something else was going on that Aunt Faith needed help with.

Interrupting her thoughts, Hannah said, "I'm sorry. I hoped you two might have hit it off."

"Me too, frankly." Cortland paused, remembering Dawson and their parting on the sidewalk. "He said he'd call, but he hasn't. But it's only been since last night. Still, I don't want to read too much into our date."

"Hmm." Hannah stretched her legs out on the floor in front of her. "I bet he will. Andrew seems to think he's got the hots for you. Speaking of which, we're inviting you both over Friday night, eight o'clock, to discuss something." Smirking, she said saucily, "You'll have another chance."

Rolling her eyes and covering her ears with her hands, she looked away again. "Enough. I don't want to hear anymore."

"Suit yourself." Hannah started to get up but fell back. "Help me. I can't get up."

Cortland giggled as she helped Hannah up from the carpeted floor. "Way to go, boss."

# COURTING CHOICES

Cortland turned her car into the small guest parking area at Hannah and Andrew's apartment building. A glance in her rear-view mirror confirmed her suspicions and ignited unease. The vehicle trailing her for the last few miles followed her into the parking lot. She stayed in her car and picked up her phone. She could call Andrew and ask him to come down and escort her. *Or am I just being paranoid? Maybe it's someone who lives here?*

She had been to their apartment before but only during daylight. Located in the outskirts of town in a heavily wooded area she was otherwise unfamiliar with, she was not feeling comfortable here at night. The quarter moon threw little light. She waited to see what the driver of the vehicle, a pickup truck, would do.

A tall, sturdy male figure got out of the truck. He paused beside his door and smoothed his hand over the top of his head. His silhouette looked familiar. *Dawson? What's he doing here?* She hadn't heard from him since the date.

Remembering Andrew and Hannah's talk about inviting her and Dawson over for dinner at the same time made her clench the steering wheel. Hannah had said she was inviting both of them over. Had they dared to try to arrange this get-together as a matchmaking ploy? A flash of anger and dismay filled her gut. She did not like the meddling if that's what was happening.

When Dawson started up the sidewalk, Cortland dialed Hannah. When she answered, Cortland lit into her. "How could you? Contriving something to get Dawson and me together? I specifically remember telling you not to do something like this!"

Hannah shushed her. "That's not what this is about. Just come into the apartment. All will be explained." And she hung up.

Cortland grumbled as she got out of the car and headed for the apartment door. It opened as she approached. Hannah took her hand and led her toward the living room.

"Beer, wine, or lemonade?" Hannah asked as Cortland set down her purse on the foyer table.

"Wine, red, please." She eyed Dawson and Andrew across the living room. Dawson's eyes met hers. He grinned as he held her gaze, Andrew talking to him all the while. Her insides fluttered the longer he stared. "Do you swear you're not playing matchmaker?"

"Positive." Hannah's hand rubbed Cortland's back briefly, then propelled her into the living room. "Have a seat." She gestured Dawson and Cortland to the sofa. Whining and barking sounds echoed down the hallway to the bedroom where the dogs, Toby and Maggie Mae, were sequestered.

"Thanks for coming, both of you," Andrew said, taking the lead after ensuring everyone had a drink. Cortland had settled on the sofa, leaving over a foot of space between her and Dawson.

Cortland glanced at Hannah and Andrew furtively. She took a gulp of her wine before asking, "What's going on?" Her eyes avoided Dawson's though she could feel his on her.

"We've decided to make it legal. And we'd really like you both to be in the wedding party as maid of honor and best man."

Dawson looked at the couple first, then his eyes slid to Cortland. "Just a maid of honor and a best man?" Dawson asked.

Hannah piped in, "I've asked Tulsi to be a bridesmaid. And Andrew's godson, Daniel, will be a ring bearer."

"Tulsi? Tulsi is coming too?" The excitement in Cortland's tone was unmistakable.

The bride-to-be chattered, "I know, isn't it exciting. All three of us together again."

Andrew interrupted his fiancée before she could ramble on, "You'll both do it?"

Simultaneously, Dawson and Cortland said, "I will."

"Perfect, Hannah and I are so happy. You'll both be helping us out."

## COURTING CHOICES

"I only have one question: what's the date? I need to know for work." Dawson said, sitting back against the sofa cushions, his arm slung along the top.

Cortland tensed slightly when he stuck his arm out in her direction. "Same for me, especially if Hannah is going to be away on an extended honeymoon."

"Fear not, my brave associate. We're only going away for a long weekend. One you are already scheduled to cover."

Cortland was silent as she sipped her wine. Dawson was also quiet.

Andrew picked up the lagging conversation. "We'll get married at St. Thomas Church at eight p.m. The reception is for family only at the Elks Club hall down the street. Well, you two are invited, of course!" He hesitantly chuckled as if afraid of what their silence meant.

Dawson asked with a tone of exasperation in his voice. "What's the date?"

"Oops, sorry. The wedding is Friday night, July 1st. We'll return Monday night."

Dawson pulled out his phone and began scrolling. "I have that day off and the day before. If there's any decorating to do at the hall, I can help, but I'm always on-call in case something big goes down."

Doing the same, Cortland said, "I'm on-call that weekend, starting Friday." She glanced up and held Hannah's eyes.

Andrew piped in. "I've arranged for Dr. Paul Tabs to cover on Friday. He's the vet in the next town over. My new assistant will handle the animal control office."

Andrew, Dawson, and Hannah chatted together as Cortland opened her phone to add the date to her calendar. "You're going to pull off a wedding in six weeks? I better get on arranging the bridal shower quickly!"

"No shower. Promise me, Cortland. I do not want a bridal shower or anything similar." Hannah's voice was full of menace, and her body tense.

"Can't say I'm not relieved about that. Are you sure? Don't say that unless you truly mean it."

"Oh, I do mean it. I mean every word of it."

Cortland looked back at her phone's calendar app. Her eyes lit up, and her voice was full of disbelief. "That's the Fourth of July weekend."

Andrew's eyes widened as he slapped his forehead with his palm. "Oh, crap. I can't believe that didn't even register in my brain."

Standing up to refill his glass, Dawson looked at the three of them. "I'll probably get called in for extra duty that weekend. Especially if the fire hazard is high. We often have small fires break out from firework cinders."

Cortland softly said, "Fourth of July weekend is a disaster for animal control and for the vet clinic. Dogs get scared of the noise and run. We get dozens of calls at the clinic for sedatives." She looked at both Hannah and Andrew. "But you're returning the night of the fourth? Right?"

"Right. We don't know when we'll be back, but—"

"You could get a phone call asking for help," Cortland smirked.

Andrew's eyebrows rose. "You can try."

• • • •

Cortland and Dawson walked away from the apartment after their goodbyes to the couple. She skirted ahead as the sidewalk narrowed, picking up her pace.

Dawson called out, "Wait up, please."

Cortland's body stiffened as she halted, turned, and watched him jog to catch up. Her eyes roamed up and down his body. His jeans were standard fare, but he filled them out as though they might be a little too small for his brawny frame. His T-shirt also seemed too small as it outlined his wide sturdy chest, broad shoulders, and muscular upper arms. Clinging to his belly, it hinted at rock-hard abs. Her mouth watered as she continued to stare, and she itched to explore his fine figure.

"I was wondering if we could have another try at a date? Maybe a hike or bike ride?" He asked, his hands now stuffed in his pockets but his eyes not leaving hers.

A flame ignited in her chest and lower. "Yes, I'd like that. But it'll have to be after next weekend. I'll be out of the state from Friday night until Monday morning."

"How about Tuesday?" When she nodded, he asked, "Can I get your phone number?" He reached for his back pocket.

A tremor ran through her gut. "You don't have it?" It became clear why he hadn't called her as he said he would. She reached for his phone.

Relinquishing it, he waited, bouncing on the balls of his sneakered feet as she punched in her number, hit send, and handed it back to him.

A cell phone rang in her purse, giving them assurance he had it. "And now I have yours as well." She smiled. She'd promised herself she'd make it up to him for cutting their first date short. "Call before Friday night. The cell phone doesn't work where I'm heading."

The statement seemed to pique his interest, but he didn't ask. She wasn't offering the location or reason.

"It was great seeing you tonight." He said, gesturing to her. "You look great."

Again she smiled. "Just jeans and a t-shirt like you."

"Yup." His beautiful broad smile emerged. "Excellent. I'll call you with details later in the week."

# CHAPTER SEVEN

Cortland had stopped at the clinic early Friday morning before her flight to Alaska. "Doctor Stewart, line two, urgent. It's your father."

Cortland sprang forward in her office chair, tossing the keyboard out of the way before reaching for the phone line. "Daddy? What's wrong?" Her voice trembled.

"Cortland." He paused, sobbing heavily. "Faith. Your Aunt Faith."

Leaping to her feet, Cortland demanded, "What? What happened?"

It was a few seconds before he could control his sobbing and speak again. "Pulmonary embolism, honey. She went fast."

As the news sank in, tears fell down her cheeks. "A pulmonary embolism? But how?"

"You know as well as I, it's a rare but possible complication of a long bone fracture. Probably a fat emboli."

Heavy with emotion, Cortland barely recognized his voice. She slumped down into her office chair. "My God. I was supposed to fly out this afternoon."

"Probably a good thing you already have plane reservations." He sniffed. "My office manager is rearranging my patient schedule and booking flights. Her attorney called to say I'm her executor, so I may be there a while."

Fear shot through Cortland's chest, rattling her further. "Are Mom and Greg coming with you?"

"I don't think so. She's taken to her bed. Greg hasn't uttered a word since the phone call."

They were both quiet, as quiet as two weeping adults could be. "I—I can't believe it. She said she had some things to discuss with me. We thought we had plenty of time."

## COURTING CHOICES

"There's no such thing as plenty of time. We both know that from previous experience, if not from our professions," her father said, his tone miserable.

The statement knocked the wind out of her lungs. He was right, of course, but the reference to Jessica's untimely death compounded the feelings of loss. "I ... I have to make some phone calls." She started to remove the phone from her ear but stopped. "Daddy, I love you."

"I love you too, Munchkin." His sobbing increased. "Keep me posted on your flight p— plans."

· · · ·

Looking over the list of available firefighter jobs on the website brought a shiver to Dawson's spine. He scanned the list as he scrolled down with his mouse. There were lots of jobs out there, but many were entry-level. Nearly all wanted at least Emergency Medical Technician certification. Some jobs wanted paramedic-level medical training. Dawson grunted. He had the EMT cert, so he was good there. And he knew he didn't want a paramedic position embedded in the fire department. He wasn't qualified for that and certainly didn't want that level of medical responsibility.

Continuing to scroll, he noticed a few industry jobs. While the idea was interesting and probably better salaried than municipal jobs, the unease in his mind led him to continue searching. *Hmm, an airport firefighter.* Clicking the posting for Homer, Alaska, he reviewed the mandatory job requirements. They wanted airport rescue firefighting training and six months of experience. *Nope, not qualified.*

He checked a few more firefighter job postings: Georgia, Louisiana, Texas, San Diego, Las Vegas, Florida, and New Mexico. *Too hot!* And the position in Louisiana was only paying $17.25 an hour.

*Screw that!* He hadn't worked his butt off in Colby to go backward. His determination to find a lateral move strengthened. The last thing he wanted was to make less money, though he was open to possibilities, provided it was still above a captain's position.

Captain. Jackson's words came back to him. He'd been fortunate to get where he was today. Unease in his gut swirled, thinking he'd only gotten so far because of his father's death. Maybe getting into the department as a rookie had been because of his father, but he'd busted his ass to measure up and excel to the best of his ability. The ache in his gut turned sour. He knew he could go further if given a chance. But as Jackson had hinted, it wasn't likely to happen here in Colby. Even if the higher-ups respected his father's sacrifice.

Dad. The anniversary of his death was coming up. Dawson clenched his teeth, thinking of yet another church service and cemetery visit with his mother. She had been so stoic during his father's funeral. Yet every year of remembrance since made it harder for her. And he and his sister were the only ones to pick up the pieces.

This year would be especially hard. His own thirty-first birthday was just around the corner. Despite the idea's absurdity, he couldn't help but wonder if he'd die this year. His father had died at thirty-one. Was he meant to as well? And if he didn't die, how would he feel living longer than his father?

His cell phone rang. It was Jackson. "Yup."

"Daw, want to come over for dinner. I bought a bunch of baby back ribs. They'll be marinating all afternoon."

"Sounds good. Can I bring anything?"

"Just yourself."

Dawson was going to hang up but thought of something. "Hey, before you hang up. How's your back doing?"

"Oh, it's as cranky as me," Jackson said. "I'll see you later."

His focus went back to the computer screen but not for long. Daggers embedded in his legs diverted his attention as Smokey climbed up into his lap. Not to be outdone, Sadie tried to join her sister. Rather

## COURTING CHOICES

than have another set of claw marks up his leg, Dawson plucked the yellow tabby off the side of his jeans and set her down in his lap.

Over the next hour, he selected a handful of job postings to respond to with his résumé. Iowa, Colorado, Pittsburgh, Illinois, Virginia, Massachusetts, and Anchorage, Alaska. All while trying to keep both kittens off his computer keyboard. At the last minute, he added a position in San Francisco to the list. It was hard to forgo the opportunity for a six-digit salary, even if it was in earthquake and brushfire country.

His frustration escalated as the kittens wouldn't sit still. Fed up with the constant distraction, he scooped up his charges and deposited them on the couch. To keep them there, he dumped out the bag of cat treats next to them. They pounced on it greedily.

Three hours later, eyes burning, he shut down the computer and stood up from the desk in the corner of his living room. He glanced over at the couch and chuckled. The kittens were snuggled together, sound asleep. Heading to the kitchen for a drink, he was diverted back to the desk when his cell phone rang.

He glanced at the caller ID. He raised his eyebrows when he saw it was Cortland. Snatching up the phone, he answered before it rolled to voicemail, "Hey."

"Hey yourself," she said but didn't continue.

He sensed a reluctance on her part. Curious at her call and hesitation, he probed. "I've been meaning to call. So, to what do I owe this ... contact." He walked back to the kitchen with his cell phone on speaker.

"Yeah, I, um, need a favor." Cortland's words came out piecemeal, like she chewed and contemplated each.

He grabbed a beer from the fridge, popped the cap off, and took a long chug. When she didn't continue, he blurted out, "Well, what do you need from me?" Immediately he regretted his gruff tone. "What can I do for you?" he said a little more gently.

"I have to leave town. Can you possibly cat-sit for the weekend?" Her voice wavered.

"If you can bring them over, sure. They're related, and what's a few more? When do you need me?" He wiped the condensate off the side of the bottle into the sink.

"Tonight. The person who was supposed to do it canceled at the last minute. I expect to be gone for three to four days. I can give you food and disposable litter boxes for them."

"Sure. That's fine." He paused. "What about your dog? Harrigan?"

"Harris. Hannah and Andrew are going to take him. He's best buds with Maggie and Toby."

*Trip?* His curiosity was piqued now. "Where you going?"

"Alaska." She sniffled. "I have a funeral to attend."

Feeling like an ass for probing, he quickly said, "I'm sorry. Is there anything else I can do?"

Listening intently now, he could hear her muffled sobbing. She must have put her hand over the microphone. "Hey, I'm sorry."

"I heard you." She sighed heavily. "Thank you. For your help. I'll bring them over in an hour or so. Is that okay?"

"No problem. Do you know where I live?" Trying to lighten the conversation, he gently teased, "Or have you been stalking me at home too?"

He smiled when he heard her chuckle briefly. His heart lightened, knowing he'd brought some levity to their conversation.

"I haven't stalked you at home—yet. But if you give me your address, it will be easier than following you home."

His chest warmed at the tone of her voice. Still grinning, he gave her the address.

Dawson glanced around the apartment kitchen and living room, two large rooms separated by a breakfast bar. Everywhere he looked, he saw detritus. By the time Cortland arrived, he'd transferred all the dirty mugs, glasses, and dirty plates to the dishwasher and straightened up the couch pillows, though it disturbed Smokey and Sadie. They immediately wanted to play while he tried to fold the throw. When he placed it over the back of the couch, the kittens started to climb it, knocking it back down helter-skelter on the couch. "Hey, ladies!" He shook them off it and replaced it only to have them scamper up it once more. Dawson rolled his eyes.

The doorbell rang. He groaned, his eyes scanning the area. *Not too shabby now.*

Cortland stood outside, a cat carrier in one hand and a paper bag in the other. "Hi." She stared up into his eyes as he reached and took the carrier for her. "Thanks."

She entered the living room, setting the bag down. "There's food, treats, and toys in here, along with those disposable litter boxes."

"One for each kitten?" He said, glancing up as he freed the two kittens from the carrier. "What's their names, anyway?"

"The yellow one I call 'Marm,' short for marmalade. The white with black spots is "Moo."

He raised an eyebrow, "As in moo-cow?" When she nodded, he added with a smile, "Very original."

She ignored his comment, glancing down to watch the four kittens reunite on the floor. They immediately started to play together. "That went well."

"Did you think they wouldn't play nice?" He smirked.

"There's always the possibility, though they've only been separated for about three weeks."

"Was it sudden?" He cringed, not believing he'd asked such an insensitive question.

Her lips pressed together, Cortland nodded, her eyes visibly filling up.

*Jackass, now you made her cry.* "I'm sorry I asked."

"No, it's okay. I should get used to it." She wiped her cheek with her palm. "It was sudden. My Aunt Faith, my father's sister. She broke a bone a week or so ago and had a pulmonary embolism. If you know what that is."

His medical training had taught him about PE. Enough to know there wasn't much an EMT or paramedic could do about it, in the field anyway. And when it struck the lungs, it tended to be fatal. "I do know. I'm sorry."

She reached down and stroked each kitten's back. "It was fast. I guess I should be grateful for that. I just wish I had been there. Maybe …" She couldn't continue, and a new rush of tears streaked down her face.

"I'm truly sorry." Stepping forward, he grasped her hand. "Do you need a ride to the airport?"

"No, Hannah is going to drop me off." She retreated hastily to the door. "Thanks for everything." She turned back toward him, her face fractured with pain. "Got to go. If you have any problems with the cats, call Andrew or Hannah. The cell phone service in Alaska is sketchy at best."

"Of course. Don't worry about us. Have a safe journey. If you want to reschedule Tuesday's hike, just say the word. We can do it another time."

"I'll let you know. Tuesday's hike might be exactly what I need after this weekend."

He followed her to the door. Snatching her hand, he pulled her gently around. As his thumb caressed the back of her hand, their eyes met. "Be careful." With a nod, she turned back, and he let her go. From the porch, he watched her drive away.

Alone again, he sat on the couch, letting the four kittens crawl and play over and around him. He'd wanted to ask her out about their date, but it clearly hadn't been the right time. Maybe he could tackle it when she returned to pick up Marmalade and Moo.

Now, he needed to get over to Jackson's for barbeque.

## CHAPTER EIGHT

Her father stood at her side just inside the door of Hope Christian Church as people filtered out. They thanked each person individually for coming to Faith's memorial service and joining them for refreshments. Last she had checked, the sandwiches, slices of homemade pie, and beverages were holding out. She was glad she had listened to the funeral home owner's recommendation. Neither she nor her father had anticipated such a crowd.

"I thought Aunt Faith kept to herself mostly?" Cortland whispered to her father.

"I thought so too. I guess not." He whispered back before greeting the next person.

Overhead, the ceiling was sectioned with darkly stained pine logs. The whitewashed walls of the large meeting room were still hung with pictures of prospectors panning for gold in nearby Resurrection Creek and the former downtown area as it had looked during the gold rush times. The sepia tone of the town images was the only clue the photos were of yesteryear. A quick look outside would not show much difference. Hope was considered one of the best-preserved gold rush communities in southern Alaska.

Cortland smiled, her heart heavy, remembering when Uncle Mayer and Aunt Faith had taken her out to the creek to try her luck. She had loved panning for gold. There were always a few tiny flakes in her pan. Somewhere, she had saved them all.

The catering staff was beginning to package up the leftover food, dodging people who grabbed paper plates and started piling them with food to take home. The five ten-foot tables still held a lot of food, much of it from the caterer but also from friends. Everyone had pitched in for the assembly.

Glancing around the social hall, Cortland was pretty sure every one of the two hundred residents of Hope was in attendance. And a bunch from the surrounding towns. It was not surprising, really. Faith had been a resident in town for over fifty years. Now, she would be forever on the homestead, resting beside Uncle Mayer in the back pasture.

"Cortland? Gracious me, I can hardly believe it's you! You're all grown up," an older woman said, reaching out to take her hand.

"Mrs. Winters?" Gently, she hugged the woman, who must be well into her eighties by now.

The woman's face lit with delight. "You remembered! That's so sweet. But you always were the sweet one." Mrs. Winters' hand shook with a tremor.

*Palsy? Parkinson's?* Cortland was too polite to ask. "This is my father, Kirk Stewart. Faith was his sister."

"The doctor? Oh, she told me all about you."

Kirk Stewart nodded with a shy smile. "I guess my reputation precedes me."

Cortland jumped in to change the subject, "How are you? I haven't seen you in at least ten or more years."

"Hmm, you may be right. It has been a while." She stepped closer. "You know, every time Faith and I got together, she always told me a story about your escapades when you came to visit."

Cortland felt the ache in the center of her chest tighten. "Oh my gosh, I always was getting into some minor mischief. Thankfully, Aunt Faith was patient. I loved every minute I was here."

"I know she was looking forward to your visit this weekend before she died, of course." Giving her hand a squeeze, she added, "I'm so sorry you missed seeing her one last time."

A lump formed in her throat as her eyes filled with tears. "I'll always regret not getting here sooner."

Mrs. Winters wiped Cortland's cheek free of teardrops. "Don't you let that regret eat you up. She understood you couldn't get here any earlier. And only the Almighty knew he would call her home before you could arrive."

# COURTING CHOICES

Patting Cortland's cheek one last time, Mrs. Winters walked out the door.

Turning back toward the room, Cortland sighed heavily. Thankfully, the hall was nearly empty. A cluster of women had helped the caterer pack up the leftover food, which the few remaining men transferred to Cortland's rented minivan. As the last of them said their goodbyes, another woman stopped to take Cortland's hand. "It's wonderful to see you back." Wiping a tear off her cheek, she added, "Faith was so looking forward to seeing you this weekend." The woman patted her hand twice before departing.

Tears stung Cortland's eyes, and she turned away to compose herself. Far more people she didn't remember had recognized her as the happy-go-lucky child of her youth. Most had stopped to speak with her and reminisce. She had maintained her composure until now, when the weight of her loss and the fatigue of the journey and time change assaulted her energy.

A couple of deep breaths later, blinking wildly, she turned back, pasting a smile on her face. "Let's get out of here. Time to feed the critters." Her father's hand settled on her shoulder, helping to guide her outside to the rental car. "See you at the house. I have some things to tell you before you leave tomorrow." He walked to his own rental car and drove off.

・・・・

Back at the homestead, Cortland tried to think of what her father needed to divulge as they carried all the food into the house. When they finished, the refrigerator was full to the rim, the counters covered with a dozen or more pies.

"You didn't eat much at the reception. Want anything now?" her father asked.

"Not really hungry. I think the long flights and the change of time zones messed my stomach up."

She ignored the dubious look he gave her before leaving the room. Instead, letting her eyes roam the kitchen.

It hadn't changed from the first day she saw it. The pine board shelving was still sturdy under the weight of plates, bowls, mugs, and old jelly jars for glasses. The white porcelain deep single basin sink still held the gray dishpan. Dish towels still hung from the handle of the gas range. The range, a relic, still perked the coffee in a percolator for their breakfast or heated tea water in a small saucepan. It felt strange to be surrounded by little technology: no dishwasher, no Keurig or Mr. Coffee, no waffle iron, no blender, no food processor. Aunt Faith and Uncle Mayer had only ever had the bare minimum and had been happy with that.

Her father's talk certainly couldn't be about money. He had already had a look at the finances. Aunt Faith had been barely subsisting, eking her way through the last years of her life. A thickness formed in her throat when she thought about how her aunt must have suffered. Why hadn't she considered Aunt Faith's circumstances? Why hadn't she sent her money? All those times they talked. Every Monday and she had never asked if she needed money. Shaking her head, she knew Aunt Faith would never have mentioned her destitute circumstances. *I should have guessed it.*

She thumped the old fridge's door with both open palms. Ashamed at her lack of sensitivity, Cortland let the tears roll as she stared out the window at the back pasture. It was still light enough to see the fresh mound of dirt beside Uncle Mayer's tombstone. Rubbing her eyes, she knew it would be another long sleepless night in the land of the midnight sun.

"Cort, you got a few minutes?" Her father beckoned her to the kitchen table with a wave of his hand. "I was hoping to speak with you before the funeral, but with all your flight delays, you got in too late this morning for me to talk with you quietly."

## COURTING CHOICES

"Yeah, that seven a.m. arrival that was supposed to be at four a.m. really screwed up a lot."

Once settled, he took her hand. "There's something I didn't tell you yet about my talk with the attorney." He squeezed her shaking hand as he tried to meet her eyes.

She closed them, took a deep breath, and then opened them, staring at her father. "I'm listening," she whispered.

"Your aunt loved you. Probably more so you than any other member of the family, excluding her husband, of course." He cleared his throat before continuing. "Her will specified the homestead is to pass to you."

Cortland slowly blinked twice as she tried to digest what her father had said. "Me? She left it to me?"

"The house, the barns, a hundred acres of land, and everything in them. All the animals, everything."

"Holy crap." Her eyes, already sore from crying, started stinging again as big fat tears filled them. "Everything?"

He nodded gently. "Yes. Everything. There won't be any money after the doctors get paid, etc. But other than that, everything passes to you."

Unable to breathe, unable to utter a word, Cortland's mouth clamped shut, her lips pressed together.

"I'm going to see about selling the animals. To give you time to decide what to do with the place."

Her head dropped back, exposing her long slender neck. "No. Don't sell them just yet. I'll pay to have Wally take care of them. If he can." She grimaced. "Can you arrange that? At least until I think it all through?"

Nodding again, he said, "I think he'll do it. Like everyone else here in Hope, he could use the extra money."

She pushed her chair back from the table, the legs scraping the floor. "I'm going to bed."

"Wait. One more thing." Her father rose from his chair. "I looked around the house for Faith's valuables. Her engagement ring, other jewelry, and any cash. I know she inherited a sapphire brooch from our mother. Except for a box full of broken and junk jewelry, I didn't find them."

Cortland thought for a moment. "Considering her bank account, do you think perhaps she sold the ring and the brooch for cash to keep the place going?"

He shrugged. "It's possible. I hate to think both are gone. But dire straits require hard choices. Someone could also have gone through her belongings before we arrived too."

"Doubt that. I find it hard to imagine anyone here in Hope would do such a thing. Especially after today's turnout."

"You've got a point there. Don't worry about it. We'll come across them eventually." He kissed her cheek. "Good night, Munchkin. See you in the morning."

Retiring to her room, Cortland pulled down the shades, blocking the glow. It was after midnight, but still light enough out that she could see everything clearly. Changing into her yoga pants and T-shirt, she settled into the bed, pulling the sheet and the handmade quilt up, despite the warmth in her old upstairs bedroom. Drifting off, she fell asleep listening to the horses and cows lowing and neighing softly to each other through the open window.

Two hours before it was time to leave the next afternoon, she made the rounds. Little had changed since her days here as a young teen. She marveled, remembering each particular: the old bird bath with its white paint mostly worn off, the line of buckets set out to catch rainwater off the barn's metal roof for the gardens and animal troughs. The ax and maul for splitting wood or making kindling when the wood stove was running. And the old wheelbarrow, now rusting profusely, made her smile with the memory of Uncle Mayer's wheelbarrow rides when she was a child.

## COURTING CHOICES

Stepping off the porch, elevated three feet to keep the house's first floor above much of the snow in the winter, she headed for the barn. Walking past Aunt Faith's herb garden, she admired the size of the plants. Everything grew big in Alaska during the summer with nearly twenty-four hours of constant sunlight. Around the corner was the cutting garden, filled with massive cosmos, Shasta daisies, dahlias, salvia, and a few irises which had just finished blooming from the looks of their light brown stalks. There were a lot of other flowers she didn't recognize. And a lot of weeds. *Who would weed the gardens?* She picked a bunch of different flowers and carried her bouquet on her journey.

Entering the front of the largest barn, Cortland said her farewells at the pen of rabbits and the attached chicken coop. Most of the hens were roosting there at this hour.

Exiting into the paddock, her pals, the horses, and the cows must have sensed her imminent departure. They gathered around her, nudging her side, arms, and hands, looking for a parting caress. Several tried to nibble the flowers, but Cortland managed to save them from consumption. Pegasus nosed her shoulder. She scratched his favorite spot, the poll, and chuckled softly as the horse closed his eyes in apparent blissful enjoyment of her ministrations. She hugged his neck, burying her face in his black mane. "Be good. I'll be back."

Wandering farther, she crossed the field of sheep and goats, finally arriving at the burial plot for her aunt and uncle. Splitting the bouquet, she laid half of the flowers on each grave. Tears welled in her eyes, spilling down her cheeks.

Her hands empty, she crossed her arms and clutched her sides, hugging herself as she wept and said her goodbyes. It would likely be a while before she could get back.

"Thank you for putting the homestead in my hands. I'll try to do what's best for it. And me."

• • • •

Standing outside Dawson's front door early Monday afternoon, Cortland rang the doorbell again. *Crap! I texted him twice to let him know I was coming by to get the kittens.* He never did answer. His truck was not in the driveway. Though it might be in the garage. *Is he on duty today at the firehouse? Should I call instead?*

Snatching her cell phone out of her back pocket, she dialed. Cortland could hear a cell phone ringing on the other side of the solid wood door. So much for that. *Maybe he's in the bathroom? Or out in the backyard?*

Walking around the side of the house, she saw a patio enclosed by a short brick wall. It was furnished with a large stainless-steel grill, a comfortable-looking table with six chairs, and a sun umbrella. Sliding doors into the house were open, showing four kittens napping in a sunbeam inside a screen door.

The comfort and perks of his house made her wish for one of her own. Not to say her apartment was small. As part of a luxury complex, the two-bedroom apartment had a spacious kitchen area big enough for a table separated from the cathedral-ceilinged living room by a granite-topped breakfast bar.

Glancing around the backyard and patio of Dawson's home, she thought how much Harris would enjoy the space. And like their siblings, Moo and Marm would enjoy that big sunny spot beyond the patio doors.

Peeping through the sliding screen doors, she caught a movement a few feet beyond the kittens. Dawson! Cortland's mouth went dry while butterflies did loopy things low in her belly. He was naked, dripping wet, a short towel slung over his shoulder. *Jiminy crickets! If he sees me* … Cortland didn't finish the thought. Afraid to turn around and draw his attention, her split-second decision was to slowly back away. Blindly stepping away from the glass, she crashed into a chair, knocking it over. Tripping, she landed flat on her back beside the toppled chair.

## COURTING CHOICES

The sun blinded her temporarily as she lay there silently assessing if she was hurt and then hoping that Dawson hadn't heard the crash or seen her tumble.

The slide of the screen door and a grunt answered her prayer. Shading her eyes with a hand, she stared up at Dawson, struggling to wrap the too-small towel around his waist. He finally gave up, just holding it before his groin.

"What the hell are you doing in my backyard?" His tone was ungracious, his eyes searching around.

Dropping her hand and lowering her eyes to look elsewhere, Cortland mustered a response. "I wasn't getting an answer at your front door, but I could hear your phone ringing when I called. I, umm, I thought maybe something happened to you like you were hurt or something."

She peeked open one eye to find Dawson standing over her, his broad, muscular chest covered with water droplets glistening in the sunlight. Every inch of him was gorgeous. Her eyes rose from his feet up his powerfully built legs to the point they disappeared behind the towel.

"I was in the shower," he growled. He sighed before adding, "Are you hurt?"

Unable to take her eyes off his magnificent body, Cortland could only mutter, "No."

"Good." He stared at her lying on the patio, looking uncomfortable as if unable to find anything to say. "Do you need help up?"

She was tempted to say yes, wondering if he'd move the small towel. Instead, she muttered, "I'm fine. Just need to catch my breath."

"Don't move. I'll be back in a minute." He turned around to head back into the house, giving her an eyeful.

Her breath stalled in her chest as she watched his firm backside flex with each stride. A shaft of light caught water droplets still clinging to the curves, and she sighed when he disappeared.

• • • •

Replacing the hand towel with jean shorts, he raced back to the patio, barefoot and not bothering with a shirt. She was struggling to get up when he returned. "I told you not to get up. You could be hurt." He held out his hand.

"The only thing injured is my dignity." She grasped his hand, letting him pull her to her feet before righting the chair and shoving it back into its place.

"Come in," he said, trying to keep his tone less grumpy. Talk about injured dignity. There was nothing like being caught naked.

"Thanks," Cortland walked through the doors as he stepped aside to let her pass. Inside the house, she stopped in the living room. "I came to pick up my kittens." Turning to face him, she added, "I texted you a couple times but didn't get a response."

"I saw your text about twenty minutes ago, after my workout. So I hopped in the shower."

Their eyes locked together, and they both said, "Sorry," simultaneously.

"Looks like they disappeared." Dawson glanced around the living room, but the kittens had long since scurried to parts unknown. He wished he had more clothes on. Maybe then Cortland would stop staring at his chest. Nearly laughing out loud with the irony of it, he covered his chuckle with a cough. He'd stared at her chest on their first date. Now he knew how she must have felt. "Can I get you anything?" He turned and headed toward the kitchen, successfully hoping that Cortland would follow him there. He poured a glass of water from a filtering pitcher on the countertop and offered it to her.

Their fingers brushed as she accepted it. A zing of awareness flashed like lightning up his arm and through his body, leaving behind a lingering heat. Turning back to the water pitcher, he poured himself a glass, hoping the few seconds would allow the heat to dissipate.

## COURTING CHOICES

"I really should get going." Cortland handed the half-full glass back to him. "Do you know where the kittens might be?"

He didn't trust his voice as a sunbeam hit the side of Cortland's head, illuminating her hair. Shiny, thick, and silky looking, he wanted to twist his fingers in it and draw her to him. He'd lift the weight of it off her neck, baring it for his lips to nibble on.

"Dawson?" She inquired, her tone hesitant.

"Um, yeah. They like to hang out on the spare bed." He set down his glass and headed down the hallway. Cortland hesitated to follow him, so he stopped outside the door. "Yup, they're all here."

Cortland joined him at the doorway. The four kittens were stretched out on the bed pillow, snoozing away. "I left my carrier outside the front door."

"I'll get it." Dawson retrieved the carrier and returned to find Cortland playing with the awakened kittens. Setting it on the end of the bed, he watched the five of them playing. *I'd like to play with her too.* The thought flashed through his mind, igniting his arousal again. "Do you want to change our outing tomorrow to another day? I won't mind."

Cortland looked up, astonishment on her beautiful face. "Umm, no. Tomorrow is good."

"Good. I know a nice relaxing place I think you'll enjoy." He stopped, not knowing what to say to make her at ease and not understanding the look on her face.

"Sounds like a good plan." She smiled, and the tension and breath held in his chest drained. "I'm not on-call. Where should I meet you?" She said as she scooped up her kittens and locked them in the carrier.

He gave her the directions and time to meet as he carried the kittens to her car.

Cortland nodded as she stood beside him at her car. "Thank you for taking care of Moo and Marm. I hope they were good."

"They were fine. All four were having a blast." He chuckled and then felt stupid. He hadn't even asked about the funeral. "How did everything go?" he asked softly.

Cortland's eyelids blinked rapidly. "As best as could be expected." She nodded. "I'll tell you more tomorrow. I'd like to get home."

"Of course," he said, feeling like an ass for not bringing it up sooner. Following her to the other side of the vehicle, he opened the door for her and stood aside. After she slid inside, he shut the door. Through the open window, he said. "Talk to you later."

She nodded before backing out and driving away.

• • • •

The morning dawned partly cloudy, which was good. The last thing Cortland wanted was to be hiking in the Hale Hollow State Forest in blistering heat. Thickly wooded as it looked, Cortland didn't want to make any more of a fool of herself than she was going to with her lack of coordination and stamina.

She looked down at her hiking boots. Bought yesterday after she dropped the cats off at home; they looked too new. Dawson might notice and question her about it. Scuffing around in the dirt beside her SUV, she kicked up a cloud of dust trying to make them look well used.

"Cripes, they hurt already," she muttered as she checked her watch one more time. *I should have worn them around the house last night to break them in a little. Or worn thicker socks.* The last thing she wanted was to stumble during the hike. Or start limping and have to admit her boots were brand new. Or that she hadn't hiked in the woods since her teen years.

Alaskan woods, actually. She hadn't gone hiking since her last full summer in Hope. She closed her eyes, trying not to think about the homestead. She'd called Wally to ask how things were going up there. Other than the miserable black flies and mosquitoes, he said everything and every one of the animals was doing okay. After the phone call she'd mailed him a check for his week's worth of work.

A crunching sound alerted her to Dawson arriving in his truck. Parking beside her vehicle, he got out of the truck with a daypack.

*Crap! I didn't bring any water!*

"Hi," she greeted him, trying to look cool, calm, and ready to trek through the forest.

"Hi. Sorry, I'm a few minutes late. I stopped to get us some cold water and snacks. Just in case." Dawson swung the pack over his left shoulder.

"Great idea." Cortland did what she thought was a runner's lunge stretch to try to distract him from the fact she wasn't adequately prepared. But she lost her balance and started to fall over, her arms flailing.

Dawson grabbed her upper arm, but his grip unbalanced her move, sending her body spinning toward him. Her chest smacked into his, and both his arms went around her. "Whoa, woman. Are you okay?" He held her tightly against his body.

*Whoa, is right! His chest is like a brick wall.* Her face flushed hotly as she maneuvered her feet steady under her body. His arms remained around her.

"Umm, I think I got a little dizzy from the heat." She straightened up, and he released her.

"Maybe this isn't such a good idea today. Last I checked, the heat index was nearly one hundred. The spot we're heading to should be cooler."

Cortland shook her head. "No, please. I'll be fine."

He eyed her outfit. "Denim shorts and a tank top? No hat?"

She quickly remembered she had a baseball cap in her vehicle. "Oops. Forgot it." She turned to head back to her SUV.

"Did you apply sunscreen?" he yelled after her.

She rolled her eyes, grateful she had her back to him so he couldn't see her face. "Of course not."

"Geez, woman."

She glanced over her shoulder to find him shaking his head and stalking back to his truck.

They met up again, Cortland with her ball cap on, Dawson with a bottle of waterproof sunscreen that he handed her.

She spread the lotion on her arms, neck, upper chest, and legs before trying to reach her upper back unsuccessfully.

"Need help?"

She glanced at him before relenting and giving him the can. His hands were warm as they spread the sticky lotion along her shoulders and upper back. She tried not to shiver at the scrape of calluses rubbing in the lotion, over and over again.

After a few minutes, he was finished and tucked the can into his pack.

Cortland gave him a sidelong look. "Are we ready? Shall we go?"

He might have started to say yes, but he stopped. "Wait a minute. I forgot to spray myself with bug spray. Mosquitoes and ticks love me." He returned from his truck with a can of bug spray. Spraying himself all over, especially his legs, he stopped to find Cortland watching. "Need some?"

"Sure. Never hurts." She closed her eyes, covering them with her hand. *What the hell? I even forgot about the insect factor.* If her eyes had been open, she would have rolled them.

Dawson turned the spray on her. Her eyes were still closed as he sprayed her front side before grabbing her hip and nudging her to turn around. The contact was unexpected, and a lightning bolt sizzled through her.

Tossing the can into the pack, Dawson slung it back over his shoulder and said, "Let's do this."

## COURTING CHOICES

Dawson led the way along the well-trod trail, frequently looking back as if she might disappear. They didn't talk much as it was only a single path. Occasionally, Dawson stopped to point out particular plants or animal tracks. He seemed to know about flora and fauna in these woods.

Cortland had to admit she was impressed. She wasn't familiar with the Connecticut woodlands, though she was more attuned to the animals. Several times each week, especially this time of year, clinic clients called or brought in hurt or "orphaned" wildlife. Especially fawns, only to be told to return it to the exact spot they found it and walk away. Fawns were often left alone by their mothers to protect them. Being scentless, the fawns could easily hide in the tall weeds while their mothers went to feed.

It wasn't long before Cortland's feet started to bother her. She could feel the blisters growing inside her boots. Try as she might, she could not help limping even if it was as slight as she could make it.

Dawson must have noticed because he pointed to a small, grassy clearing beside a babbling brook after nearly an hour of hiking. "Let's have a rest."

She settled down in the enchanting scene. Lush, cool grass speckled with wildflowers and dappled sunlight from the newly leafed trees surrounded the glade. The brook wasn't deep, but the bottom was stony, giving it a gurgling sound as the water passed through.

Reaching into his pack, Dawson handed Cortland a can of water. It was still cool, the outside wet with condensate. "Thanks," she said, popping the top and gulping its contents. As she watched, Dawson pulled out a thin blanket he spread over the grass and then a can of water for himself.

After they both sat down, he pulled a bunch of snacks from the pack before laying them out on the blanket. There were cookies, a can of peanuts, potato chips, a small container of red pepper hummus, and a box of crackers. "Help yourself," he said, opening each package and placing them before her.

"Wow. You certainly come prepared." She shook a handful of peanuts into her palm and started munching them one at a time.

Scooping a wad of hummus onto his cracker, he smiled. That brilliant, sexy smile warmed her thoroughly. Brushing the salt residue from her hands, she reached for a cracker and dipped it into the hummus. "Mmm, that's good. I've never had hummus before."

He raised an eyebrow. "Never?"

"Never."

"What else have you never done?" He smiled.

Cortland chuckled. "Let's see ... I've never gotten a speeding ticket. Never been skinny-dipping and, hmm, oh, never forgot a credit card payment."

"My, my, you don't live very dangerously, do you?" He was teasing her, but she didn't mind. Between the view and the cooler climate beside the shady brook, it was lovely where they sat.

"What about you?" She eyed him as he contemplated his response.

"Well, I have done all those things you haven't." He grinned and munched a handful of peanuts before continuing. "But I have never broken a bone, never been skydiving or bungee-jumping. And I've never ridden a horse."

Surprise shot through Cortland. She couldn't keep the suspicion from the tone in her voice. "Really? You've never ridden a horse?"

"Nope."

Feeling bolder, she asked, "How about your love life? Girlfriends? Engaged? Previously married?"

"My love life has been very tame. One or two girlfriends, never engaged and thus, never married." He looked her in the eyes as he answered as though he wanted to be sure she knew he wasn't joking. "And you?"

"None of the above." She admitted with a shrug.

## COURTING CHOICES

It was Dawson's turn to look suspicious. "I find that hard to believe."

"It's true. I've dated once in a while. But I never had time for a boyfriend."

He cocked his head. "Why is that?"

She shook her head and raised her eyes to the sky briefly. "It takes four years of undergraduate college plus another four years of veterinary school. I didn't have time between all that studying."

"How about before college? Nothing in high school?"

Her mind searched back to those years, all those terrible years. "None."

• • • •

Dawson watched Cortland's expression change from happy and relaxed, even amused, to something dark and painful. Remembering the same look from their first date, he was curious but knew he'd have to tread lightly. "Your tone suggests those years were not the best. What was wrong?"

Closing her eyes with a quick exhale through her nose, she was silent a moment. "My family life was difficult."

"If you don't mind me asking, how so?" He focused his full attention on her face and her body language. There was something very traumatic hiding there. He could hear it in the tone of her voice and the tension that invaded her body.

She was silent again for a few moments. "My elder sister died in a car crash when I was young. My family never got over it." She looked into his eyes. "And there you have it."

Dawson was silent for a few minutes. "I know what that feels like. To lose someone you love. When my dad died, everything changed in an instant. No matter how much people tried to make it so, it was never the same again."

She nodded, dropping her head, her chin hitting her chest, her fingers twisting a blade of grass.

*Time to change the tone of the conversation.* "I have an idea. My feet are hot and tired." He unlaced his battered hiking boots, tugged off his thick wool socks, and dug his toes into the soft, cool grass. "Come on. Take your boots off." He leaned over and pulled the shoestring.

"No, that's okay, you go ahead." She pulled her booted feet out of his reach.

His gut told him something was wrong. Why was she hiding her feet? "Come on, it will feel great." When she didn't relent, he added, "Okay, so I won't either." He reached out for his socks and started to put them back on his feet.

Grimacing, she said nothing but unlaced her boots and slipped them off. His breath caught in his chest as she peeled off her red-blotched cotton socks.

Her feet were angry red, blistered, and bloody in some places, especially the heels.

"My God, your feet."

A heavy veil of embarrassment covered her face. "Don't look. They're hideous."

"Don't look? You can't put those back on. Are they the wrong size?"

She sighed heavily. "No. If you must know, they're brand new. I bought them yesterday afternoon."

"I take it you haven't been hiking for a while?"

She winced. "Not since high school."

Shaking his head, Dawson stood up. "I have a first aid kit in the truck, but it's too far away. You'll just have to numb them up in the cold water." Then he bent down, picked her up in his arms as though she were a small child, carried her over to the brook, and set her down on the bank. She slipped her feet into the cool water. The expression of relief washing over her face lightened his heart.

## COURTING CHOICES

He sat beside her and stuck his into the water also. His size thirteen feet dwarfed hers. "What size do you wear? Two?"

Laughing, she nudged her side against his upper arm. "Six."

They sat quietly like that for some time, watching the water slip by, caressing the heat and swelling from their feet. Slipping his arm around her, he tucked her head against his chest. She fit perfectly.

The unpleasant weekend, the food, the exercise, or maybe the quiet and comfort of his arm around her lulled her eyes to close briefly.

"Let's go take a nap on the blanket. It's a perfect day for it," Dawson suggested.

Nodding her head, Cortland stirred languorously, leaving the shelter of his arms. They lay on the blanket on their sides, facing each other.

His hand cupped the side of her face, his thumb feeling its smooth, delicate curve. "Close your eyes and rest. You're safe with me."

Dawson rolled onto his back. Cortland snuggled up to his side and promptly fell asleep.

The afternoon was fading by the time Dawson awoke. Side by side, Dawson cuddled her in the flattened grass as she snoozed. The dappled sunlight through the cottonwood and red maple trees highlighted her auburn hair, the curve of her eyebrows, and the lips he had hoped to feast on more times than he could remember. Her beauty stirred him.

Her lack of experience unnerved him. At thirty, he was at least five years older than she. It hardly seemed possible she was still a virgin. Not that he doubted her word. Her single-minded drive to become a vet had probably been the focus that saved her from her bad home life. Between that and those trips to Alaska, she'd turned out okay. Sensitive and hesitant at times, but still okay.

Allowing him that close would be an honor if she chose to have sex with him. It would have to be on her terms, at her initiation. Until then, if it came, he'd hold back and concentrate on making her feel comfortable and happy.

Glancing up at the sky, he noticed it was getting late, and they still had to get back to his truck. It was a good hour's hike back to the parking lot ahead of them. And there were Cortland's feet to consider.

"Cort, babe, wake up. It's time we head back." He gently nudged her, speaking softly in her ear. An ear he wanted to bite, but he didn't dare.

"Mmmm," she replied, turning into him and draping her arm over his chest.

"Cortland, time to go," he tried again.

Her eyelids blinked open, her hand rising to block out the rays of sunlight peeking through the leaves. "Oh-kay." She sat up. "Where are my boots?"

He shook his head. There was no way she was putting those on again. Not for a couple of weeks anyway, if he had any say in the matter. "You'll have to ride piggyback."

"Piggyback? You'd do that for me?" She looked at him, her eyes wide. "I'm no feather."

He winked. "I noticed that in the last couple of hours." He chuckled when she elbowed him in the side for his comment, then took her in his arms. "Seriously, you're lighter than an air pack. You can't put those boots back on, and I don't want you hobbling barefoot. Your open blisters will get seriously infected."

"I like being barefoot."

"Another time." He extracted himself from her arms, his heart and body suddenly aching with the absence of her touch. He knew he was attracted to her and she to him. That was clear from their banter. Holding her curled in his arms while they slept beside a babbling brook wasn't what he'd thought would happen. She'd trusted him, and that was a good first step.

Pulling her to her feet, he deftly swung her onto his back in one smooth movement.

## COURTING CHOICES

"Where'd you learn how to do that?" She said into his ear, her arms locked around his shoulders.

"I'm a firefighter, remember."

# CHAPTER NINE

"Welcome back. How did everything go?" Hannah asked as the two veterinarians caught a moment at the end of their first work day together since her trip.

"Once I finally got there, it was a mad race to get from Anchorage to Hope in time for the memorial service and reception." Cortland flounced down on the couch, brushing tendrils of her hair out of her eyes. "At least they had my rental ready at the airport and didn't give it away to someone else."

Hannah sat in her desk chair and slung her feet up onto the edge of the desk after kicking off her shoes. "Were you able to bury her beside her husband?"

"Yes, there are still no state rules about interment outside of a cemetery. She's resting beside Uncle Mayer."

"Everything else went well." Hannah started rearranging papers on her desk.

"It all went according to plan." She swung her legs up onto the couch. "It was weird to see so many people who remembered me from my summers up there. Most I didn't recognize."

"How's your dad doing with the estate?"

"It's going okay." She frowned, then continued, "Aunt Faith's will specified I'm to inherit everything."

"Everything?" Hannah sat up, putting her feet back on the floor.

"Yup, everything. Now I have to decide what to do with it all: the house, barns, animals, land, and all the contents."

Hannah's eyes widened and she asked, "What are you going to do?"

Before Cortland could answer, there was a knock on the door jamb.

Andrew stood in the entry. "What's who going to do?" He strolled over to kiss his fiancée.

## COURTING CHOICES

Cortland started blinking rapidly. "My aunt left me her estate. So now I have to figure out what to do with it. In the meantime, I have someone looking after the house and caring for the animals."

"Wow! A place in Alaska. Too bad it wasn't closer, like the next county." He sat on the edge of Hannah's desk and looked from Cortland to Hannah and back.

"Yeah, that certainly would make it easier. But it's over forty-five hundred miles away."

"Makes sense to sell it. Or are you considering keeping it as a vacation home?"

Cortland stood up, adjusting her scrubs. "I haven't thought about it much." *Liar, Liar.* The truth was her mind kept focusing on it. She rolled her eyes. "Well, I have, but all the options keep swirling through my brain." She headed for the door. "I keep trying to think what Aunt Faith would want me to do with it. She loved the place with all her heart. Even though she had quite a few big offers, she never considered selling after Mayer died." Tapping the door frame, she added, "I'll see you tomorrow. Hope you have a quiet night on-call."

• • • •

Hannah called, "Me too!" as Cortland disappeared out the door.

"Well, are you free for dinner tonight?" Andrew asked, walking to the window. "It's hot out, so I don't suggest dining al-fresco."

She walked over to the office's only window, surrounded by plants courtesy of Barbra Pari. "I don't like going for a sit-down meal when I'm on-call. Half the time, I get called away before my food arrives, the other half just after it arrives." She walked back to Andrew and gathered him into a hug. "How about Indian takeout? Or Chinese?"

He ignored her question. Andrew brought up the subject that was silently waiting in the room. "What do you think Cortland's going to do? Any idea?"

Hannah shrugged. She didn't want to say what she thought would happen so it didn't entice the universe to cooperate if that was Cortland's choice. But she couldn't help herself. "Frankly, I think she'll move up there."

Andrew put his arms around her and held her close. "Leave you? Leave Colby?" He sighed as Hannah tucked her head into the crook of his neck.

"She's not handling the time here well. Some of the clients have given her a hard time, and some of the patients have hit her harder than they should have. She might decide to pack it all in and move to Alaska. The place is very dear to her. I doubt she could sell it."

"Does Dawson know about her predicament?"

Hannah rested her chin on his shoulder. "I don't think she's told him. Yet."

· · · ·

Shutting the dishwasher door, Cortland hit start. It had been a long week already though it was only Thursday. It was the tail end of calving season at the dairy farms on the outskirts of town. Most of the time, the farmer took care of the calf's birth. But sometimes, something went wrong or didn't look right, so the clinic would get called for assistance. The busy large animal service kept her occupied which was a good thing; otherwise, she would have let her mind wander to Dawson. A shiver ran down her spine just thinking of him now.

Unlike before, true to his word, he'd called her on Monday night even while on duty. They had spoken for over an hour before he had to hang up to go to a fire call. Before the alarm rang, they had made a mountain biking date for later in the week. Today, the jingle of his particular ringtone came at a terrible time. Up to her elbows, applying lubricant to assist with the passage of a nearly born calf was not the proper time to answer. *Why do I always get important phone calls during work?* Ignoring the call, she continued with the difficult delivery by

## COURTING CHOICES

"walking the calf out". In the back of her mind she prayed Dawson wasn't cancelling their biking adventure.

It was another thirty minutes by the time the calf was finally born and breathing, and its umbilicus was treated with iodine. The heifer still acted restless, so Cortland checked for another calf. Sure enough, a second smaller calf was delivered within minutes. But the calf didn't breathe. After cleaning out the airway, she tried stimulating respiration with a piece of straw, tickling its nostril. When that didn't work, she moved to another tactic. Vigorously rubbing its back didn't stimulate a respiratory response either. Cortland had to resort to inserting her gloved finger into the calf's rectum. That simple move started it breathing. *It'd start mine too, buddy,* she thought with a sense of relief.

Taking care of the second calf until it was treated and stable took up another hour. When assured everything was as it should be, she cleaned up as best she could with fresh water and liquid soap in a bucket, packed up her equipment, and headed home.

His voice message said he was at work and knew she was on-call for large animal emergencies that night, but if it wasn't too late, she could try to call him back. *What's too late to call back?* He hadn't said. Glancing at her watch, she bit her lip. Nine-thirty. Much as she wanted to hear his voice, she decided it was too late to return his phone call.

Her stomach growled, but she ignored it, rationalizing she would be going to bed shortly and didn't want to eat so close to bed and antagonize her acid reflux. Besides, she needed a shower.

A half-hour later, her shower over and her summer pj's on, she poured herself a lemonade and sat down on the couch. Letting the cold liquid soothe her throat, she propped her feet up on the coffee table. A second later, the doorbell rang. Her spirit leaped as she struggled to the door. *Dawson?*

A glance through the peephole surprised her. Flinging the door open, she called out, "Daddy? What are you doing here?" Her palms grew damp as he walked over the threshold without saying a word.

"Daddy, what's going on?" A tightening in her chest and abdomen accelerated as he silently dropped a small gym bag on the floor beside the couch and sat down. Finally, he lifted his eyes up to hers. "Can I stay the night?"

Her throat tightened, strangling her voice. "Yes, of course, you can have the spare room as long as you like. But what's happened?"

His face crumbled, and Cortland could see his eyes water before he wiped them. "I—I've left your mother." He jumped up. "I'm sorry, Munchkin, I couldn't stand it another day, not another hour."

Rushing to her father, she threw her arms around him and hugged him tightly. "Oh, Daddy, I can't believe you held on this long." Holding him as he cried, the tension in her torso eased. When he finally pulled away, she gestured for him to sit down and poured them a glass of whiskey. Handing one to him, she set the bottle on the coffee table.

He gulped it back, scrunched up his face, and coughed before setting the glass down on the table. Then he poured more from the bottle. He swiftly drank that as well, not even trying to speak. When he regained his composure, he said, "When I met your mother, what drew me to her was her resilience and stability. She knew what she wanted, and nothing was going to stop her. Now—"

"Now?" Cortland fiddled with her glass before taking a sip. She knew she had to be patient with him. She had a strong enough notion of the hell he'd been going through for so long.

He wiped his lips with his shirt sleeve. It was a gesture she could remember her father yelling at Greg for doing. "She's nothing like that woman anymore. Since Jess died, I've spent the last fourteen years watching her become less than a shadow. I used to think she could continue, that her work and practice would keep her going." His eyes locked on her. He took another gulp of whiskey. "I'm sorry, Munchkin, but I can't take it anymore. I've filed divorce papers."

# COURTING CHOICES

The news felt like a gut punch. Cortland stared at him, her face no doubt showing surprise. After putting up with his wife's nonsense for fourteen years? She blurted out, "Why now?"

"Did you know she closed it? Up and shut down the office. Transferred all her patients to other obstetricians." His voice crackled with fresh pain. "She said she couldn't concentrate on other people's problems anymore. Nor could she see more girl babies being born."

Another punch in the gut. How was it her mother was deteriorating? Wasn't she going to therapy? Wasn't any of it doing any good at all? "What did her psychiatrist have to say about that?"

He waved his hand. "She blew him off ages ago. Said she'd been seeing him for years and wasn't feeling any better."

Cortland bit her lip before continuing her questioning. She hated to give him the cross-examination, but she had to understand, had to know how, after thirty-two years, their marriage, such as it was, was over. "So her quitting her job was the last straw? The one that tipped the scales?"

"That, and I—" He took a deep breath and let it out, not meeting her eyes. "I met someone."

This time the gut punch took her breath away. Her hand flew to her erratically beating heart.

"I know this shocks you, probably more than everything else." He took her hands in his two large ones and squeezed them tight. "On my way back to Rochester, after Faith's funeral. She was sitting in the window seat beside me on the plane. We got to talking. We talked the entire non-stop red-eye flight from Anchorage to La Guardia. About everything. She is the gentlest of souls, and her eyes are stunning. It's like they can see into your heart, into your spirit." He chuckled lightly. "I missed my connection to Rochester just to stay and have breakfast with her at the airport."

"LaGuardia? Isn't Chicago closer?"

"It was the only flight available on such short notice."

Cortland's immediate reaction eased as she listened to her father's words. She hadn't seen him so uplifted, calm, and free of tension since before Jess's accident. "Where's she from?"

He smiled. "She's from downstate. Lives outside of West Point in Highland Falls. We've been teleconferencing for the last week. I went to visit with her over the weekend." He adjusted his hold on her hand. "I love that she wants to spend time with me, and she's everything I need. Everything I've needed for a very long time."

She squeezed his hand back and asked, "How does she feel about you? I mean, geez, you two haven't known each other for more than two weeks at best." When she saw his face fall, she quickly added, "I'm just worried this is a rebound relationship."

"She lost her husband to cancer three years ago. I worry about that too. For both of us. But I suddenly feel alive again. Not just because of Allegra but because she's opened my eyes to the living I've been missing for years. Your mother hasn't wanted to go on living since Jessica died. Her entire focus and the focus of this entire family became treading water." He grinned, "Except for you. You kept going, kept looking and moving forward." He paused as though contemplating his next words. "You were the only one in the family who kept living. I see that now. And I'm so proud of you for that.

"All this time I thought you, Mom, and Greg felt it was disrespectful of me to move on with life. Mom especially. It was one hell of a guilt trip. But I moved forward anyway. I had to."

"I know, Munchkin. I know the struggles you've had. But you persevered." He kissed her forehead. "My friendship with Allegra has made me see that it's not too late to live again. Sometimes the choices in life are hard ones. But you have to do what makes you happy."

"Allegra, huh?" She smiled gently. Eyes filling with tears, she hugged him tight again. Whispering into his ear, she said, "Welcome back to the land of the living."

## COURTING CHOICES

In the middle of the night, Cortland rose. Anxiety had kept her awake again. She worried about her father and her father's new woman. What kind of relationship was it really? Could it be she was a stalker or maybe looking for a sugar daddy? Being a urology doctor in an extensive, successful practice, he made good money and had great benefits. Maybe this woman was after his money? Maybe she was a total scammer, hoping to win his trust and wipe out his bank accounts.

Her stomach growled again. It had been doing that since before she got home, but it was much worse now. *I can eat something and then fall asleep sitting up on the couch to prevent heartburn.*

Silently, her feet carried her to the kitchen. She poked in the food cabinet, scrounging up a bag of almonds, a large sleeve of buttery crackers, and a jar of peanut butter.

*I know what you're doing;* her mind's eye called her out, but it wasn't strong enough. Pouncing on the food, she ate the entire bag of almonds, the crackers, and half of the peanut butter. Mechanically, she went searching again. Pulling out a box of breakfast cereal and a box of popcorn bags. Digging into the cereal box, she poured out a big bowl. Not waiting for milk, she grabbed handfuls and shoved them into her mouth. Compulsively eating, unable to stop herself, she pulled a popcorn bag out of the box and popped it in the microwave. Shoving handfuls into her mouth as she popped another bag, she hardly had time to swallow.

"What are you doing?" Her father's incredulous voice stopped her binging episode.

She stared at him, trying to blink the tears away. Nausea rose from her bloated stomach while her body trembled. She'd been caught.

Her father walked over to her, put his arms around her, and hugged her tightly. "I've upset you," he said while holding on to her. "I'm so sorry I did this to you. You were doing so well."

Cortland hung on as tears streamed down her face, dripping onto her pajama top. "No, this is my weakness, my disease. You aren't responsible for it any more than I can control it." She hated herself for binging again. A persistent war, this urge made her eating out of control. Embarrassed by her relapse, she clung to him until her tears ran out.

When she had calmed down, her father said, "Cort, darling. You have suffered so much since the night Jess died. You know—you must know, you were not responsible for what happened. You could never have prevented it. And there wasn't anything anyone could have done to save her. I know this as a doctor. It makes it easier for me. Maybe knowing that will help make it easier for you too."

She looked at him, her eyes swollen and red, misery swimming in the pools of tears. "I did feel guilty at first. Guilty for surviving the crash, guilty for not preventing it somehow. Maybe I could have prevented Greg from distracting her if I had been sitting in the front passenger seat. But I wasn't, and I couldn't let the guilt take over and rob me of my life. Not when I had been spared in the accident somehow."

"And now? How do you feel right now?"

"I feel so out of control. Like everything is a parade of steamrollers knocking me down." She rested her forehead on his chest. "I'm tired of getting back up. I'm tired of staying strong. I'm tired of everything being out of my control."

"I know, Munchkin. I felt much the same way since the accident. From my point of view, the only way to combat it is to decide what is best for you and throw everything else under the proverbial bus."

"Do you know what your father did to me?" A loud, harsh voice demanded over the cell phone, without the courtesy of a "hello."

Cortland knew better than to say she did and that he had talked to her four days ago and stayed with her the entire weekend before leaving for Allegra's house in Highland Falls, New York. "What did he do?"

"He's up and disappeared since last week, and I was served divorce papers this morning!"

## COURTING CHOICES

"Wow, that's pretty serious."

"Is that all you have to say?" Her mother huffed.

Knowing she was treading on thin ice, she said, "I just don't know what to say, Mom." Then her mouth took over before her brain could stop her. "At least you still have your practice."

"I do not. I closed the office weeks ago. I'm so sick of listening to all those people complain about this ache or that symptom. Made me sick. I've given up being a doctor," she announced. "I have more important things to worry about."

Ignoring her whining, she replied, "How are you going to get along?"

Her mother quickly replied, "Well, that's what I wanted to talk to you about. I want you to come home."

*Crap!* "I have a home here in Colby. And I have a job here too."

"You could find a job here at home. I need your help." Her mother said forcefully over the phone. Then her voice softened. "I'm sorry I haven't been here much for you. I'd really like you to come home so we can ... umm ... you know ... re-establish our relationship."

"Haven't been here for me *much*? Are you kidding? You completely tuned me out."

"I said I was sorry. Please come home. I want to make it up to you."

She didn't believe it for a second. It was money. Now that her practice was closed and her husband, the only breadwinner of the three of them, was gone, her mother was freaking out about money. She paused, trying to figure out how to say what she wanted without being insulting. "I understand your predicament, but I'm not coming home to financially support you. Or Greg, for that matter. Does he have a job yet?"

"Never mind Greg. He's still broken up. When he's emotionally ready, he'll get a job."

"No, he won't. It's been fourteen years, Mom. You both need to get your lives together and move on." Cortland cringed, hearing her mother suck in a heavy breath.

"Don't you tell me how to live my life. How could you, after your sister died, how could you be so insensitive? To me and to your brother. He was in the vehicle when it crashed. He's traumatized. PTSD."

"I was in the car too when it rolled over. All six times. I remember distinctly what happened. I managed to move on with my life. He can too." *And so can you if you let yourself.*

"Like I said, insensitive." Her mother was silent for a few moments before softening her tone to plead her case. "Look, Honey, I need you to come home. Your father's gone to heaven knows where. Who's going to take care of us? Pay the bills, buy the food, do the laundry? We're too grief-stricken."

"Sorry. You and Greg made your beds. I'm not bailing you out."

"I see. You're a big shot now that you've inherited that property in Alaska. How could you steal that from your brother?"

The tips of her ears must have been flaming red because she felt heat rising in her neck and face. "I did not steal anything from anyone. Aunt Faith left that property to me because she knows how much I enjoyed it. How much I enjoyed going there. Greg only went once. Then he refused to go."

"Nevertheless, Faith should have split it down the middle."

"Aunt Faith did what she wanted. It was a perfectly legal will. If Greg was so hot for the property, he should have visited more often."

Cortland could hear her mother screaming for Greg at the top of her lungs. The noise of the phone being dropped came over the speaker, then she heard her brother say, "Hello?"

"Greg. It's Cortland."

"Yeah?" He paused.

Her mother prompted him in the background. Then he said, "We need you to come home."

## COURTING CHOICES

"No can do."

This time she could hear the two of them bickering in the background. After a minute, she said, "Hello?"

Greg came back on the line. "If you can't come, can you send money? Maybe a couple thousand a month?"

She hadn't planned on it and couldn't stop herself. Cortland started laughing hard at the absurdity of their request. When she could speak again, she said boldly, "No," and hung up the phone.

# CHAPTER TEN

Cat carrier in hand, Cortland got out of her car at Dawson's house, heading for the bright red front door that stuck out like a sore thumb against the white cape. It opened long before she got there. He stood in the door frame, watching her approach. "Thanks for your help."

He broke into a grin. "I was having too much fun watching. Do you know you have a sort of sexy swagger?"

"That 'sexy swagger' is me struggling to carry these kittens. They're bouncing around in the carrier, playing, I think." She held it out, relinquishing it to Dawson before following him into the house.

He set it on the floor in the living room, his own two kittens immediately bounding up to it. Paws from the inside poked out the air slits, causing paws from outside to attack. Dawson laughed as they watched them play.

"For God's sake, let them out." When he didn't move, she unlatched the carrier's door. Dawson's cats scrambled inside, and a scuffle ensued.

"Do you think we should split them up?" Bending over, he tried to see inside the slits.

"No, they're fine. They need this play date." He stood, ignoring the kindle of kittens. She watched him saunter over to her, a gleam in his eye.

"I need a play date too."

The look in his eyes took her breath away for a few minutes. She busied herself petting each cat to hide her growing attraction to him.

"Hey, let's get going while we still have daylight."

His face fell, keying her into his disappointment. "I'd rather stay. Screw the bike ride."

Cortland backed away, giving herself space. "No way. I've been looking forward to this since we discussed it. I haven't ridden a bike since I was a kid. I'm not sure I still know how."

## COURTING CHOICES

"It'll quickly come back to you." He picked his day pack up off the couch. "I have snacks and a bottle of wine."

"Where are you leading me, besides into ruin?" She winked as they headed out the front door.

"You'll see."

They piled into Dawson's pickup, the two mountain bikes in the back bed. "Where did you get the second bike?"

"Andrew's. Or should I say, Hannah's based on the pink paint." He smiled mischievously. "Or maybe it's the bike he uses when no one's around."

"Andrew? In the closet?" Cortland sputtered. The very thought was ridiculous. Mirth bubbled up from her core, spilling out as giggles. Dawson glanced at her as if surprised by her childlike laughter. His chuckles joined hers in the cab as he reached out to hold her hand. The warmth of it brightened her mood and made her heart beat faster.

They chatted as they drove along for a half hour. She was surprised how relaxed, how natural their conversation went. Until he asked her about her day. Cortland filled him in on the emergency that had delayed her arrival. She could see by the look on his face she was making him wish she'd change the subject. Medical procedures, even veterinary ones, seemed to make him uncomfortable.

"Are you squeamish?" She asked him outright. "Haven't you seen worse?"

He nodded at her before looking back at the road. "I have seen far more gruesome things than you can possibly imagine. Things I'd rather forget but can't." He glanced out his window. "I'd rather not discuss such things. It brings back the nightmares."

Cortland was stunned. She hadn't thought he'd be so sensitive. She was an idiot for being crass and insensitive. "Sorry."

"It's okay. Now you know." He nodded as he took a right, following the signs for the park.

## DIANA ROCK

Finally, Dawson pulled into the gates of Wilkesbury State Park. Before them, a single narrow road led deeper into the park. On either side of the road were open fields of recently mowed grass. Scattered about were picnic blankets occupied by couples and families, some with dogs enjoying a chance to play fetch with their owners.

The road ended at a large cluster of white pines under which were picnic tables, grills, and lots of visitors. Dawson parked the truck. "We're here."

Rolling her eyes, Cortland snickered. "No. Really? I thought maybe you ran out of gas at the end of the road."

Dawson smirked and shook his head but didn't respond to her sarcasm. He fetched the bikes while Cortland followed with the pack. Dawson swung the pack onto his back before mounting his bike. "Follow me."

Cortland struggled at first to get her bike going. This bike was far different from the old bike with butterfly handles and a banana-shaped seat from her younger years. "I'm not sure I can do this," she called out, her voice trembling, hoping he could hear her from behind him.

"You'll get the hang of it. Follow my trail. I'll try to avoid obstacles," he called over his shoulder.

She was quickly out of breath, her legs pumping the pedals and her thigh muscles beginning to ache. "Is it much farther?"

"Almost there."

It was another ten minutes or so before Cortland couldn't take the searing burn in her thigh muscles and stopped. "Hey!" she called out as Dawson continued on the trail. He didn't seem to hear her and kept going.

She contemplated her choices. Get back on the bike and suck up the pain. Or stay there until Dawson realized he was alone and returned to find her. Fortunately, he returned before she could make up her mind.

## COURTING CHOICES

"What happened?" He asked, his eyes scrutinizing her from head to toe.

"I got tired, so I stopped to rest." She dismounted, setting the bike down, before walking over to him. "Is it much farther? My legs are complaining."

"Just around the bend up there. Maybe a football field away."

Shading her eyes, Cortland stared down the trail. "Okay, I can probably make it that far."

He raised an eyebrow. "We can walk if you'd like."

Shaking her head and returning to her bike, Cortland tried sucking it up. Not much farther. Mounted at last, she nodded for Dawson to resume the lead.

In minutes, they reached the spot beside the lake. Off a side shoot, the trail ended in what appeared to be a marshy area. As they passed through the reeds on either side of the path, it opened into a small sandy beach about sixty feet long. And it was blissfully empty.

"Wow. I'm impressed. I would have thought someone else might be here." She dropped the bike on the soft sand and walked up to the water's edge.

"I wasn't sure. Few people ride the mountain bike trail. Fewer still check out this side path. A few times, I've found other people enjoying the spot. Most of the time I come here, it's empty and quiet."

Cortland could feel the peacefulness of the place. The gentle lapping of the water onto the shore and birds chirping in the surrounding trees were the only sounds. Looking down at the water, she could tell it was shallow for at least ten feet out. Nearer the reeds looked mucky, but the sandy bottom beckoned directly in front of her.

Dawson stood beside her. "Take off your boots and wade. It's not deep. The water is cool, and the minnows kiss your toes."

"Minnows?" She looked harder, trying to spot them. "I don't see any."

"They're there." He walked back to the pack and removed the small blanket and the food. He took off his own boots before returning to her side. "Well, I'm going in."

Shuffling forward, he eased his feet into the water, his hands lifting his pants legs to keep the hems out of the water. "It's nice and cool." He waded farther, about twelve feet from shore, before stopping.

Not wanting to be left out, Cortland returned to the blanket, shucked her boots, and waded in after him. The water was cool but not so cold it numbed her toes and feet. "I still don't see any fish."

"Patience. And you have to stand still. If you move your feet, they scurry away."

Side by side now, Dawson took her hand to stabilize her as she watched the water around her feet.

"See? There's one off to your right, about six inches from your pinky toe."

A beam of sunlight gleamed off a silver fish. Cortland startled. "Oh! I see it."

He squeezed her hand. "Don't move."

A thrill zinged through her body as the fish swam closer and touched its mouth to her little toe. "He did it!" she exclaimed, her movement scaring the little fry away.

Laughing, Dawson hugged her to him. "I told you. You didn't believe me."

"I did." She returned to the blanket, trying to keep her wet and sandy feet off it, as Dawson did the same.

They dug into the snacks and wine, sipping from paper cups. Unlike their hike through the woods a week before, only Dawson devoured the little feast. He noticed.

"You're not eating very much." He gestured to the hummus. "I even brought more hummus since you seemed to like it so much last time."

"Thank you for that. It was very kind of you." *Crap, I sound way too formal.* The tone of her voice was rather curt. Fortunately, Dawson

## COURTING CHOICES

ignored it, or at least, he didn't say anything in response. The last thing she wanted was to explain her eating eccentricities.

"How are your legs doing?" Dawson asked, finishing his wine and setting the cup aside. He laid back on the blanket, his hands cradling the back of his head, his elbows splayed out.

"They'll be okay. But I'll probably be hurting tomorrow." She settled beside his relaxed figure, and he curled an arm around her, pulling her against his body.

With her ear against his chest, Cortland could hear his heart beating slow and steady. Glancing down at her watch, she counted for fifteen seconds, then multiplied by four. Fifty-six. He was in great physical shape to have a heart rate that low. On the other hand, her heart rate sounded like a field of horses galloping in a derby. Her insides trembled to the rapid beating. *Should I let him be my first? Even if it might never happen again? Even if I might decide to go live in Alaska?*

Dawson's hand lifted her chin, bringing her eyes up to his. His lips brushed hers once, twice. On the third brush, they settled on hers, pressing gently at first, then more insistently.

She turned, facing him directly to meet his glorious lips full on. Pressing back into his kiss, her insides melted and quivered with excitement she hadn't known was buried inside. Her fingers threaded through his short hair, the sweat-dampened strands feeling cool to the touch. When they broke apart, she asked the question lingering in her mind. "You have protection?"

"I do. Are you sure?"

At her nod, he cupped her face pulling her closer still, their legs willy-nilly between them. They broke apart briefly, his chuckle rumbling deep in his chest. She giggled as they disentangled their legs before nestling hers between his.

She scrambled onto her knees inching forward to get closer. Full upright on her knees, her chest was at his chin level. Dawson drew her down, teasing her collarbone with kisses.

He pulled the band from her hair, freeing it to splay around her shoulders. She gasped as his tongue played lazy circles, then his lips bore down, sending shivers running through her body.

Instinctively, her head lolled back, her upper body arching slightly, giving him full access to her breasts.

He accepted the invitation, and she sighed.

• • • •

For a long time, they snuggled together, Dawson's arms surrounding her, keeping her close.

Rolling onto his side to face her, he took her hand. "I—want you to know something,"

Cortland's stomach clenched. She didn't like surprises, never had, and never would. Remaining silent, she nodded for him to continue.

"I like you. A lot. I feel good about us. And I'm hoping you're feeling the same."

Cortland blinked a few times. *Am I really hearing this?* "Can you be a little more specific?"

It was his turn to pause. He looked at her, his face scrunched into a WTF look. He reached out to pull a coarse blade of grass. He ran it between his thumb and index finger. After a moment, he replied. "I'm glad we had a tug-of-war at the food truck. I'm glad you stalked me at the firehouse. I'm glad we had our first date, even though it was … difficult for both of us. I'm glad you let me take you out last week." He stared into her eyes, "And I'm glad we're together again right now." He threw the blade aside. "I'm super glad Hannah is your best friend because Andrew is mine, and we can look forward to hanging out together."

The bottom of her gut fell, leaving a hollow sensation. How was she going to tell him? Her throat tight, she tried. "There's something *you* need to know."

# COURTING CHOICES

As she watched, his eyes widened. "I'm glad for all that too. But something has happened, is happening." She stopped, looking out into the lake, wishing she could jump in and escape this conversation.

"Hmmm, go on." His voice was not gentle. Rather impatient sounding.

She took a deep breath and let it out before continuing. It was a good thing she was sitting down because her knees were trembling. "I told you about my Aunt Faith. The one who died up in Alaska. And I'm pretty sure I told you about spending summers there as a kid, up into my high school years."

He nodded, his eyes not leaving hers, his breathing slightly faster than normal.

"My aunt left me her home in her will. The entire homestead, really. The house, barns, animals, one hundred acres of land." She glanced away again. "I have to decide what to do with it all. I love being here in Colby. But I also love it up there in Hope. Those memories are the stuff I dream about. If I could go back to any time in my life, I'd go back to those endless-feeling summers on the homestead."

Dawson stared at her, not breaking eye contact. "So you haven't decided yet?"

She shook her head. "No. Not officially. But there's a reasonable chance I'll go. It's free land, a free house. Surrounded by hills, fields, and marshes I roamed with exquisite pleasure. I don't think I can let it all go. Not for any amount of money."

Silence engulfed them as the promise of the day dissolved away. She hated to disappoint him. He was a good man. Incredibly handsome and strong, and he enjoyed life. He was active, athletic, and a terrific lover. He checked every box on her list of a perfect man. But he was welded to his career and his community. She knew that in her soul.

Dawson had been staring out over the lake. At last, he said, "Thank you for telling me. When do you have to decide?"

"As soon as possible. The court wants us to settle it as quickly as possible."

He nodded his understanding, his face dour looking, a tension in his jaw, his lips no longer smiling as they had just fifteen minutes ago. "We should get going."

They picked up their gear and rode back to Dawson's truck without further conversation.

The radio filled the silent space between them on the bench seat. When Dawson shut off the engine in his driveway, he turned to her. "Can you do me one favor?"

Mashing her lips together a few seconds, she nodded.

"Tell me when you decide. I don't want to find out from anyone else."

"Of course. I understand."

Cortland retrieved her exhausted kittens, pulling them out of their nap all curled up with their siblings. Dawson carried them out to her car for her.

"Thanks for a beautiful day," she said. "It was great."

He nodded, a little too curtly for Cortland's liking, and walked back into the house without a backward glance.

• • • •

On the other side of the front door, Dawson leaned against it and sighed heavily. The weekend was blown. He wandered the living room, ignoring the cats who had come to greet him. Entering the kitchen, he paused in front of the refrigerator. He opened it. Pulling the bottle of champagne out of the fridge, he set it on the counter with a thud. Kittens on his heels, he retreated to the bedroom. Lying down on the bed, a bed he had hoped to share with Cortland that night, his jaw muscles ached with tension. "So much for that idea," he said as he shut his eyes, a heaviness filling his body as he surrendered to his misery.

## CHAPTER ELEVEN

Andrew and Dawson walked out of the Formal Wear shop just after noon. Their appointment for measurements had been quick, considering no one else was in the store at that time.

They blinked rapidly in the dazzling sunlight. Heat radiated off the asphalt parking lot of the strip mall. Inside they had been comfortable in the air-conditioned store. Outside, Dawson could feel his pores open with sweat. He glanced at the other stores looking for an escape from the heat. But he didn't need yarn, books, cigars, or jewelry. Not yet, anyway.

Standing on the sidewalk, the two men glanced around. Dawson could feel something was bothering Andrew. He looked tense. Inside the shop, his manner had been reserved and quiet. Dawson had no idea what exactly, though it could easily be anxiety over his upcoming wedding. Somehow, he felt it was more than that. Perhaps since they were both free earlier than expected, they should hang out. Maybe Andrew needed to get something off his chest.

Andrew cocked his head toward the store. "Thanks for meeting up with me to settle this. Hannah was starting to get anxious about our suits."

"I'm glad I had the day off. I have to say I'm thrilled you didn't go for the full tux or morning outfit. I love you, man, but that might be above and beyond."

Clasping Dawson's arm, Andrew spoke more than he had in the last hour. "I get that. And I'm just as glad Hannah wasn't expecting a full tuxedo. I had to wear one for my sister's wedding. It was hot and tight and overall suckdom."

The feeling Andrew had something on his chest stayed with Dawson. Wasn't this part of his best man duties? Keeping the groom from bailing on his bride?

Snickering loudly, the two men walked back to Dawson's truck. "Got time for lunch?" Dawson asked after the two were inside the cab.

"What did you have in mind?"

"The Irish Harp. You game?"

Andrew rubbed the back of his head. "I've got time, but I can't drink. I'm going back on duty at three."

"Good enough." Dawson started the vehicle, and they raced to the pub a couple blocks away.

The two men sat at a small wood-topped table beside a front window, allowing them a perfect view of whoever was going in and out of the building.

"I didn't realize they renovated," Andrew said, glancing around at the wooden tables and chairs.

*He's not meeting my eyes. What the heck?* Dawson nodded. "Me neither. It feels more like an Irish pub now. Between the wainscot on the walls, the darker interior, the wood-carved bar in the back." He picked up the menu left behind by the waitress after they had ordered lunch.

"Yeah, looks much better," Andrew said as he took a long sip from of his soda bottle. Setting it down, his eyes locked on Dawson. "How's it going with Cortland?"

Dawson noticed Andrew's tension evaporate with his question. He raised his eyes to the ceiling. "It was going pretty good. We've gotten a lot closer. But—" He shrugged, his beer bottle halfway to his lips. "There's a complication."

Andrew glared at him, his face serious. "What?"

"Did you hear about Alaska?"

"I walked in while Hannah and Cort were discussing something about Alaska. Tell me what she told you."

"Don't trust her to tell the same story twice?" Dawson raised an eyebrow.

# COURTING CHOICES

He shook his head. "No, that's not it. I didn't get the whole convo, so I was hoping she might have told you more than what I overheard."

He set his beer bottle down on the table, crossed his arms over his chest, then leaned forward on the tabletop. In a softer voice, he said, "Her aunt bequeathed the entire place, house, farm animals, and 100 acres of land to her. She says she's torn about whether to sell it or not. The tone in her voice indicated to me she doesn't want to." He sat back in his chair. The beer churned in his stomach. He really didn't want to talk about it.

Andrew stared back at him across the table. "What will you do?"

"Me?" Dawson balanced the wooden chair on its two back legs. "I'm here. I still have my career here." He mashed his lips together and wrinkled his nose before adding, "So far."

"What's that supposed to mean?" Andrew's eyes opened wide with surprise.

Dawson glanced around the room as though scoping it out. Then he leaned forward again and gestured for Andrew to do the same. "Remember our conversation on our last bike trip together?" When Andrew nodded Dawson continued. "Don't say anything, but I've decided to look for a new job." He sat back in his chair.

"Can't say I blame you. I'd be pissed too."

Nodding, Dawson declared, "There's nothing to hold me back. My mom has my sister here in town. So it doesn't really matter what Cortland decides to do. I may not be here anyway."

"What if she asks you to go with her?" Andrew asked as their meals arrived.

"She hasn't, and she might not. I'm not sure I'd go." He picked up a curly-fry and chomped on it.

His eyes widening again, Andrew asked, "Why not?"

"It's a long ways away. Besides, I did check for jobs up there. I'm either underqualified, or the position is below my current level. I don't want to be fighting wildfires. I'm looking for a management position."

"Find anything yet?" His friend took a huge bit out of his Reuben sandwich.

"I applied for a few. No responses yet."

Andrew stared at him. "You'll still be here for the wedding at least, right?"

"Yes, of course. I won't bail on you. It will take me longer than four weeks before I manage to find something."

• • • •

Over the next few days, he and Cortland met up after she got off work.

They had hiked and kayaked in the nearby Hale Hollow forest. Each time ended at Dawson's place, where they made dinner together and ate before Cortland left to go home and care for Harris, Moo, and Marmalade.

Wednesday night, they went to the Mexican restaurant downtown for dinner and drinks and then went to the top of the treeless hill in the Hale forest to do some star gazing. Dawson had realized she was quite an astronomical fanatic, always gazing up at the stars outside at night. He thought she would enjoy lying on a blanket and checking out the stars, planets, and constellations. She had.

"Reminds me of a few visits I made to Alaska in the late fall and winter when the stars are visible there."

Dawson asked, "You didn't see them in the summer?" He slapped his forehead with his palm. "Never mind. Twenty-four hours of daylight in the summer, right."

Cortland giggled. "Right."

The wind sighed gently around them as they lay side by side, their near hands clasped together. Cortland tried to explain the constellations she knew to him. It was difficult to point them out. Eventually, she switched to telling the stories associated with some of them: Hercules, Draco, Aquila, Cygnus, and Lyra. "That one there," she pointed, but while he looked, he couldn't find it, "is Pegasus." She was silent a few moments before adding, "Did I tell you I have a horse in Alaska named Pegasus?"

"No! Tell me more," Dawson replied, turning on his side to look at her.

Cortland also turned to face him. "My aunt and uncle's mare had a foal while I was there one summer. I got to watch the birth. Once they were assured the foal would live, they gave him to me. He's still at the homestead, though sixteen years older now." She looked back up at the constellation she named him after. "In Greek mythology, Pegasus was an immortal white-winged horse that sprang from the neck of the Gorgon Medusa when Perseus beheaded her. The brightest star in the constellation is named Enif, which comes from the Arabic word for nose."

"How do you remember all this stuff about constellations and stars?" Dawson's tone was filled with amazement. "I can't ever find the big or little dipper."

Cortland giggled. "There's not much to do in Hope. We spent a lot of time whenever I was there in the fall and winter just like this but wrapped up in parkas. Lying out on a blanket at night to gaze at the heavens. It's enjoyable to hear all the stories behind the constellations when you're a kid. Uncle Mayer knew them all like the back of his hand." She sighed.

His eyes softened, and he kissed her lightly on the forehead. "You lived an idyllic childhood up there. Most kids today couldn't find Polaris. Their eyes are buried in video games and social media. No wonder you love the place so much."

"It was idyllic. Those weeks up there were the best times of my life."

They stayed as long as the mosquitoes would allow and then went to Cortland's apartment.

Dawson had been there a few times. He liked her sense of style. The sparsely decorated rooms had a French country flair. A mix of rustic and refined pieces. It was comfortable and had a casual elegance with softly patterned fabrics in muted shades of yellow and cream, distressed painted furniture, and a few natural items: a conch shell, a bird's nest, a geode, a whale's tooth, and a lichen, among them.

They entered her apartment foyer, where the kittens appeared to greet them. Like his two kittens, they had grown considerably into slim, lanky young cats that raced around the living space, hiding and jumping out to ambush anyone or anything passing by.

Then Harris came around the corner with his tail wagging excitedly, his eyes radiating happiness at their arrival.

Cortland froze. "What the heck?"

Following her gaze, Dawson saw what had stumped her. And his curiosity was aroused.

Harris had a string hanging out of his closed mouth. It was about two inches long and a tan-brownish color.

"What the heck is that?"

• • • •

"It's his habit to always meet me at the door with something in his mouth. Didn't I mention that?"

Cortland's mind raced, her heart pumping wildly, her nerves on high alert. There was only one type of item in the house that had a string attached to it. *But it's not that time. Where would Harris get a tampon? Did he get into the bathroom closet and ....* Her nerves skyrocketed as she had a sudden thought. She had to get it out of Harris's mouth before he choked on it.

She bolted forward and dropped to her knees in front of the dog. He wasn't displaying any sign of choking or breathing difficulty. Just to be safe, she grasped the end of the string. *This isn't string! Holy crap! It's a tail.* She let go of it, recoiling. Cortland felt her entire face flame red. It might be less embarrassing if it were a tampon. There was no getting around the moment. Dawson would have to witness the unveiling.

"Harris. Open."

## COURTING CHOICES

The dog instantly complied, opening his jaws to reveal a dead mouse attached to the tail.

Cortland gently pulled the mouse out of Harris's mouth by its tail. The body hung limp and lifeless as Harris sat on his haunches, grinning and panting proudly.

Dawson laughed hysterically.

"Excuse me," Cortland said as she passed by him, opened the front door, took the offending vermin outside, and tossed it into the shrubs. *At least Dawson is finding the episode funny rather than gross.*

When she came back inside, Dawson still stood in the foyer, one hand over his mouth as he tried unsuccessfully to stop laughing.

"Stop laughing."

He continued to cackle like a chicken around his words. "You … should have … seen the look on your face!"

She ignored his statement while bypassing him again on the way to the bathroom to wash.

As she shut the door, she could hear Dawson congratulating the dog on his fine catch. "Good boy, Harris. Good dog." Harris gave a light bark in reply.

Returning to the foyer, Cortland found Dawson petting the grinning dog. "Where do you think he got it?" He asked, merriment sparkling in his eyes.

Cortland shook her head. "I have no idea. Maybe the kittens found it?"

Dawson walked over and took her in his arms for a hug. "I have to say, you were as cool as iced tea when you took it out of his mouth." He nuzzled her ear, lightly nibbling on her earlobe.

"It's not the first dead mouse I've ever handled, but I sure hope it's the last I find between Harris's jaws."

Dawson cracked up again, hugging her to his broad, sturdy chest. His laughter was infectious, and she joined him, feeling the tension release. She let herself melt into his arms.

He held her so tight against his body his arousal was evident. Cortland sighed, resting her head on the front of his chest. When Dawson pulled away from her slightly, she looked up. His lips found hers, teasing, nibbling, exploring them as her heart pounded so hard she thought he must be able to feel it. Their lips still together, she ran her hands down his sides to his buttocks.

Dawson's hands did the same, stroking her, kneading her backside, fanning the flames of her passion.

Her breath caught in her throat as his hands smoothed over her. Stepping back, she took his hand and tugged him toward the bedroom. In the doorway, he pressed her against the wall, kissing his way down the column of her throat. Gently at first, he grew bolder, enticing her passion.

"Dawson," she whispered, her breath coming hard and fast, her knees weakening.

An alarm sounded, startling her.

Dawson reached for his off-duty pager. He read the message and groaned loudly. "It's a four-alarm. I have to go." He kissed her swiftly and headed for the door. "I'm sorry. I'm being recalled to duty for a massive warehouse fire in the industrial park. I'll call you tomorrow."

# CHAPTER TWELVE

Hannah sat in the break room with Barbra Pari and Valerie, finishing a slice of pizza. "I can't believe someone actually gave us three large pizzas and five pounds of Italian cookies from Russifano's bakery."

"Did someone tell Cortland? Did she get any pizza?" Barbra asked Valerie, the only one to have been there in the last half hour.

"Oh, yes. She was here. Scarfed down like five slices of pizza and took a handful of cookies back to her office."

Barbra and Hannah shared a glance. Hannah had told Barbra in confidence about Cortland's former eating disorder. Especially with all the pressure she had been under at work and in her private life. Having another pair of eyes that could alert Hannah to any return problem was deemed necessary. She wasn't always in the clinic, having to make on-site appointments at various county livestock farms.

"I'll go check on her," Hannah said, heading for the door.

She walked into Cortland's office when there wasn't any answer to her knock. "Cortland?"

Her chair was empty. The only sign she had been there was a napkin full of cookie crumbs sitting in front of her computer keyboard. Hannah's eyes scanned around again, noting the bathroom door was shut.

Hannah knocked on the bathroom door. "Are you all right? What are you doing in there?" The muffled sound of spitting was the only thing she could hear through the door.

"Cortland? Are you all right?" She knocked again and tried the door handle, but it was locked from the inside. Then she heard Cortland call out, "I'll be out in a second."

"One, two, three ..." They had always teased each other when they lived together about saying one of them would do something in a second when it always took much longer than a real second. Their banter had developed into counting the seconds out loud in jest.

The door opened, and her friend looked miserable. Her eyes were red, her face gaunt. Cortland's arms hung as though lifting them required too much energy.

Hannah took her in her arms and hugged her. "My God, what is going on?"

"I—I was sick."

"At eleven-thirty in the morning?" Hannah's eyes widened. She grabbed Cortland's upper arms, looking her in the eyes. "Oh my God! Are you pregnant?"

Cortland shook her head. "I don't think so. Maybe I ate too much for breakfast."

"Hmm, maybe a few too many pizza slices and cookies?" Hannah glanced past her into the bathroom. A toothbrush and toothpaste rested on the sink counter beside a bottle of mouthwash.

"Umm, I didn't have that much." She rested her palm on her forehead as if checking for a fever.

"Maybe you should get a pregnancy test. Maybe you and Dawson—"

Cortland swept past her into the office proper and sat at the desk. She crumpled up the napkin. "I don't need a pregnancy test," she glared at Hannah, "as you well know."

Hannah knelt down beside her chair and took her hand. Cortland didn't meet her eyes. "I'm worried about you."

At first, she didn't reply. Hannah continued, knowing her best friend was feeling as ashamed as the look on her face foretold. "You're dealing with a lot of stress right now. What can I do to help you?" She paused, then added, "I can cut back your hours if that would help."

Tears spilled from Cortland's eyes, streaming down her cheeks. She stared at her blank computer screen for a time before answering. "I don't know. Coming to work helps keep my mind off my problems. I need to make a commitment to stay or to go."

"What are you fearing most?"

# COURTING CHOICES

"Making a choice I'll regret for the rest of my life."

Pulling her to her feet, Hannah led Cortland to the couch. They sat down side by side, and Cortland talked while Hannah listened. It wasn't anything she hadn't said before about the steady stream of patients, unkind clients, and the homestead that was her refuge each summer after Jessica's death. What surprised her was Cortland adding Dawson to the list.

"I think I finally found a man I can have a relationship with. And I would have to leave him behind if I moved to the homestead. Not to mention leaving you in a lurch."

"Don't worry about me. You are irreplaceable, Doctor Stewart, but I'm sure I could hire a temp until I find the right candidate.

A knock on the office door sounded. "Doctor Woodbridge, your next appointment is here in room two."

Hannah huffed as she turned toward the door. "Thanks, Alissa. I'll be there shortly." She focused on Cortland, saying, "We can continue this conversation tonight after our Zoom meeting with Tulsi about the wedding plans."

Cortland's face brightened ever so slightly. "I forgot about that."

"Why don't we have dinner together tonight. Just a quick bite at my place before our meeting?"

Nodding hesitantly, Cortland agreed. "Okay. But please don't mention this to Tulsi. She has enough problems."

Hannah froze. "What's going on with Tulsi?"

"I'll tell you over dinner. Go take care of your client. Mine will be here any minute."

• • • •

Over their takeout eggplant parmesan dinners, the women discussed Tulsi's predicament at the apartment Hannah and Andrew shared.

"She says getting to work with the exotics has been wonderful, except that's all they let her do. No routine domestic animals. No farm livestock. Only amphibians, reptiles, and an occasional bird," Cortland reported. "She tried talking with the manager and owner about the situation, but they told her that was what she was hired for. *Exclusively.*"

Hannah's face registered her surprise. "No wonder she's unhappy. I can't wait to talk with her."

While Cortland cleaned up the leftovers on the coffee table, Hannah connected with Tulsi on her laptop in the kitchen.

"Hey, Tulsi! So good to see you," Hannah exclaimed when Tulsi's image popped up on her computer screen.

"Ditto!" said Cortland, who was zooming in on her cell phone. "How are you, girlfriend?"

Tulsi grinned her gorgeous full smile. "Oh my God, you have no idea how much I miss you guys!"

"We miss you too. I can't wait to see you at the wedding," Hannah replied. "I have so much to tell you guys about it."

"Well then, get to it so we can chit chat afterward." Tulsi laughed.

"Okay, first off, this is going to be a small, unconventional wedding. Andrew and I are keeping it simple. No flowers, no music, and the reception will be simple fare. No DJ or band. Just enjoying one another's company. Also, I don't want a shower, not of any kind." Her voice got stern, "You hear me? No naughty-nighty party, no kitchen gadgets, etc. We have everything we need and then some as it is since we moved in together."

Tulsi frowned. "Are you going to wear a wedding dress?"

"Yes, that's one convention I am keeping. But Andrew, Dawson, and Andrew's nephew, Daniel, will have regular suits. No tuxedos. You two can decide on your own dresses. They can be official bridesmaids' dresses, or you can choose something off the rack or online."

"Any particular color scheme?"

Hannah replied, "Pastel. They should be the same, but whatever color works best for both of you."

## COURTING CHOICES

"Cortland, I'll do some searching and let you know if I see anything," Tulsi said.

"Excellent, I really don't have time to browse."

"The honeymoon will be short. Just a couple days. And it being the Fourth of July weekend, I've asked Barbra to contact owners who routinely call for calming drugs for their pets to come get them a week in advance, to lessen the problem on the actual day."

Relief washed over Cortland, lessening her anxiety over the event. "Thank you for doing the pre-emptive work on that. I appreciate it."

"Anything else?" Tulsi asked. "What about favors, wedding cake, and seating arrangements?"

"No favors, there will be a wedding cake, and it's already ordered, and no assigned seating. The food will be a hot and cold buffet, and we're going with an open bar."

"Nice! I like the sounds of this non-traditional reception." Cortland quickly added, "I take it the church service will be traditional?" It didn't sound like she and Dawson would have to dance together. The sinking feeling in her chest made it clear she might have been looking forward to that chance to get into his arms again.

Hannah nodded vigorously. "Yes, a traditional wedding ceremony without the nuptial mass. So, quick and easy."

"Thank you!" Tulsi feigned wiping her brow. "How are you doing, Cortland? I'm so sorry your aunt died. How's it going?"

Cortland wrinkled her nose. "It's okay. She left me her house and everything. Now I have to decide what to do with it."

Tulsi's eyes widened. "Wow! What's your gut say?"

She sighed. "I think I have to sell it. I do love the place so much. It was such an extraordinary time in my life. It became my home, my refuge after Jess's accident." She nodded as her eyelids blinked rapidly to dispel the tears. "It makes the most sense to sell it, but I'm really not sure I want to. But what else can I do with it? I can't commute from there." She shook her head. "But I have to decide quickly. The probate court is anxious to see the process completed."

The two other women chuckled lightly at her comment.

"No way to commute for that." Tulsi scratched her head. "Maybe you can take it for now. You can always sell it later. That way, you won't do something you might regret after a hastily made decision."

"Great advice, Tulsi," Hannah interjected. "Now, what's this I hear you aren't happy there in Louisiana?"

Tulsi rolled her eyes, flicking her deep dark brown hair out of her face with the wave of her hand. "Ugh. I took this job under the assumption it was vet service for exotics *on top* of seeing the regular companion animals. You know, cats, dogs, rabbits, etc. But they have me doing exotics exclusively. Nothing else. It kind of sucks. I'm missing all the rest."

"Can't they give you some more routine clients?" Hannah asked.

"They won't. I've asked. I know exotics were my specialty training in vet school, but I had no intention of doing it solely."

Cortland asked, "What are you going to do?"

"I guess I'll be job hunting." She shrugged. "It's just as well. The community doesn't like me, and I don't like their racist attitude."

Both Hannah and Cortland simultaneously blurted, "What?"

Again, Tulsi shrugged. "I'm constantly getting comments. Nothing overt of course. But more than one person has asked me where I'm from, and when I say I was born in New Jersey, they snicker and say, 'No, I mean, *where* are you from?'" She rolled her eyes. "I don't understand it. Louisiana even had a governor of Indian heritage for eight years! They should know better than to ask those kinds of questions."

Both Hannah and Cortland knew how much that type of questioning irritated Tulsi. It was like asking a Black person which part of Africa they were from. Some people could not get their heads wrapped around the fact skin color didn't determine one's authenticity as a US citizen. And some people used it to subjugate a person of a different race."

"I'm sorry." Hannah sighed.

"That's the milder of the things that have happened. I had one client ask me to do a dance in the exam room. She wanted a full Bollywood dance. I tried to explain I didn't know any Bhangra or Garba dance forms, but she kept insisting it was 'in my genes.'"

"Oh my God!" Cortland exclaimed. "What did you do?"

"I left the room. The exam was over. I was finished with her pet iguana and herself."

"We'll help get you out of there. If we hear of anything, we'll let you know." Hannah frowned. "Looks like our time on Zoom is nearly up. Goodbye, Tulsi! We'll talk again soon. Call me if you have any questions. Cort, I'll see you in the kitchen."

Cortland disconnected from the Zoom meeting. Walking into the kitchen where Hannah was closing her laptop, Cortland asked, "Do you know of any openings?"

"None. I'll check the vet listserv. We can't leave poor Tulsi to those miserable people and that job." She grasped Cortland's hand and steered her to a ladder-back chair at the table. "Now. It's your turn."

She rolled her eyes and crossed her arms over her chest. "I know what you're going to say. Save your breath."

Hannah sat down beside her and retrieved her friend's hand. "Look. We both know stress brings on these—episodes. What can we do to get you some help?"

Cortland shook her head slowly, a look of sadness on her face.

"You were in therapy before you started vet school. You told me that. Maybe you should consider another round," Hannah said softly.

"And add more time crunch to my daily schedule?" Her eyes blazed with fury.

Holding up her hands in surrender, Hannah replied, "I know. I know. You could try telemedicine. It's like Zoom meetings only with a therapist. You can do it right in your office at work. I'll make sure Barbra clears your schedule for the time." Exasperation filled her, and she blurted, "You can't continue binging and purging. It's so bad for your health. And Dawson—"

Cortland's eyes flashed with anger. "Don't you dare tell him." Her voice was low and threatening.

"I won't. But you know what he would say."

Cortland turned her head to stare at the wall in an effort to tune out Hannah.

"Cortland, you told me this all started with Jessica's death. And losing your aunt has contributed to its return. That along with the stress of your work schedule and your feelings for Dawson—"

"Dawson has nothing to do with this."

Hannah raised an eyebrow. "Are you sure about that?"

"Positive."

• • • •

Cortland's father said over the phone, "You know, you don't have to fly all the way to Hope. We can do this transfer with a power of attorney."

"No," Cortland answered. "If I'm going to put the property up for sale, I want to have a last look around. Maybe box up some things to bring to my place. I know there are items that will always remind me of the homestead. I would hate to see them go."

"All right, but don't save too much, or you'll have to rent a trailer to haul it back across the continent."

"I always wanted to drive to Alaska. But I don't have time. I guess it will never happen."

"Don't say never. It's just not the right time." Her father grunted. "Speaking of which, Allegra is going to join me there this weekend. If you don't mind?" His voice got soft. So soft it was almost a whisper.

The request left her speechless for a moment. Raging emotions battled it out in her gut. She didn't get to see her father often, so having to share him during this emotional transaction was not what she wanted. On the other hand, she hadn't heard her father this happy in years. She didn't want to deny him some measure of support and happiness. Aunt Faith was his sister. His last living sibling. Faith's loss cut him to the bone as surely as it did to her. "That's great, Dad. I'm looking forward to meeting her."

He sighed as though he had been holding his breath. "Excellent. Thank you, Munchkin. And don't worry about cooking at all this weekend. Allegra is an awesome cook."

*Greaaat. Good food. And someone else I'll have to hide my secret from.* With only one bathroom in the house, and it being tiny, it would be difficult to keep her father and Allegra from discovering the truth: she was still binging and purging at least once a day.

• • • •

Cortland set down her pen and looked around her aunt's attorney's sparsely decorated conference room. One wall of shelving filled with official-looking tomes was the only visual distraction in the room, with the shades drawn against the afternoon sun. Her father sat beside her, silently offering his supportive presence. He patted the back of her hand when the attorney said, "And that's it. The whole shebang is in your name now."

As she started to rise from the solid wood conference table, the attorney held up his index finger. "Hang on a couple minutes while we ensure you have a complete copy of all the materials you signed and reviewed." He handed the pile of papers to his assistant. She disappeared out the door, closing it behind her. His kind eyes crinkled at the corners when he smiled at Cortland. She liked his well-worn and tanned face. He must enjoy outdoor sports.

He slid an envelope across the table toward her. "Oops, almost forgot. Your aunt left a letter for you. I wasn't supposed to give it to you until you accepted the property."

Cortland raised an eyebrow as she took the thin envelope. "So, if I didn't accept it, I wouldn't have received it?"

He smiled. "Not really. But I might have given it to you anyway."

Keeping her emotions in check, she stuffed the letter into her purse. She would read it when she was alone.

Cortland's father asked, "Can you recommend a real estate agent for the area?"

"Hmm, I mainly work with Anchorage area agents, but if you can give me a couple days, I bet they could suggest someone closer to Hope."

"That would be helpful. You can call the house. The cell phone doesn't work well in that area."

"I'm not surprised. Less than 9 percent of the population in the entire state has cell coverage." He chuckled.

The blonde assistant returned with two bound folders of papers. She handed them to the attorney. "You hang on to this," he said, handing one to Cortland. "And you will need this in probate," he stated, giving the last copy to her father.

"Thank you for seeing us on the weekend. We appreciate your help." Cortland rose from the table as her father did as well.

"Yes, we do appreciate your making the appointment for a Saturday morning." They walked to the office door.

"My pleasure. I've worked with Faith and Mayer for a lot of years. I was sorry to hear of her sudden demise. You have my condolences." He shook their hands. "If there's anything else you need, please let me know. And I'll be here for the real estate closing when you're ready."

# CHAPTER THIRTEEN

Captain Dawson and Lieutenant Korth stood beside the engine, hot and sweaty from making an exterior attack on the building. The abandoned four-story brick mill was around the corner from their station, so it had taken only minutes to arrive. They'd knocked down the fire somewhat, holding back the blaze that threatened to advance to a conflagration, with their engine alone. Long before Station Three's ladder and engine could arrive.

Korth was slamming compartment doors as he put away equipment. Dawson knew that meant he had something he was angry about and wanted to get off his chest.

"Lieutenant. What's the problem?"

Korth wheeled on him, his hair sweaty and messed up, his eyes flashing with malice. His soot-stained face gave him a sinister look as he advanced on Dawson, hands fisted at his side. "You're expected to follow department policy. You were supposed to wrap a hydrant, lay in the line, and pump the sprinkler system."

*He's trying to ream me a new hole.* Dawson wanted to look suitably contrite, but the facts of the situation dictated otherwise. "The fire was on the roof. There's no sprinkler system up there."

"We need to be following standard operating procedures, *Captain* Michaels."

"When the situation fits the policy, *Lieutenant*, we will. In the meantime, you follow orders from your superior officer," Dawson barked. "That would be me, in case you've forgotten."

Lieutenant David Korth turned abruptly and started to walk away, muttering what might have been obscenities as he went.

"Lieutenant," Dawson called him back.

Korth paused but didn't turn around for a few seconds. When he did, he looked as though he tasted bile. When Dawson didn't say anything, waiting to be acknowledged, Korth finally ground out between his clenched teeth, "Yes, sir?"

"Do not forget to replace any used air tanks. I want all air tanks inspected, full, and ready for the next call."

Korth nodded before stalking off to the other side of the fire engine.

Dawson turned back to the scene to find Battalion Chief Lonny Greg watching him from ten feet away. His stomach fell as he was gestured to approach.

"Did you wish to speak with me, sir?"

"You thought fast and decisive. This could have been a five-alarm fire if you hadn't stopped it so quickly. Smart move, Captain." He lowered his voice and leaned forward. "Glad you stood your ground with Korth. There was a reason you got the promotion to captain, and he didn't. Don't let his sour grapes get to ya."

*Yeah, maybe. But not smart enough to earn a further promotion.* Dawson's jaw was tight as he replied, "Thank you, sir." He knew no one liked Korth, not even the upper command. Still, if they knew Korth was an ass, why did they promote him to lieutenant?

Dawson heard Greg relaying the message to dispatch over his communication radio that the fire was out and Engines Four and Five could return to quarters.

He retreated to his engine to size up the packing of the line back into the hose bed. Lucas was up on the rig, folding the hose as it should be. At least until they returned to the station and could hang it to dry. Then they would pack another line of hose on the rig in case they received another emergency call. "Lucas, let me know when you're ready to leave. We should probably stop for more fuel on our way back to the station."

"Aye-aye, Captain."

The cool air from the A/C sent a shiver down Dawson's spine as he entered the cab's passenger seat. He hadn't realized how hot he

## COURTING CHOICES

was until he'd removed his helmet. Though it felt good, his sweat-dampened hair chilled him to the bone. *Korth. He's got to go.* Picking up his run sheet, he began to recount the details of the call for department records.

They were on a fuel run when their station was dispatched to a fire at a manufacturing plant. Since the engine was only two blocks away when dispatched, they arrived first on the scene to report smoke showing and flame on the roof, possibly from the HVAC unit. While Lucas and Bob Merrill laid the hose line, Dawson positioned a ladder against the building's outer wall to gain access to the roof. Bob took the line up the ladder to report it was indeed the HVAC unit, and he and Lucas promptly put the fire out before it could spread along the flat roof.

While it was over in less than five minutes, a second alarm had been called automatically as the plant used flammable chemicals to clean aircraft parts and assemble them. Had the fire gotten away, the conflagration could have been historic.

"Ready, Cap?" Lucas said, climbing into the driver's seat.

"Let's go home."

Back at the station, Korth remained out of sight. He was supposed to be changing out the air tanks used at the last call. Not that they had used any. Still, it was his job to ensure every air pack had a full tank. The most important duty he had, but it was the one he resisted doing. Just as well he was staying out of sight because Korth's words were gnawing at him. The lieutenant quickly found fault in his fellow firefighters but never looked at his own failings.

The men cleaned up the apparatus, hung the wet fire hose in the hose tower, packed the rig with dry hose, and then cleaned themselves up.

In the duty officer's private shower, Dawson sudsed head to toe. He hadn't been in the fire or smoke's way this time, but the day's ninety-degree heat was made worse by the forty-two pounds of turnout gear he and every firefighter had to don for each call. The lukewarm water rolled over his skin. He leaned against the tiled shower wall to let it do its magic. It was nearly dinner time, and his stomach was reminding him to eat soon. With any luck, their dinner of Crockpot pork roast with sauerkraut and apples would go undisturbed.

Once dressed in his spare work uniform, he gathered his sweat-soaked one and hustled it to the laundry machine before Bob started it. He'd need that dirty set cleaned just in case they had another call. Sometimes Dawson wondered why he didn't keep more sets in his duffle bag, so he didn't have to re-wash them as they got soiled.

In the kitchen, he was greeted by Lucas. "Hey, Cap. Korth booked off the rest of the shift. He spoke with District Chief Hood while you were in the shower. Jerry Nost from Station Three is being sent over to cover."

Dawson's teeth clenched as flames rose up in his body. "He didn't notify me of his departure according to department policy." What a prick for busting his balls when he turned around and refused to follow procedure. He knew it was Korth saying, "fuck you, I don't consider you my superior officer."

Pulling a disciplinary report form out, he sat staring at it. Korth deserved to be reported. Most of him wanted to report the lieutenant as AWOL. But if he really had received approval from Hood, there was nothing Dawson could do. He crumpled up the form, threw it in the recycle bin, and walked back to the kitchen.

The other firefighters were already seated at the table, their plates heaping with pork and all the fixings, including fresh dinner rolls. Dawson picked up an empty plate beside the Crockpot and reached for the serving spoon. The box alarm bell went off.

"Shit." He dropped the plate on the countertop and grabbed a couple of dinner rolls from the basket on the table on his way to the engine's cab. He donned his gear, mounted the apparatus, belted himself in, and quickly consumed the roll. Swallowing hard, he nearly choked on it as he tried to answer the dispatcher on the radio.

The alarm was for a supermarket two blocks over. The dispatcher relayed witness information reporting flames showing. Heavy smoke could be seen billowing from the doors and off the top of the building as the engine and tanker approached the scene, parting a crowd of people to the far side of the parking lot.

Bounding out of the cab, Dawson was met by the store manager. "Is everyone accounted for?" Dawson asked.

"For my employees, yes. But I don't know how many shoppers were inside. Someone thought they heard a dog barking." He shrugged. "I don't know. Dogs aren't allowed in the store."

Lucas and Bob grabbed a hose line off the rig while Engineer Randolph pulled the levers on the pump panel. Pressure increased in the hose line giving the crew water to start their attack. They could hear small explosions inside the building, probably aerosol cans exploding. Dawson put on his air pack and followed them into the building to assess the extent of the fire. With the line under his arm to keep him oriented and with his men, he advanced, finding heavy smoke but little actual fire among the market's shelves and aisles. They moved deeper into the store. It was hard to tell how far back they were. Dawson suspected they were getting closer to the rear of the building. The smoke had become thicker until they could barely see one foot in front of their masks.

Suddenly Bob's air pack tank sounded the low air alarm. Dawson tapped him on the shoulder and took his place behind Lucas. Even though the hose wasn't spewing water, it was heavy. It would take a minimum of two men to advance it further into the building. Bob headed back to the front of the building, his hand staying in contact with the hose as it indicated his only way out.

In minutes, Lucas's tank sounded a low air alarm. Dawson tapped hard on Lucas' shoulder, taking over his spot at the nozzle so he could return outside the building before his tank ran out. Glancing over his shoulder, he made sure the rookie was following the hose line out.

The hose line was heavy, and advancing it further into the building would be even harder for one man. He couldn't see in front of him, and a feeling of danger and dread crept through his gut. If Lucas's and Bob's tanks were running low, his might be next. No sooner had he finished the thought than the low air alarm sounded on his pack.

*Shit, full air tanks should have lasted a lot longer. Korth. He didn't replace the tanks after the last call. I'll have the bastard fired for this.*

Grinding his teeth together, he dropped the nozzle but held on to the hose as he turned around. The smoke was too thick to see the way to the front doors. Instinctively, his hands followed the hose line he couldn't even see, heading to the front of the store.

Nearing what he thought were the checkout lanes, a crash sounded overhead. What must have been the suspended ceiling grid knocked him to the ground. He twisted and lost his grip on the hose line, the thick gray smoke enveloping him like a smothering blanket. Blind and breathless, he struggled to stand but collapsed as pain lanced up from his ankle.

Despite the killing pain, he frantically searched on his hands and knees for the hose line but became more entangled in the debris. Partially broken metal grid sections and fragments of ceiling tile fell off his back as he struggled to free himself. His air tank was caught on a long metal section, preventing him from getting to his feet and finding his way out.

Not that he could stand. He wasn't sure if the stars he saw were from the intense searing pain in his left ankle or if his air had completely run out and he was hypoxic. He sank back down to the floor, sweat pouring from every inch of his body as he swiftly contemplated his options. If he could locate the hose line, he could ditch the air pack and make a go for the store's front doors. Disoriented and shrouded in smoke, he had no idea which way to go, even if he found the hose. Choosing the wrong way would be a disaster.

*You can lie right here and join your father. He was thirty-one when he died. You almost made it that long.* The thought was tempting, and his chest heaved with a sob at the thought of seeing his father again. He broke down for a few seconds. The air in his tank felt thinner. The feeling spurred him to grab his radio and hit the transmit button. He called out. "Mayday. Captain Dawson. Mayday."

He lay still, waiting for the thirty seconds necessary to activate the automatic distress signal device on his air pack. The ninety-five-decibel alarm blared from the air pack into the darkness.

*Help will be on the way.*

It was like a foggy nightmare. Orange flames danced overhead as he lay unable to escape. His hands continued to search around him for the hose line. It couldn't be far. But the debris hampered his search.

Men shouted from what seemed to be far off. The thick smoke prevented him from seeing anyone approaching, but he could hear them. He knew they were coming.

His air seemed even thinner now. A dull halo of light gleamed. *Is it a flashlight? Or is this it? The light at the end of the tunnel?* He knew it was a silly thought and fought the urge to laugh. Sleepiness was also coming. He knew the giddiness, the silly thoughts, and the drowsiness were all caused by the diminishing air.

He tried to control his breathing, the phrase slow and steady repeating in his mind. The sounds of crashing close by, then something or someone stepped on his hand. The weight of materials lessened as if being removed from his back. He gasped for the last ounces of air in his tanks.

He closed his eyes as his arms and legs were gripped hard, and he felt himself being dragged; heart racing and gasping for breath, he tried to claw off his mask to get air.

When he came to, he was out on the sidewalk, his pack gone, his turnout coat and helmet gone, and an oxygen mask trying to force air into his lungs. He grasped the mask, pinning it to his mouth and nose, breathing hard and fast as his body tried to make up for the airless minutes.

"Cap, where do you hurt?" A paramedic shouted in his face.

Dawson ignored the medic until his breathing slowed and the muscle aches from oxygen deprivation subsided.

A cluster of firefighters stood immediately behind him, intently watching as they stripped off their helmets and unfastened their coats. Bob and Lucas were among them. Thank God! They'd made it out. All were sweating profusely, their labored breathing proof of their emotion. His men must have rescued his ass.

As his wits reawakened, Dawson pointed at his left ankle, buried deep inside his boot. When the medic lifted his foot to remove the boot, searing pain erupted, and he cried out.

Gently returning his foot to the ground, the paramedic said, "Okay. Let's get you on the gurney and into the ambulance instead. We can work on your boot in there, then your bunker pants come off."

"I don't think you need to take them off. Nothing else hurts except the back of my skull." If he remembered correctly, the ceiling grid had hit his helmet hard, dropping him to the floor. Well, that and the weight of the grid and ceiling tiles.

Lucas and Bob helped him get on the stretcher as the medic tried to stabilize his foot. Again, the stabbing pain returned, then settled down to an ache so intense he thought his foot was going numb. Fear gripped him tight around the chest.

"Hey, Doc, my foot feels numb."

When the gurney latched into the back of the ambulance, paramedic "Doc" Simon, as his name badge indicated, gestured for the guys to hold his left leg. "We'll have to get the boot off sooner rather than later. Brace yourself."

## COURTING CHOICES

Dawson could feel the blood draining from his face and his teeth clenched hard as Simon reached for his boot with one hand and cut-all scissors in his other hand. Dawson held the stretcher's metal rails in a white-knuckled grip. The searing pain continued as his boot and his sock were cut from his foot. Simon immediately felt for a pedal pulse. "You have a pulse." With a careful flick, he exposed the entire foot. Shaded an angry red color already turning purple, Dawson managed to wiggle his toes despite the pain.

Simon nodded. "Another good sign." He reached down and squeezed the nail bed of the big toe and the little toe. "Capillary refill isn't compromised." He looked Dawson straight in the eye and said, "You might be able to keep it."

All four men seemed to sigh with relief in unison. No pulse would have meant it was not getting any blood supply, thus jeopardizing the life of his foot so much it might need to be amputated. *Nightmare.*

Lucas Campbell poked his head over the paramedic's shoulder. "Want me to call anyone for you?"

"You know the Chief makes those kinds of notifications in person. You go tell him not to notify my mother. She's had that visit one too many times already. I don't want him scaring the rest of her life out of her by knocking on her door again."

Lucas looked stunned.

"When you get back to the station, you check all those air packs and the tank logs. Make sure they were changed out with full air tanks before we left."

Lucas looked at him again, his eyes wider, understanding the implications. The firefighter stepped back and hesitated, obviously not knowing what to do first.

"Get my phone first and hand it to me," Dawson barked. The pain in his ankle was spreading up his lower leg and intensifying.

Would Cortland dump him if he only had one foot? Cortland. He wanted to have her called. But the last thing he wanted was her hysterical and trying to fly back to Colby, even though he didn't think she was the hysterical type in an emergency. Thanks to her medical training. His phone. Where was his goddamn phone? Probably in the engine.

Dawson called out to Lucas again. "Luc, get my phone from the cab."

Lucas had been on his way to the rig but turned back when Dawson called him.

*Just shut up and let the rookie get your phone.* Dawson watched Lucas jog off from the open back doors of the ambulance.

The ambulance waited for to Lucas returned with Dawson's phone. Then the back doors were slammed shut, and the ambulance departed for Colby County Hospital.

# CHAPTER FOURTEEN

The house phone rang. She struggled to wake at first, and then a jolt ripped through her body. No one called her in Alaska except her father, who was just down the hall. There had to be an emergency. Was it her mother and Greg? Were they going to pester her about the money they needed? She glanced at the clock. It was two-twenty-six in the afternoon, according to the antique clock on the wall. Which meant it was 6:26 in the evening back east. Her two-hour siesta had left cobwebs in her brain. Cortland rolled over in her bed and struggled to reach the old-fashion dial-faced phone on the nightstand. She shook the cobwebs out of her head as she answered, "Hello?"

"Cort?"

As a siren screeched in the background, she could barely hear Dawson's voice. "Dawson? I can hardly hear you." Her gut twisted, and her body tensed. She knew his schedule and that he would be working today. "What happened?" She said rapidly, steeling herself for what surely would be bad news.

"I think I broke my ankle. I'm on the way to the hospital to have it examined." His voice quivered.

*Crap!* "Oh Dawson, are you all right other than that? How did it happen?" Her words were delivered like bullets, hard and demanding. She wasn't sure if she should celebrate it was only his foot or if there was more to it than that.

"I—" he hesitated as though trying to decide how to say it. "I got knocked down at a fire. The suspended ceiling fell."

She sat up fully with both hands cradling the phone receiver. "Are you okay?" She shook her head, trying to focus and sound coherent. "I mean otherwise? What about your head?"

"The helmet took the brunt of it." His voice sounded tinny, and the line crackled loudly.

"You're breaking up. What did you say?"

"I gotta go. We're at the hospital." He said something else but his garbled speech was indecipherable.

"What did you say? Please, Dawson," She yelled through the mouthpiece before the line went dead.

She bounded out of bed and ran to her cell phone on the dresser. Her fingers nimbly found the number she was looking for as she sat down on the edge of the bed. She dialed the number on the house phone.

"Colby County Veterinary Clinic," Alissa Grainger said.

"Alissa, it's Cortland. I need to speak to Hannah. It's an emergency."

She waited an eternity. At last, Hannah answered the phone.

"Cortland? What's wrong?" The tone of her voice was stern and demanding.

"Hannah! Dawson's been hurt on the job. He's at the hospital. Can you call Andrew and ask him to check on Dawson for me? He might have broken his ankle, but he also mentioned getting knocked down by falling debris."

"Of course. I'll call Andrew right away. One of us will get back to you as soon as we hear anything."

"Thanks, Hannah. Love you." Cortland's heard her voice waver while tears filled her eyes.

"Love you too, Cort, and don't worry. If he could call you, it can't be too bad."

As Cortland, her father, and Allegra sat down to dinner, Cortland heard back from Hannah. "His ankle is broken but not too badly. They put it in a cast. Everything else checks out fine."

The tension left her body like a fifty-foot wave. "Thank you, God. Does he need help? I can move up my return plans."

"No, he's got Jackson, his mother, his sister, and Andrew to wait on him." She chuckled. "Don't worry. He'll be fine."

## COURTING CHOICES

The two women hung up, and Cortland returned to the table where dinner was underway.

"Thank you for a wonderful dinner, Allegra. I wish I could cook as well as you." Cortland stood up from the kitchen table and stretched. "I think I'll go for a walk to the barn to let everything settle." She picked up her empty plate and utensils and placed them in the sink. "I'll do the dishes when I get back."

"I'm so glad you liked it. I'd be happy to show you how I made it." Allegra also rose, taking her own plate and Cortland's father's plate to the sink with her.

"Don't you two worry about the dirty dishes. I'll do them," her father said as he grabbed the bowl of leftover spaghetti with sliced fresh zucchini, fresh basil, and Parmesan cheese.

"I'll help dry them," Allegra said as she put the leftovers in a lidded container and popped it into the fridge.

Cortland stepped out the kitchen door onto the wooden veranda. It was nearly seven thirty, but the sun still shone brightly in the sky. *No star gazing here tonight.* She descended onto the small walkway as her eyes caught movement in the herb garden. It was a mouse hiding under the basil plants that had flavored supper.

She heard the chatter between her father and his girlfriend. *She's nice.* Cortland felt warm inside. She hadn't realized how young Allegra was. The woman was slim and tall, with long dirty-blonde hair and bangs cut over her forehead. Her wide, friendly smile left deep etches and exposed dimples on her ovoid face. Natural-looking brows framed her almond-shaped eyes, and a smattering of freckles highlighted her cheekbones. She wore no makeup, simple clothes of stylish jeans, a solid-colored cotton T-shirt, and sturdy sneakers. Allegra exuded friendliness, laughter, joy in her demeanor, and determined walk. Cortland sighed, realizing her father was quite smitten with a lovely lady she approved of wholeheartedly.

Walking through the barn, Cortland checked on all the animals. Pegasus must have sensed her presence because he started whinnying, his hooves sounding on the wood floor as he stomped around his stall.

She walked over to him, her white horse. He was the first animal she ever owned. Their many summers together exploring the surrounding land were indelibly etched in her heart. Rubbing his nose how he liked it, he settled down. His big dark brown eyes seemed to look at her with love. Wrapping her arms around his neck, she hugged him fiercely to her. "Don't you worry. I'll find someone to take good care of you. *You* especially." She pulled an apple from her pocket. "You knew it was there all along, didn't you, boy?" He nickered a response, bobbing his head as though nodding in agreement. His lips gently took the offering from her upturned palm. After a final pat for the night, she continued out the barn's back door.

She stopped outside the old outhouse and glanced over her shoulder. No one was in sight. She purged her dinner. It had tasted wonderful. Not so much now. But this was the only way, the only place she could do it without Allegra or her father hearing. She spat the yuck from her mouth several times, wishing she had her toothbrush, water, or even a breath mint.

Finished, she stepped out from the few shadows. Her eyes searched for stars that wouldn't be visible until the fall. Her bones were weary. Her mind felt scattered after a long drive to the attorney's office in Anchorage and back. The property had been transferred into her name. The probate judge had accepted the paperwork. And tomorrow, a real estate agent would be stopping by with the paperwork to put the homestead up for sale. The very thought had Cortland tearing up and feeling hollow inside. She kept moving, trying to distract her thoughts from tomorrow's task and worry about Dawson. His disoriented phone call and the broken ankle brought home the danger of his work. He'd lost his father in a fire and could have lost his life today. She shivered. She couldn't deny he was an important man in her life. Her first partner, someone she had grown to care about deeply. One she hoped would stay even if it was just a friendship in the end. Based on the power of his professed feelings, she wasn't sure that could happen.

She found Wally at the pig sty and helped feed them, filling their water trough while he dumped vegetable scraps and grain in their food bin.

"Excuse me? Is this Faith Watson's house?" a thick Texas-twang from behind her.

She spun around to find a weathered man in cowboy boots standing behind them. His hands held a ten-gallon cowboy hat at his side. She felt Wally sidling up beside her. Had he sensed this was trouble too? "Yes. Who's asking?"

"I'm Hancock Cartwright. I'm looking to see if you folks are selling the property." His graying mustache twitched as he spoke, his salt and pepper graying hair sloping to the right on his head. He looked like a real estate agent in dark-colored, neat-looking jeans, a white button-down shirt, and a dark brown suit-style jacket.

Crossing her arms over her chest firmly, she said, "It's not on the market yet. Not until tomorrow."

Mr. Cartwright grinned. "That's excellent news. I heard about the property. One hundred acres, much of it waterfront. I'd like to make you an offer." He pulled a checkbook out of the inside pocket of his jacket.

Stunned for a few seconds, Cortland finally said, "It's not really waterfront. More like salt marsh."

The man scribbled on a check, tore it off, and held it out to her. "My deposit. Two hundred thousand dollars. I'm offering you one point eight million for the property right here, right now."

Cortland's heart nearly stopped beating as her breath was knocked out of her chest. "Dollars?" she sputtered.

Mr. Cartwright smiled broadly. "Yes, Ma'am. I've been looking for waterfront property and a lot of acreage not too far from Anchorage. Someone told me about this place. I like it."

He was too slick, too sure of himself. Cortland had no doubt there was a cocky attitude underneath his polite facade. "What are you going to do with it?"

"Build of course. I want to build my wife and myself a rustic log cabin big enough for our family to all visit at once if they want."

"What about the farm? The barns?"

He glanced over at the fences, the paddocks, and the barns. "Once the animals are gone, they'll come down easy. Pretty old anyway, don't you think."

*Yeah, pretty old. Uncle Mayer and Aunt Faith built them in the first ten years they lived here ... over forty years ago.* "I don't know. I'll have to think about it." She gnawed on her lower lip.

He held out his check again. "I can give you four hundred thousand if that will make up your mind quicker."

Cortland stared at the proffered check but didn't move to take it. She glanced at the barns and paddock, way off into the distance to the spot where her aunt and uncle were buried. "My aunt and uncle are buried on the property."

"I know. I heard as much. They can be easily moved to a real cemetery, so you can visit any time. I'd be happy to pay for it."

Wally nudged her.

"Okay, I'll think about it." She started to turn away. "I'll talk to the real estate agent tomorrow."

"I don't want to involve an agent. That would cost a whole lot extra that isn't necessary." He held out the check again. "I want you to take this for now. You think about it tonight. I'll be back at eight tomorrow morning."

Cortland took the check and stared at the sum. When she looked up again, Cartwright was gone.

## COURTING CHOICES

The rest of the night, Cortland walked the property like she hadn't since she was a teenager. The bright night sky helped her navigate outcrops, marshes, and ravines with creek water all running to the Cook Inlet. Everything came flooding back to her as she explored the acreage. The spot where they had found one of the sheep stuck in marsh mud after it had gone wandering. The glade where she'd watch a fox family skulk outside their den inside a hollowed-out tree log. The time she found a couple elk fawns hiding in the marsh reeds. There were so many memories tied to this land. She would love to be able to introduce Dawson to it. With his love of the outdoors, he'd appreciate it. This homestead she had called home all those summers ago. Her heart grew heavier with her steps.

Steps that took her to the gravesites. The brightening rays of the morning sun found her seated on the rustic wooden bench her father had built beside Aunt Faith's and Uncle Mayer's graves. She pulled Aunt Faith's letter from her pocket, the one the attorney had given her after signing the paperwork. Her name was written on the outside of the envelope. The writing was squiggly, but Cortland could still tell it was her aunt's hand. She'd put off reading it. Several times she had patted the pocket it was stashed in. Once or twice, she had pulled it out. But she was afraid of what it might say. Staring at it now, she realized her aunt deserved to have her last words heard.

Cortland cautiously ripped the thin envelope, removed and opened the neatly folded letter.

My dearest Cortland,

I have no idea when you're going to get this letter, but it doesn't matter. It's safe to say I will be gone to meet my husband when you do get it. And you have decided to accept the homestead as your own.

I'm so very, very proud of you, apple pie. Proud of the woman you have become and proud you are taking on this endeavor. I wouldn't want everything your uncle and I built to fall into any other hands than yours. You love the place as much as we did, that much is clear. I know you'll take good care of the critters and all that was bequeathed to you. Always remember we loved you as if you were our own child. And we trust that you will do what's right with the legacy we leave you.

With love always,

Aunt Faith

PS: check the last page in my journal.

Tears slid down her face as she tucked the letter away. Wiping them with the back of her hands, she sat staring into the fading night sky, a tumultuous battle raging in her chest. How could she do this? How could she give up this space, this land that felt so sacred to her very existence? And to dig up these graves so some rich man could tear everything down. So he could sell the animals that had made this place their home from the day of their birth?

A car horn blared off in the distance toward the house. The agent must be here. Or was it Mr. Cartwright? She glanced at her watch for the first time since she'd arrived. It was five after eight.

Striding through the fields, her weary mind cleared. Ten minutes later, she entered the homestead proper. Mr. Cartwright stood beside her father, watching her approach.

Cortland walked directly to him, a fire burning in her gut. She stopped a foot from him and his leather tooled cowboy boots and locked eyes with him.

"Goo—" he started to say.

She pulled his check out of her jeans pocket. Without looking at it, she tore it in two and held it out to him. "I'm not interested in selling."

# CHAPTER FIFTEEN

Waving at the computer screen, Cortland said, "OMG! Look at your hair!"

Tulsi Anthony smiled back from the screen, her hair a peachy pink color. "Isn't it awesome?"

"That color looks great with your skin tone." Her lovely light brown skin blended well with the new coloring. "Has Hannah seen the color yet?"

"God, no. I'm afraid she'll have a fit. It would clash with the light gray bridesmaids' dresses we'll be wearing. By the time she sees me, it will be back to my natural dark brown, almost black color." Tulsi took a sip from a ceramic mug.

"Did I arrange this call too early? Are you just getting up?" She glanced at the clock. If she figured correctly, it should be only one hour behind. "Eleven o'clock there?"

"Yes, it's eleven. And no, it's fine. It's just tea." Her friend put the mug down. "Where are you? I hear a PA speaker or something?"

"No, I'm stuck here in Minneapolis/Saint Paul airport. My plane was delayed."

"Did you have lunch?"

Tension filled Cortland's body. "I ordered it, but it hasn't arrived yet." *Two can play that diversion game.*

The tone of Tulsi's voice became stern. "An unlikely story. Are you still binging and purging? Have you contacted your therapist?"

Cortland closed her eyes and shook her head slowly, "Hannah told you."

"Yes, she did. She's worried about you, and so am I. Please tell me you've sought help."

At least Cortland could tell her the truth about that. "I have had several telemedicine sessions with my old therapist."

"Thank you, God. At least she knows your history and what helped last time." Tulsi added, "Is it any better?"

"Yes. And I'm getting help. Can we leave it at that?"

"Okay, but I'm here if you need me. You know that."

"I do. Thank you. Now, what about you? How's your job going?" Of the three women, Tulsi came from even more dire financial circumstances than Hannah. Her poorly paying summer internship after graduation had been cut short. Instead, she jumped right into the first job offer she received.

"Not much better. But I am enjoying learning more as I handle the different exotic species here. Last week I had an emu from the Alexandra Zoo. It was pretty cool. Massive bird though. Did you know they have a tracheal sac for communication?" she said, but Cortland noticed the pleasure in her tone didn't reach her dark brown eyes. "What did you want to talk about?"

*Is it really working out?* Based on Tulsi's lack of enthusiasm, she thought maybe not. Cortland noted the rapid change in the subject but decided to let it go. For now. "Hannah hasn't given us much time, but do you think we should arrange a bridal shower? If so, we'd have to get it together quickly."

"She said no shower."

"Maybe she did, but did she really mean it?"

Tulsi nodded. "I really think she did. She and Andrew are living together. I would imagine they have most everything they need."

Cortland bit her lower lip. "People could just give them bigger wedding presents if they wanted."

"Exactly my thought too." She giggled her infectious giggle, which made Cortland join her.

When they both caught their breath, Tulsi asked, "What about a bachelorette party the evening before? You know, after the rehearsal."

"I like that idea. I'm sure a lot of the clinic staff would want to go. It's all women."

# COURTING CHOICES

"Any ideas where?"

"There's a restaurant in town she likes called Roberto's. Maybe there? They have a small party room. We could order a bunch of appetizers."

"Heck yeah. As long as they can make margaritas." Tulsi ran her fingers through her hair. "Anything else to discuss?"

"I wanted to tell you. I'm moving to Alaska." Cortland said it almost as a low whisper so no one standing nearby could hear.

"What! I thought you liked it in Colby?"

"I do, but something has come up," Cortland explained her decision about the homestead and Aunt Faith's will again. Then she told her about Aunt Faith's final letter and the odd message at the end of it. When she finished, she bit her lip. "What do you think?"

"Did you check her journal?"

"Yeah, just the last page. It had a long list of sums. Like she was adding something up as it grew. I don't have a clue what it's for."

"Maybe it will come to you if you give it time," Tulsi replied before inquiring, "What about that hot firefighter you were seeing?"

Cortland rolled her eyes. "He had an accident while on a fire call. Broke one of his ankle bones."

"So you're dumping him because of that?" Tulsi asked, incredulity in her voice.

"Of course not. I'm just telling you. He was hurt on the job, so now he's out of work until he's healed."

"Okay, but how does he factor into this decision?"

Cortland shrugged, her heart heavy at the thought of Dawson. "I like him a lot. We actually get along really well. And he is hot." She smirked and winked when she said the word "hot." "But I can't give up the homestead. Not even for Mr. Light My Fire."

Nodding her understanding, Tulsi agreed. "You have to listen to your heart. If it likes Alaska more than your firefighter, well?" She paused a moment. "What will you do for work when you move up there?"

"I don't know. Hang a shingle on the house, maybe. Anchorage is almost two hours away, so it's not really a feasible commuting distance."

"Are you anywhere near Girdwood? I think it's on the Kenai Peninsula."

"It's about an hour away. Why?"

Tulsi started scrounging for something on her desk beside her computer. "I was reading this pet-vet magazine and flipped through the employment ads in the back. I think the wildlife sanctuary there is looking for a part-time vet."

Cortland's heart rate sped up. "Really? Can you send me the ad? That might be the perfect solution. I don't need to make much money since there's no rent and no mortgage."

"I'll scan it after we hang up and email it to you."

"Great, thanks." An overhead speaker announced the imminent boarding of her flight. Turning back to the screen, Cortland scrunched up her nose. "I've got to get going. They'll be boarding in a few minutes. It was great talking to you. We should do this more often."

"It was. Let me know what you find out about that restaurant. I'll be waiting to hear."

Four hours later, Cortland checked her cell phone's email service. Finding Tulsi's email, she opened the scanned document and skimmed its contents. As she read, her excitement grew. It was a part-time job at the wildlife sanctuary. It sounded like the answer to Cortland's prayers.

# CHAPTER SIXTEEN

His house was quiet. He didn't like being at home with his foot up on a hassock, even though it did make it feel better. Lord knows they didn't give him anything strong enough to alleviate the pain. The prescription strength Naproxen was helpful, but the dull ache was still there. *Probably a good thing. Otherwise, I'd be trying to do too much.*

Dawson had filled out the paperwork to have Lieutenant Korth discharged from the service. The paperwork indicated Korth had left that day without performing his duty of changing the air pack tanks after their previous use. Deputy Hood said Korth had told him all his duties were fulfilled. It was one thing for Korth to have deliberately neglected his duties. But in lying to Hood, he'd sealed his fate. His failure to perform his duty nearly cost three firefighters their lives. David Korth was fired. The fire department did not tolerate such behavior. Every firefighter had a job, and everyone relied on that job being done without question or delay. Firefighters and the public's lives depended on it.

What pissed Dawson off the most was that the entire crew could have died at that scene; Lucas, Bob, and himself. Luckily, no one else had used one of the unfilled tanks.

His mother and his sister visited every day. They brought him meals and groceries he didn't need. Protesting their ministrations had done no good. At least having someone to talk to kept his mind off all the other things he could be doing rather than keeping his duff in a comfortable seat. Especially in this unseasonable June heat wave. Most everything he liked to do required two good feet, and he was short by one.

Cortland. She was supposedly on her way back by now. The ache in his chest wouldn't subside until he held her in his arms. If she let him. He knew they were on shaky ground. He wanted the relationship, yet she seemed unsure. They had fun together hiking and biking, and the sex was awesome. But he had to cool his heels until she decided about the homestead. He started to get up to wear off the restlessness in his legs. The heavy cast and the sharp pain reminded him to stay where he was. He glanced at his watch. He was supposed to pick her up at the airport in another six hours. Maybe then he could get some answers.

As he sat sipping his morning coffee, Dawson realized he hadn't heard from Jackson. Usually, he reached out once a week. But he hadn't heard from him since before he broke his ankle. He pulled out his phone and speed-dialed his surrogate father. The house phone rang for a long time before it was answered.

"Hello?" A feeble-sounding voice answered.

Confusion swirled in his brain. Did he have the wrong number? "Hello? Jackson, is that you?"

"Yes. Dawson?" the voice came a little stronger but still not sounding like his friend.

"Are you OK? What's wrong?" An unsettling feeling filled his gut.

"Ah, nothing. I think I got the flu or something."

"I'll come over. Is there anything you need? Soup, Gatorade, ginger ale?"

The man cleared his throat hard. "Yeah, all of the above. I've gone through what I had."

"Why didn't you call me?"

"I didn't want to bother you. I heard about your broken ankle."

Dawson rolled his eyes and sighed. "Well, come on, man. You know me better than that. You know I would do anything for you. Hold tight. I'll be over in an hour."

Fifty-two minutes later, Dawson arrived at Jackson's house. Hobbling up the sidewalk, he saw four newspaper rolls on the front doorstep. His heart rate kicked up at the sight. Dawson's stomach turned when the man did not greet him at the door as he usually did. *This is not good.*

## COURTING CHOICES

He tried the doorknob and found it unlocked. Crutching awkwardly, afraid of what he might find, he entered the living room, his eyes searching for Jackson as his nose wrinkled at the smell. Despite the summer heat, no air conditioning was turned on, and it was stifling hot in the house.

His eyes scanned the mess. The coffee table was filled with empty plastic soda and water bottles, soup bowls crusted with dried remnants, and a large Tylenol bottle with the cap off. A pile of newspapers on the couch sat beside a rumpled blanket and a pail reeking of vomit.

He dropped the bag of groceries on the floor and proceeded to search. "Jackson?"

Silence. He'd spoken with Jackson not more than an hour ago. The man had to be here.

His mind swirled with horrid thoughts. He had underestimated Jackson's condition, and he was too late. *Why did I go to the store first? I should have come here to assess the situation.*

Maneuvering down the hallway with his crutches, he glanced into the bathroom, steeling himself in case Jackson was on the floor. The toilet seat was up, the hand towel crumpled on the floor beside it. But no Jackson.

He plodded down the hall to the bedrooms. Pausing outside the spare room doorway, he noticed it still looked the way it had when he had stayed overnight as a kid. Pictures of his father and he dotted the walls. Interspersed with pictures of his father and Jackson, in turn-out gear, some in action on a fire scene. A wall shelf over his old twin bed still held his favorite Hardy Boys books. Not long after his father died, he had helped Jackson put the shelf up. Beside the books was Jackson's ceremonial engraved speaking trumpet, a parting gift for every Colby Fire Departments retiree.

Dawson closed the door, turned, and crossed the threshold of Jackson's bedroom. A figure was in bed, huddled deep beneath the covers. He rested on his crutches beside the bed observing Jackson's gaunt face, pale yellowish hue, and closed eyes. *He looks ...* Dawson shook his head. He took the man's wrist to feel for a pulse. There was one, but it was weak. But he noted the wrist and hand were limp, and the skin turgor was poor, suggesting dehydration. Another pail reeked of sickness.

"Jackson, can you hear me?" He fumbled to his knees beside the bed, getting as close to the man's ear as he could. A foul smell wafted up through the sheets striking him in the face. It smelled like fecal material and the acrid ammonia of urine. "Jackson, can you hear me?"

His eyes fluttered open. Jackson stared at him, his eyes unfocused and darting about as though he didn't recognize where he was or who had spoken. The whites of his eyes were eerily yellow.

He placed a hand on his friend's shoulder and said, "Don't worry, I'm going to get you some help." Reaching for his cell phone with a trembling hand, he dialed 911.

## CHAPTER SEVENTEEN

Dawson waited for her at the baggage carousel. At first, he started by standing, leaning on his crutches. Then when his ankle began to throb, he sat in one of the chairs. When that got too boring, he clenched his teeth and stood before hobbling about a little. No matter his position, standing, sitting, or even lying down caused a searing pain that felt like ice picks hammering into his ankle joint.

It had been a crazy day of waiting, only to find out her flight was delayed by hours. She had called him about the delay, offering to just take an Uber home, but he couldn't wait to see her again. It didn't matter to him; she had been gone four days. He needed to see her again and get answers.

As he waited, watching the ebb and flow of travelers, his blood pressure rose. He fingered the jewelry box in his pocket. The one with the necklace, a token of his—dare he say it?—love. Her absence and his broken ankle had shifted his world into wait mode. A mode he wasn't used to doing. His life was action, whether work or play. He needed, no, he wanted Cortland with him. Wanted to hold her, and as corny as it sounded in his own brain, he wanted to love her.

She had gone out to Alaska to get the homestead signed into her name and then list it with a real estate agent. She was coming home. Coming home to him.

A fluttering in his chest made him laugh out loud. Some people passed him by, their eyes wary as he stood on metal crutches beside the conveyor belt, waiting for the woman he knew was the love of his life.

A tap on his shoulder drew him to turn around. Like magic, there she was. Like he had conjured her out of the air. "Cortland!" He slung his arms around her to pull her tight and dropped his lips to hers for a hearty kiss.

She bent over awkwardly, trying not to kick his crutches or step on his casted left foot. Her lips barely responded. And she said nothing.

Looking at her critically, he noticed she was haggard. She had been crying. "Ah, darling. Don't worry. It will be okay. Look, I have something for you."

His right hand dug into his jeans pocket, pulling out the jewelry box.

Eyeing the box, she struggled, so he loosened his hold on her. Her eyes tore into his.

"I'm sorry. I couldn't do it."

His hand dropped away, the box still in it. "What do you mean?" Another crowd approached, and he tried to pull her to the side of the room. "You couldn't take the house?" Fumbling with the box in his hand while trying to maneuver the crutches, he finally gave up and shoved it back into his pocket.

Shaking her head, she said, "I can't sell it. Not even for over a million dollars. Literally."

He looked around, bewildered to his core. Behind her, one lone suitcase still revolved on the carousel. "Yours?" He asked as he pointed. She nodded and fetched it before it disappeared again. "Let's go."

He wanted to swing his arm around her shoulders and guide her out to his truck. But it wasn't possible with the damn metal sticks that helped him walk. She secured her luggage in the back bed of his truck before they headed for her home.

The only sound between them was the radio which Dawson turned off immediately. The music only stirred the turmoil roiling throughout his chest. Silence engulfed them as he tried to find a way to ask why without sounding like a dick. "Tell me what happened."

Cortland told him about the offer, about spending the night wandering the property. Ripping up the check and sending both Mr. Cartwright and the realtor packing back to Anchorage. Her voice was thin, sometimes wavering so soft he had to ask her to repeat herself.

"So, you're keeping it as a vacation property? Or a rental?" He scratched the back of his head as they sat in the parking lot of her

# COURTING CHOICES

apartment building. He was confused. She said she didn't want to give it up. Okay then. But she hadn't clarified what she was going to do with it.

"No. No to both. I—I'm going to live there. Take care of everything."

Dawson felt like he'd been hit by that ceiling again. He looked away, staring out his truck window. "So you're quitting your job and moving?"

She nodded, her eyes teary again. "I'm sorry. It's the only place I've ever been truly happy. It's the only place I've ever felt was home."

"What about us?" He blurted out, his tone more forceful than he would have liked. But the pain in his ankle was nothing compared to the pain in his chest right now.

"You can come with me." She whispered. "If you want."

"I don't want, damn it." He brushed his fingers through his hair angrily. "I don't want to lose you. But I can't move. Not now."

"Why not? Your family?"

He nodded. "Yeah. And Jackson has cancer. Pancreatic cancer. He's failing fast. I can't leave him." He shifted his weight in the seat. "And my lieutenant is being fired in a hearing in a few weeks. He's on paid administrative leave right now, but he'll be fired from the department."

"Wow." She closed her eyes and dropped her chin to her chest as if in resignation. "I'm sorry about Jackson. When did you find out?"

"Yesterday afternoon. I hadn't heard from him. I found him at home very sick. He went to the hospital by ambulance. His blood work was way out of whack, and he's jaundiced. All the signs and symptoms suggest pancreatic cancer. And tests have confirmed it." Dawson looked up at the ceiling inside the truck's cab and cleared his throat before adding. "He doesn't have much time."

"I'm so, so sorry. Everything you told me about him ... He's a good man who doesn't deserve this suffering."

They sat silent for a few minutes; Dawson lost in his thoughts, his face turned away from her in case the water in his eyes spilled. Losing his substitute father and his girlfriend within two days? It was unthinkable. For the first time since his father died, he wanted to scream or kick something until it was pulverized. Or cry all the tears pent up inside because he was too proud to let them out.

Abruptly, Cortland said, "I better go. Hannah's waiting for me inside."

He nodded, not meeting her eyes.

She got out of the truck. When she turned to slam the door shut, he called out, "Can we talk about this later? Can I call you?"

Nodding silently before shutting the door, she grabbed her bag and disappeared through the apartment door. Dawson's gaze pinned to her back as tears threatened to spill.

On the drive back to the hospital, Dawson let them go.

• • • •

Cortland walked into her apartment. "I'm home," she called out. The rumbling of the kittens running veered her attention down the hallway to her bedroom just in time to see Moo and Marm sprinting toward her. They looked like they'd gotten bigger in the days she'd been gone.

"Hannah?" She gave the cats a scratch before heading for the bedroom.

The apartment door opened, and Harris rushed in, his tail swinging in circles, yowling his happiness. Cortland dropped to her knees to accept his kisses.

"My goodness, I wish Andrew greeted me like that," Hannah joked.

"With sloppy licks?" She giggled.

"Whatever I can get." Hannah laughed. "How was your trip?"

She stood up. "I have so much to tell you. Maybe you better sit down. Wine?"

# COURTING CHOICES

"Oh, God. If you think I need a glass of wine, this is not going to be good."

Cortland poured them both a few ounces. Settling on the couch, she told Hannah about her time in Alaska. Everything from the attorney, Allegra, and her father, Mr. Cartwright, and the real estate agent.

Hannah sat quietly, letting her tell all before speaking. "So, you're giving notice? You're going to leave Colby?"

Cortland's heart squeezed as she saw the disappointment on her best friend's face. She gave a nod. "I'll fill out for up to three weeks. But I need to get back. Wally can only do so much for so long."

Hannah brushed a tear away before shaking back her shoulders. "I was expecting you to go in the first place. When you said you would sell, I kind of rejoiced." She sniffed loudly. "But you're really going to live in Hope."

Cortland gathered her into her arms and rested her chin on Hannah's shoulder. "Yeah. And you know what?"

"Don't tell me. Let me guess. Dawson is going with you." Hannah pulled back, grinning like a jack o'lantern.

"No. He's not." Cortland palmed her forehead. "I asked. He said no" The ache throbbing in her chest wouldn't allow her to continue. "I won't ask again."

This time Hannah engulfed her in a tight hug. "Maybe he'll come to his senses?"

"I don't think so." She cleared the lump from her throat. "One of his best friends, his mentor, Jackson, is dying of cancer. He won't leave him. Jackson is like a father to him."

They both gulped back the last of their wine.

Hannah's eyes widened with fear. "You'll still be my maid of honor?"

"Yes, of course. I'll come back for your wedding." They bumped shoulders playfully.

"Well, I guess I should start the hunt for your replacement," Hannah said, setting down her glass.

Cortland grasped her arm, her eyes wide and sparkling. "Start by calling Tulsi."

• • • •

She stared back at Harris. He sat before her, his tail sweeping the floor, a grin on his silly face as his tongue lolled out one side. "You know I'm out of boxes again, don't you?" Cortland crossed her arms over her chest. "And you want to go—."

Harris raised his paw and swatted at the air, almost as if he were trying to give her a high five. Behind him, the kittens chased and pounced on his tail.

"Out?" She asked him. He immediately headed for the door.

Gathering his leash, she clipped it on, and they left the boxes behind.

The air was still humid from a mid-afternoon shower though the temperature had dropped to a more comfortable seventy-eight degrees Fahrenheit. Harris frequently stopped to sniff as they walked the woodland path.

Her heart gave a squeeze. She had only been in Colby for a year, but she had come to enjoy it. The town was far bigger than Hope, providing many food and entertainment options. Hope had its own one-room library, but other than a couple restaurants, there wasn't much to do except fishing, hunting, hiking, and riding the white-water rapids on Six Mile Creek. There was snowshoeing, snowmobiling, and skating on the few inland ponds in the winter. Otherwise, it was shoveling snow and chopping firewood to stay warm.

She glanced back at her apartment door. For the first time, Cortland was glad she didn't have much as far as personal possessions. Otherwise, she'd have more to pack. The kitchen was the worst. She wasn't much of a cook or a gadget fanatic which was a good thing.

## COURTING CHOICES

Packing what she did have required ten boxes. And that was only the kitchen. She needed to get more empty, sturdy boxes from the liquor store. *And maybe something for my nerves.*

Initially, she had wanted to tow everything behind her car in a rental trailer. Her father had dissuaded her from doing that. She had agreed when he offered to pay for the moving company. On the downside, it meant she would be without those possessions for three to four months if she was lucky. Either way, she still intended to drive her car with Harris, Moo, and Marm.

Technically, she didn't need her furniture. Aunt Faith's house was still furnished. The age of some of the furnishings and their condition was troublesome. When she got there, she'd decide what could stay and what Wally could haul away.

Based on the moving company's delivery estimate, she was planning to cram as much into her car as possible. All of it around Harris in his crate and the kittens in theirs. It would be a long and arduous journey across the United States, over the Canadian Rockies, and up the West Access Route.

"Hey," Dawson's voice came from behind her.

Whirling around, her nerve endings igniting, she said, "Hey." She gave Harris's leash a light tug to get his attention. He wandered over to Dawson, who gave him a couple of pats on the head while the dog sniffed at his crutches.

"I came to talk. And see if you needed any help." He stood, cocking his hip out.

"I'm done for the night. I'm out of boxes." She strode to her front door, with Harris reluctantly in tow.

Dawson hobbled up beside her. "I can get more for you. Fill the bed of my truck if you think you could use that much."

She gave him a stare. "Good God, I hope I don't need that many." She continued walking, reaching out to open the door.

Dawson's hand grasped her arm, stopping her. His crutch fell to the ground with a clatter. But he said nothing more.

"What?" She stood still, her eyes searching his face. It looked haggard. Had he been by Jackson's side all day?

"I'm—" He stopped, turned his face away, then back. "I'm going to miss you."

Cortland gave a short chuckle. "You came all the way over here to say that?" She knew the instant the remark was out of her mouth that she was being cruel and heartless. They were friends and had enjoyed a lusty and what promised to be a deep emotional bond. Yet she couldn't help but try to make light of their relationship. To cope. To protect herself, she had to put distance between them. Otherwise, she wouldn't be able to pack up everything and leave him behind. She held the door open for Harris, then tipped her head to gesture that Dawson could enter if he wanted.

He did. He couldn't use his crutches inside past the pile of boxes in the living room. He looked around as though trying to memorize the scene. He turned back toward her, his face pale, his shoulders slumped. "I'd like you to reconsider."

She frowned and shook her head. "I can't. It's a done deal. My apartment lease is being taken over by Dr. Anthony. The moving company is coming tomorrow. And I leave with the dog and cats three days later."

"Can't or won't?" He hitched out his hip again, the cast protecting his mending ankle looking big and clumsy.

She ignored his question. "Would you like to sit down?" She started to turn away toward the kitchen, but his hand on her arm stopped her.

"I asked you ... can't or won't?" His face darkened.

Standing a little taller, she pulled back her shoulders. "Won't." The misery filling his face broke her heart. "I asked you to come with me. You declined."

## COURTING CHOICES

"What am I supposed to do with the rest of my life? Milk cows and feed pigs? What about my career? Am I not entitled to have a job that makes me happy? That makes me want to get out of bed in the morning? That provides for my needs and wants?"

Cortland sighed heavily and tightly closed her eyes. "Look. I understand you need all that. I understand why you said you wouldn't move to Alaska with me. But don't ask *me* to change my plans for you either. Because I won't." She locked her gaze on him. "When I was in session, the therapist said something that I thought was very profound. She said I should make plans for my own life, and if a man loves me, he will follow."

Dawson staggered to the living room window that looked over the parking area. He pulled back curtains she had yet to take down and pack. "I thought we had something special." He turned back toward her. "I thought we had something to work toward together."

"Maybe we did." Her self-preservation attitude kicked into gear. "We've certainly had fun together. But it's over. I have to go my way, and you have to go yours. It's that simple."

His eyes dimmed. "You're right. It is that simple." He staggered to the door and opened it before turning back. "I want to drive with you."

"What?" Cortland's eyes widened.

"Let me go with you. We can share the driving. And I'll fly back when we get there."

Cortland paused, her mind racing with the pros and cons of Dawson's offer. It would make the drive easier on her, but they would be stuck alone in a car for four to five days. Would they sleep together at the hotel at night? Or have separate rooms. She crossed her arms over her chest. "Why?"

Dawson shrugged before sweeping his hand down toward his casted ankle. "What else do I have to do? I'm on comp because I can't work. Jackson's family, what's left of them have kind of booted me aside." The tension in his face, around his eyes, softened slightly. "And

I'll worry about you the entire time. Besides. It will give me a chance to see the place you call home."

It wasn't a good idea. Twenty-four hours together for four to five days? Could they stand it? What if it didn't work out? What if they end up hating each other in the end? She didn't want to lose his friendship. But she also didn't want to prolong their separation for all the hurt it would cause.

"Well?" He asked, impatience on his face.

She shook her head, but her mouth said, "Okay."

He looked relieved. "Good. I'll call you tomorrow, and we can pre-plan our trip."

And he was gone.

From the window, she watched his halting progress to his truck. He awkwardly maneuvered inside and drove off.

She hiccuped, then broke into heavy sobs as tears poured down her cheeks. She flung herself on the couch and cried until her throat was sore and her tears had run out. She was going to miss him. Miss him more than she could have admitted to his face. The aching throughout her chest led to a hollow spot where her heart should be. *I love him.*

Closing her eyes tightly, she kept thinking of all the time they had spent together. Their relationship had been an easy, natural feeling. It was the most comfortable she had ever been with anyone except Hannah, Tulsi, and her father. *Maybe I should stay. Stay and see where this takes us?*

The thought of leaving the homestead to fend for itself strengthened her backbone. No. She was going to Alaska. Going to the only place she had and could ever call home. Maybe when he saw it, he'd decide to stay. Maybe he wouldn't be able to leave her. Maybe—

She shook her head and sighed as she glanced at the chaos around the room. A whine redirected her attention to the dog nestled beside her. She reached out and patted Harris's head as he sat beside her, his chin resting on her thigh, his eyes sorrowful, as though he understood

## COURTING CHOICES

everything swirling in her mind and heart. "You're a good boy, Harris," she whispered. "It's going to be a heck of a trip."

# CHAPTER EIGHTEEN

Their car inched along in afternoon rush-hour traffic outside Chicago on Route 90. "We should have gone 94 to 290 up to Milwaukee," Dawson muttered, his head resting on his fist, his elbow braced on the car door.

"Too late. Spilled milk," Cortland replied, trying to keep the agitation out of her voice.

Yesterday had been fine as the first of their five-day trip across the continental United States. They had discussed everything from music, concerts, childhood memories, and school memories from kindergarten through high school. Dawson had told her about some of the things he'd seen in his firefighting career thus far: the baby boy he had delivered, the drowning victim, the old lady passed out in her bathroom who regained consciousness after letting loose a huge, loud, stinky fart so bad that it sent everyone scurrying out of the room.

Neither of them had slept well the night before. The air conditioning in the hotel room outside Cleveland had not worked properly. The desk clerk would not do anything about it, and there were no other rooms he could move them into. Rather than repack the car and go to another hotel, they stayed. They shared the double bed, with Dawson's ankle propped up on an extra pillow. Cortland kept to her side of the bed for fear of hurting his ankle during the night. By morning they awoke in each other's arms anyway. This morning, they had to deal with short-fused tempers caused by a short and fitful sleep.

Once cleared of the traffic beyond Chicago, they had stopped for a bathroom and lunch break. Cortland walked Harris around the edges of the rest area property. He always enjoyed stretching his legs. Though his travel crate was large, he rarely stood in it while the car was in motion. The cats also got a walk on leashes, though that was more frightening for them. Time had been so tight she hadn't had a chance to acclimate them to the harness and leash before they left Connecticut.

## COURTING CHOICES

When everyone was fed, watered, and stretched, they continued on with Dawson at the wheel, complaining about everything. Was it the pain in his ankle? The frequent stops for the animals and for him? Cortland insisted they stop so he could stretch his legs to keep the blood flowing. The very last thing she wanted was the sedentary car ride causing *him* to have a pulmonary embolism.

"I'll make a hotel reservation just beyond Madison, Wisconsin," Cortland said, picking up her cell phone to find a place to stay that allowed animals.

Dawson glanced over at her. "I think we can get farther. Maybe before Minneapolis?"

She glared at him, feeling the heat rising in her chest. "We planned this out before we left. I think we should stick with the original plan. Besides, if anything, don't we want to be beyond a major city, so we don't end up in morning rush-hour traffic?"

"Madison is only a couple hours away. We could stop there for dinner and drive farther afterward."

Cortland bit her lip and checked the navigation app on her phone. "Minneapolis is four hours beyond Madison. That would get us in at midnight. Assuming we don't hit any traffic or construction delays."

She checked for other cities between the two. There had to be a compromise. "How about Eau Claire?" She suggested. "It's about an hour and a half outside of Minneapolis. We'll get plenty of sleep tonight. I'll make sure the hotel has A/C."

Dawson shrugged, then winced. "I guess that's okay."

"Pain?" Cortland asked. She knew it was pain. He refused to take pain medication when he was driving. Even though it wasn't narcotics, only prescription strength Naproxen.

He nodded, his eyes not leaving the road.

"You know, I'm capable of driving my own car. Having you along for the ride is helpful even if you're only a passenger."

"I'm fine. The seat doesn't go back quite far enough for my legs. That's all."

She rolled her eyes. They had discussed this before, and he refused to give up driving. Picking up her phone, she started looking for a hotel. His inflexibility was getting on her nerves. The change in tonight's stop threw off the rest of the plans they had previously made. "With the change, tomorrow we can go as far as Minot, North Dakota. There's an air force base, so there should be plenty of hotels."

"Can't we get across the border? Isn't there a town on the border? Wasn't the name Port-something or something like that?" Dawson said, eyeing the rear-view mirror. "Is it too far away?"

"Let me check." Cortland buried her head in the cell phone again. "It's an hour and thirty-five minutes from Minot. And yes, it's called Portal."

"How very original." He interjected, his tone laced heavily with sarcasm.

Cortland ignored him. " Let me see what they have for hotel rooms tomorrow."

It was a long time and a lot of heavy sighing before she spoke again. "There are no hotel rooms available in Portal. In fact, there's only one motel. Booked solid for months."

Dawson's jaw tightened. "You're sure?"

Cortland felt her head exploding. "Of course, I'm sure. Do you think I would lie to you about it?"

Dawson shrugged and grimaced.

"Pull over," she grunted. Really, this was unbelievable. *He screws up all our pre-planned stops and now doesn't believe me when I say there's nothing available.* Harris whimpered from the back of the vehicle.

"Don't get testy. We should keep going," Dawson said, making no effort to pull over on the highway.

"Harris needs a walk." Cortland's voice was curt and forceful. She felt her blood pressure jump to new heights.

# COURTING CHOICES

"Harris isn't the only one," Dawson barked back. The car slid over a lane and eased onto the shoulder of the highway. It came to a stop near a clump of trees. Dawson staggered with his crutches over the uneven terrain toward the trees while Cortland got Harris out on his leash. She met Dawson on his way back to the car.

"Can you hold onto him? I should get the cats out of the car for a few minutes." She held out the leash. Dawson scowled as he took it. Harris tugged at the leash, wanting to check out the tree line. Dawson followed the dog, stumbling slightly until Harris stopped to sniff.

Returning to the vehicle, Cortland got the cats harnessed and out into the grass. She looked around for Harris and Dawson. They were in the shade on the side of the clump of trees. Harris was rolling in the thick, tall grasses while Dawson's nose was in his cell phone.

"What's he rolling in?" She called over as she approached.

Dawson's head snapped up. He tugged on the leash, but Harris wouldn't come. Dawson hobbled over, bent down to grasp the dog by the collar, but drew back quickly. Curse words flew out of his mouth as he tugged harder on the leash.

By then, Cortland was nearly beside him, and the smell coming from their direction wasn't pleasant. Still dragging the cats along, she reached Dawson. The smell hit her squarely now. Decomposing dead skunk with a ruptured stink gland. She stomped over to Harris, grasped his collar, and yanked him off the putrid remains.

"What the —hell—" Dawson started to say. "You can't put that dog back in the car with us."

Fury raged through her entire body. She ground her fists on her hips. "Are you suggesting we leave him behind?"

He gripped the end of Harris's leash, grumbling loudly though unintelligibly.

"Look, buster. Your nose was in your phone, and you weren't paying any attention to your charge. Don't blame Harris. He's just a dog." She snatched the leash from Dawson and pulled all three of her critters back to the car.

Dawson stood there. His hands on his hips.

She turned around. "Are you coming with us or hitchhiking?" For a moment, she thought he was going to hitchhike, and it wouldn't bother her one bit. She was tired of his bullshit, his complaining, and his commanding attitude.

He pounded his fist on his forehead and walked away in the opposite direction. It was only a few steps before he did turn around and headed back to her, the stinking dog, the curious cats, and a packed-to-the-roof SUV.

They made it to Eau Claire without stopping for dinner anywhere. Once in town, they found a supermarket where they bought snacks, paper towels, hydrogen peroxide, baking soda, and dishwashing detergent. Everyone gave them a very wide berth as they stalked the aisles, looking for items.

Back at the hotel, Cortland mixed the formula together and bathed Harris with it in the bathroom. Because the cats' fur also smelled like skunk due to their proximity to Harris, they got the same treatment, howling so much the entire time that the next-door neighbor pounded on the bathroom wall.

While she did all the bathing, Dawson cleaned Harris's crate with paper towels soaked in the mixture. By midnight even Dawson and Cortland had showered with the formula, getting the offending smell off their skin. The critters slept as the humans ate snack foods to satisfy their hunger.

· · · ·

Later that night, Dawson awoke to the sounds of retching in the bathroom. His hand felt over to her side of the bed, but the spot was empty. His feet hit the floor, and he staggered to the bathroom door.

## COURTING CHOICES

He tried turning the knob, but it was locked. "Cort? You okay in there? Unlock the door."

"No, I'm okay," she replied. "I think something I ate didn't agree with me."

"Unlock the door, please. Let me see you." His heart thundered. Andrew had said something about Cortland's reaction to food, but it had been vague, cryptic, and almost nonsensical. Is this what he meant? Did she have a weak stomach?

"Not yet. Let me clean up and brush my teeth."

"Let me help. Please." He begged this time. He didn't like the helpless feeling of not being near to help her. "Please." When she still did not respond, he added, "I'm not leaving this door until you come out."

A click and turn of the knob and the door flung open to Cortland standing in the doorway. "See, I'm okay. Just let me be. I want to clean my mouth, and I'll be back to bed in a few minutes."

Dawson relented, returning to stand by the bed where Harris sat, his eyes wide and fearful. "It's okay, bud." He patted the dog's head. Harris lay back down on the bedcover, but his eyes remained intent on Dawson. In a few minutes, Cortland joined him.

Her face was tense. Her eyes wary as she headed for the bed. "Must have been something I ate."

"We ate the exact same things. I'm not sick." His gut told him she wasn't being truthful, that she was hiding something. He tried to gather her into his arms, to soothe her, but she was having none of it. She dodged around him to her side of the bed.

"You have a cast iron stomach." Cortland laid down with her back to him.

He couldn't beat it out of her. But it was rather suspicious. He watched her small, tense form until sleep overtook her, and he placed a protective arm around her, drawing her back against him. And pulled the covers up over her shoulders.

They pulled onto the dirt road to the homestead four days later. Cortland drove, giving Dawson the chance to check out the layout. Pulling into the yard, Cortland parked the SUV and shut off the engine. It was eight at night, and the sky was still bright.

*Thank God we made it.* Dawson got out of the car, feeling the muscles in his legs protest standing after the last four hours in the vehicle. They had made good time. From Minot, they had crossed the border the following day, getting as far as Dawson Creek in British Columbia. The following night found them in Whitehorse, Yukon. There hadn't been any other incidents along the way. Yet, the skunk episode wedged between him and Cortland.

He knew his attitude was getting on her nerves. He couldn't help it. They should be having a fun time together. He should be enjoying her company. Instead, the tension in his gut and chest escalated with each passing day and each night in bed. As part of their pre-trip planning, they had agreed to share a bed to save money but decided there'd be no intimacy. Each night he lay beside her, wanting to reach out and wanting to break that promise. The close proximity and his memories of their previous intimacy left him with a tightness in his balls that grew each day. Though they fell asleep exhausted, as far apart as the bed would allow, each morning, they woke intertwined.

They finally arrived in Hope. The scenery was breathtaking. Behind the homestead was a mountain that overlooked the area. Mount Alpenglow, Cortland called it. All through the drive once they got into Alaska was rather spectacular. Cortland was driving then so he could look around. It seemed every direction he looked, he could see a glacier. The forests were thick with conifers, the fields with pink-purple flowers Cortland called fireweed. She also explained most of the rivers and streams had milky-bluish white water from glacial run-off.

He was surprised by how peaceful and relaxed he felt, enjoying watching mountain after mountain slide by them.

## COURTING CHOICES

Standing in front of the house, Dawson paused, setting the cats' crate down on the ground. The gardens were a mess. Choked with weeds and flowers. "I guess Wally doesn't weed," he said as Cortland stopped beside him with Harris in her arms.

"What do you think?" She glanced from him to the house.

"Looks sturdy enough. Needs some paint. Maybe repointing the chimney." He crutched forward toward the kitchen door. "Got the key?"

Cortland opened the door and walked into the kitchen, where they set their charges down on solid ground and let them go. "They'll be busy exploring for the next couple hours."

Cortland took his hand, introducing him to every room in the house. They visited Aunt Faith's large bedroom with windows overlooking the back meadow and paddock. He paused. "Are you going to move into this room?"

Cortland bit her lip. "I should. But I don't quite feel comfortable doing that yet." She pointed out the window and said, "You can see their graves, way back on the edge of the meadow."

Dawson looked, following her finger off to the right. "Yup. I see them. Could you take me there?"

She glanced down at his cast. "It won't be easy walking. Maybe Pegasus will let you ride him there?"

His face scrunched up. "Sounds like a great way to break the other ankle."

She shook her head and walked out of the room. "Let me show you the rest of the structures." He followed behind as she led him to the chicken coops, the sheep and goat barn, the sty, and the horse and cow barn. She walked stall to stall, greeting the animals, her smiles and laughter easy and sincere. Dawson felt the warmth in his chest. Cortland was clearly coming home. It showed in her body, now loose and vibrating with excitement. Even the tense lines on her face had disappeared. And the animals responded to her presence with nickering and lowing. Each called for her attention. Even the chickens had gathered around her feet to greet her. All except the big white rooster who pecked at Dawson's cast.

In an end stall, next to the rabbits, was a large gray-white horse with a black mane and tail and expressive dark eyes. Cortland scratched his nose. "This is Pegasus." The horse nickered when she said his name, nosing her hand for more scratching.

"Wow, he's handsome. And tall." Dawson stretched out his hand, palm up. The horse sniffed at it, exhaled something moist, and stepped back. "Does he like me?" he asked as he wiped the horse's snot on his pants.

The horse's ears turned backward. "Well, not so much. But on the flip side, he didn't bite you." She laughed, and they returned to the house. The house phone rang. It was Wally. She chatted for a few minutes, then hung up. "Wally and his wife, Belinda, are coming over to greet us. And help feed the animals their evening meal."

The older couple greeted him with enthusiasm before they began the feeding chores. Dawson and Cortland followed, with Cortland helping them. Even he got to help, filling the water troughs with the hose and dumping the five-gallon bucket of grain and food scraps into the pig trough. It felt good to him, helping out, seeing the livestock respond to his pats. But this wasn't for him. He could feel it in his bones. There wasn't enough excitement. He reckoned he was a type A personality. Always looking for the next adrenaline rush. This homestead had a lot of work to keep him busy, but it didn't make his heart scamper like a rabbit.

As the older couple prepared to leave, Cortland asked, "Have you had any problems? Anything I should be aware of?"

Wally shook his head. "I cut hay in the back pasture but haven't got all the bales into the barn loft yet. The hay elevator has been givin' me grief. Sometimes it's okay but not always working right. Keep your eye on it if you use it. But you might want to get it looked at soon."

## COURTING CHOICES

Cortland and Dawson eyed each other. "I guess we know what we're doing tomorrow," Dawson said.

After Wally and Belinda left, they settled down in the house for the night.

In the wee hours of the morning, Dawson awoke to find his arms and Cortland's side of the bed empty. He got up, curious as to her whereabouts. She wasn't anywhere in the house.

He stepped outside and headed for the barn. Maybe she had a case of insomnia and had gone out there. When he silently crutched through the barn door, he heard her retching again. *What the hell?* He strode over to Pegasus' stall and found Cortland kneeling over a bucket, one hand holding her hair back, the other resting on the floor to support her upper body.

She glanced up and groaned when she saw him. He didn't care. He was worried. What was wrong with her this time? He crouched down beside her. "Cortland. Are you all right?"

She looked at him, her eyes so full of pain and sorrow it nearly knocked him over. His pulse throbbed in his neck, his heart felt like it was tearing in two. He took her in his arms and rocked her as she cried her heart out. "Tell me what's going on. You ate very little for dinner."

A thought dropped into his mind, and he froze, his arms still around her. "Are you pregnant?" The tone of his voice had hiked up a notch.

Cortland shook her head very slowly. "No."

"Then *what* is going on?"

She stared into his eyes. A silent tear rolled down her cheek. "I have an eating disorder."

# CHAPTER NINETEEN

The shock on Dawson's face could not have looked more astounding if a grizzly bear had walked up to him and asked for a cigarette. His mouth opened to say something, but nothing came out.

Cortland felt her tether to him, whatever they had left together, slipping away, leaving behind a hole in her chest nearly as big as the one left by her aunt's death. "When I get over-stressed or have an out-of-control feeling, I can't help myself." She cupped her forehead with her palm. "I—I overeat, binge out of control until I feel sick. And then I purge it by vomiting." Her resolve to tell the truth to this man was firm. This man she felt close enough to share a bed with repeatedly. A man she could love and did love more than any other man besides her father. "I'm not proud of my bulimia, but I want to be honest with you."

Dawson's face softened. "How—why?" He couldn't get the words together. It occurred to Cortland that he might never have known anyone with such a disorder and didn't know what to say.

Cortland stared at the barn ceiling, trying to decide what to say. "My brother and I were in the vehicle. We both were wearing a seatbelt. Jessica was driving without one. She had just gotten her license the week before. It was raining, she was driving too fast, and the SUV hydroplaned off the road, rolling six times before it stopped." Silent tear drops rolled down her cheek.

"Hey, you don't have to tell me," Dawson said, wiping her tears away with a finger.

"No, it's okay." She dabbed at her face with her shirt sleeve. "Jessica was partially thrown out the window. Her upper body was crushed underneath the Jeep." She paused, took a deep breath, and let it out slowly.

She'd stunned him into silence. When he found his voice again, he said, "I'm sorry."

# COURTING CHOICES

She nodded silently. "My mom had been the one to tell Jess to take Greg and me to the movies. She blamed herself. Went kind of religious cuckoo. Her depression infected the entire household. My dad tried to keep things going, keep everyone pulling together. It didn't work. Mom was always in mourning for Jessica, to the point of neglecting her two surviving children. Dad sent me and Greg here for the rest of that summer. Greg never came back, but I loved it from my previous visits. I spent every chance I could here.

"Binging and purging wasn't something I knew about and took on intentionally. It started slowly. I'd eat, then eat more until I'd feel so sick I'd vomit to feel better. It was the only thing that made me *feel*. It made me feel in control of my life, gave me a sense of wholeness I couldn't find in the months after Jessica died." She rubbed her face, not knowing what else she could say to explain why she did what she did. "I know it doesn't make sense how I could feel in control while eating uncontrollably until I chose to make myself sick. But it did."

"So it started because of the accident?" Dawson settled into a more comfortable position and took her hand, holding it firmly. "How have you kept it secret all these years?"

"It hasn't been much of a secret. My father recognized it pretty quickly. And he sent me here, to Aunt Faith and Uncle Mayer, to get me out of the stressful situation at home. They helped me. Being here helped me. I felt loved still. The chores made me feel competent and effective. It gave me a new start. Back home, I saw a therapist for many years. It hasn't been a part of my life for the last five years."

"But this situation with the homestead brought it back?"

"Yeah. It came back with a vengeance between feeling overwhelmed at the clinic, losing my aunt, and having this life-changing decision to make. I started seeing my therapist a few weeks ago. It's helping some, but it will take much longer to overcome this and get back into remission."

He held his arms open, an invitation to nestle into them. She took that invitation.

"I'm sorry," she said softly. "For everything. This isn't what I wanted to have happen. None of it."

He shushed her. "It's okay. I understand. It's not what I would have wanted, either. But we can make the most of the next few days before I leave."

She pulled out of his arms slightly. "Promise?" The look on his face gave her a warm feeling in the center of her chest. He still cared for her despite not wanting to move here permanently with her. She concentrated on being grateful for his support. She would not have thought he'd understand. But he surprised her. And she would always thank her stars for that faith.

"Always." Dawson went to pick her up in his arms but stopped. He shrugged. 'I'd carry you if I could." His glance swept down to his casted ankle.

"That's okay. I'd rather walk beside you." She smiled, her heart lifting, feeling lighter than she had in weeks.

· · · ·

They rose at six, heading out to make the morning feeding rounds after their own breakfast of toast, thick-sliced bacon, and scrambled fresh eggs Dawson found in the coop. Not to mention all the different jelly and jam condiments made by Aunt Faith's own hands.

Dawson couldn't help much around the barns. He filled the water troughs and spread feed for the ducks, turkeys, and chickens. Most of the time, he watched Cortland as she did the work. She greeted each animal by name. They responded eagerly to her voice and her touch. He remarked that, other than the kittens, he'd never seen her in action caring for animals and that she was a natural with them. His open admiration further reduced her tension.

## COURTING CHOICES

They took a short half-hour break before tackling the hay bales. Cortland got the tractor running and instructed Dawson on how to drive it. Despite his cast, he didn't have any problem. He said it was ornerier than a fire engine but not nearly as big. With the flatbed trailer attached, they headed out to the pasture to bring in the last two dozen hay bales.

"Why do you have square bales here versus the large round ones back in Connecticut?" Dawson asked as she brought one over to the trailer. "Is there any difference besides the shape?"

He took the bale and swung it up onto the flatbed. They stopped periodically to stack them neatly, two high and two deep. "Yes and no. It's different machinery. The equipment here is old. It makes bales. We can carry and load the bales. Those huge round ones need to be lifted and carried by a tractor to move them. And they're harder to stow in the barn loft because of their size and weight. I think that's why they're left in the fields. These bales go up into the loft with the hay elevator. It's a huge help. I can remember as a kid watching Uncle Mayer and his farm help throwing the bales up to the loft. That was before they bought the hay elevator."

"Throwing?" Dawson's face filled with admiration. "They're pretty darn heavy and clumsy," he said as he hefted one up on the flatbed.

"These are small. About forty pounds each dry. Those big round ones can go up to two thousand pounds."

He swung another one on the trailer bed easily. "I'm glad these are the small ones."

Back at the barn with the last of the bales, Cortland set up the hay elevator. She plugged the extension cord in the outlet in the barn's first stall.

"This electrical wiring doesn't look too healthy," Dawson said, his eyes following the old wiring from the stall up throughout the barn.

"It's original. Probably when the barn was built in the seventies by my aunt and uncle." Cortland watched him scrutinize the wiring, her spirit flagging. Add one more item to the list of things to upgrade. It seemed everywhere she looked, something needed to be fixed. And she was only going to be working part-time at the sanctuary. Her heart sank, thinking it would not be enough to keep the homestead running.

Dawson nodded. "Keep an eye on it. But you should consider rewiring as soon as possible."

The engine started up. It sputtered several times before humming steadily. It seemed louder than she remembered it should be. And it sputtered every couple of minutes.

"I'll go up into the loft and stack them. You throw them on the elevator one at a time. I'll tell you when I'm ready for the next bale to come up." She disappeared into the barn, hoping he remembered to wait for her signal.

From the open loft window, she could see Dawson waiting below. When he looked up at her, she gave him a thumbs up.

Dawson hauled a bale onto the elevator, hit the button, and the bale rose up like it was riding an escalator. At the top, Cortland stopped the action by pressing her button. Then she hauled the hay bale off the machine and stacked it with all the other bales already stored there. Going back to the window, she gave him the thumbs up again. They continued their chore for nearly half the bales when Cortland realized something was wrong.

She got to the window, and Dawson wasn't below. Suddenly she heard him yelling at the top of his lungs. "Get down! Get out! Fire!"

Cortland's mind raced, her heart pounding. Making her way to the loft ladder, she caught the scent of smoke. *He's not joking.* Not that she expected a firefighter to cry fire when there wasn't any. But the suddenness of it surprised her.

As she descended the ladder, she saw Dawson below, opening stall doors and shooing the horses and cows out the back door into the paddock. The smell got stronger, and Cortland saw flames in one stall where the extension cord had plugged into the wall.

## COURTING CHOICES

*Extinguisher.* She ran to the opposite stall, which housed an assortment of items. In the far back corner was a large fire extinguisher. She hefted it over her shoulder and raced back to the fire. The flames were licking their way up the old wood barn walls. *Oh God. Where do I start?*

Dawson yanked it out of her hands. "Go get the rest of the animals out." He yelled, pulling the pin and squeezing the handle. A spray of ABC yellow powder shot out the nozzle onto the outlet. "Shut the electrical service off. I'll get the water hose." He ordered, swishing the last of the powder up the wood boards the fire had risen.

She ran to the utility stall across the barn and pulled the electrical cut-off switch. Running to help Dawson with the water hose, she tripped over a goat in the doorway, observing the emergency. Covered in mud, she picked herself up and kept running. She grasped the hose and pulled to extend it as far as it would go, hoping it reached as far as Dawson needed. Running back to the spigot, she turned it on and raced back to his side.

With the nozzle in hand, he immediately began spraying at the flames, the wood sizzling as water hit it. "Get the rest of the animals out," he ordered as he continued to battle the rapid progression of the flames up the side of the barn.

Cortland checked every stall, even if the door was open, to make sure the livestock inside had fled. She heard a loud whinnying at the end stall. Pegasus.

She continued methodically but quickly until she was sure everyone else was out. Everyone except him. Opening the stall door, she grasped his collar and tugged him forward. She saw his eyes swivel to the other end of the barn where flames still chewed at the wood siding. He drew back, fear in his eyes. "Trust me, Peg. Let's go!" She hauled on the harness, but he would not move. Spinning around, she looked for something. An empty burlap sack hung over the nearby stall. She ran for it and returned to Pegasus, throwing it over his eyes. Blinded, his only choice was to trust her.

Yanking him in the direction of the rear barn door, he started slowly, then gathered speed as she praised him. "Good boy, Peg. Come on. We're almost out."

She pulled the burlap off when they cleared the door and smacked his hindquarter hard. He galloped off deep into the paddock away from the barn.

Cortland turned and re-entered the barn. Running up the center aisle, she found Dawson still dousing the wall with water. No flames were visible though the smell of burned wood filled the air. Cortland breathed a sigh as her limbs continued shaking.

He must have been satisfied because he dragged the hose outside and drenched exterior surfaces that had been burning on the other side. It was only a few minutes before he shut off the nozzle and dropped it in the dust.

Drenched in sweat and water, he gathered Cortland in his arms. She clung to him, thanking him for being there to help save them. Save the barn, the critters she loved as family, and them both.

The next afternoon Cortland drove Dawson to the airport. Neither of them said much during the two-hour drive. Dawson kept his eyes focused outside the window. There wasn't much unusual to see along the way. At times, the two-lane Seward highway sliced through the sliver of space between the water on their left and a sheer rock outcrop more than five hundred feet high on their right side.

Dawson perked up with interest as they passed one rest area along the Turnagain arm.

"What's going on there? Seems like a lot of people out watching the water."

"People wait there at Beluga Point to see the bore tide," Cortland said quietly.

"Bore tide? What's that?"

## COURTING CHOICES

"It's a rush of tidal water as low tide ends and starts returning. It can be as high as six feet, so they say. It's sort of like the Bay of Fundy between New Brunswick and Nova Scotia in Canada. Except it's much smaller." Her eyes remained glued to the road as she explained.

"Hmm. I had no idea. Have you ever seen it?"

She could feel Dawson's eyes on her. It was already a hot day for Alaska, but his scrutiny had her sweating even more. "I did once. My aunt and uncle took me when I was a kid. It didn't impress me except as a waste of time."

He chuckled. "Sounds like something a kid would say."

They continued on wordlessly. As they crossed the bridge over Bird Creek, Dawson interrupted the silence again. "Wow, there must be fifteen fly-fishermen out in that creek. What's running? Salmon?"

"Mmm, I think it's probably early Pink Salmon considering the time of year."

He was quiet for a few moments. "I've always wanted to try fly-fishing."

"You're in the right spot for it, especially for salmon." She frowned. "Until your flight leaves in a few hours." She pressed her lips tight together, afraid to say anything else. Afraid of what she might say. Her chest ached already with his imminent departure. She wanted him to stay. To move here and be with her. But his choice had been made.

He cleared his throat as though he were going to say something. Instead, he focused out the door window again. And tense silence filled the SUV.

They entered the airport zone, and Cortland pulled up to the drop-off curb. It didn't make sense for her to park the car and go in with him. She couldn't go to the gate; besides, she preferred to say goodbye in private. She gazed forward, not watching Dawson but acutely aware of his stillness when he should be getting out of the vehicle. When he didn't move, she turned to look at him.

He turned his body to her. "Thank you for everything. I enjoyed seeing the homestead and seeing how much you love it." His hand scrubbed at the scruff on his face. Cortland saw his hand shaking. "I—I'm sorry."

Her head bobbed sharply. "I guess I understand. Doesn't mean I like it." Her voice was monotone, and she pressed her lips together again. "You can change your mind and come back. If you decide to."

Nodding curtly, he said nothing.

She couldn't stand it. She struggled to hold back her tears. He needed to leave before she embarrassed herself. "I'll see you at the wedding."

"The wedding. Yup, I'll be there." He reached for his duffle bag. "See you then."

Cortland wanted a kiss, one last kiss, but she wasn't going to ask for it.

Dawson hesitated as he reached for the door handle as though he was going to kiss her. In a split second, he ducked his head and got out of the vehicle. He shut the door. His hand rose as if to wave, his eyes still on her.

Cortland gave him a nod, put the vehicle in drive, and pulled away from the curb. In her rearview mirror, she could still see him standing on the curb, watching her leave.

She cried all the way back to the house in Hope, where the ticking of the kitchen clock was the only sound.

# CHAPTER TWENTY

"I'm glad you declined the bachelorette party, but I think the office staff would have liked a night to let loose and relax together," Tulsi said as she sipped her Mai Tai through a straw. She looked around fervently, nodding her head. "This place may become my favorite restaurant in town."

"It is for me," Cortland said. "Cinco de Mayo is great. Authentic Mexican food and great drinks. I can't get enough of their margaritas. But they sure get enough of me quickly."

The three women chuckled at her insinuation. They all knew Cortland didn't drink much; hence it didn't take much to inebriate her.

Hannah looked up as she tried pouring two glasses of margaritas from the pitcher. Some of the cloudy lime and tequila liquid spilled as her hand shook. "Everyone can let loose tomorrow at the reception."

"I thought it was going to be family only," Tulsi said.

"After everyone griped about not being invited to the wedding and reception, Andrew and I decided to change our plans."

"Did you hire a band after all?" Cortland knew the affianced couple had been debating that issue as well.

"No, but we did compromise on a discreet DJ. One who will not play certain songs and who will cut out the BS. Every event I've been to with a DJ, they act like they're center stage. You know, the main event." She licked the briny edge of her glass before adding, "I want music and nothing more. Or he doesn't get paid. It's in the contract."

"Thank you for that in advance. I do hate the games and the theatrics."

Tulsi piped in, "No chicken dance, hokey-pokey, or electric slide?"

"That's right. And a bunch of others. He has a Do Not Play list. If he plays any of them, he's DJing the event for free."

"You drive a hard bargain." Tulsi sipped at her drink, her eyes closed. "I don't have these often enough." Turning to Hannah, she added. "Thank you for hiring me. And giving us all the night off so we can celebrate together."

"Doctor Plat didn't want to cover tonight. But Andrew convinced him to do it so we could go out. He's missing out on Andrew's stag party. Which makes Kimberly, Andrew's sister, happy." A devious smirk on her face made her friends laugh. "Cortland didn't need to have the night off. She doesn't work for me anymore. Well, not officially until after July 5th anyway." Hannah gave Tulsi a sideways hug. "But you do, and I couldn't be happier."

Tulsi giggled and cleared her throat. "At least until the part-timer starts."

Cortland cut in. "When does that happen?"

"Soon enough," Hannah and Tulsi said simultaneously, giggling together.

"What's so funny?" Cortland looked at the two women sitting side by side across the table.

The waitress appeared with their orders, the white peasant top with short, puffy sleeves hanging off her shoulders. Her red, three-tiered skirt swished as she walked away.

Tulsi looked at Hannah. "Didn't you tell her?"

Hannah shook her head before locking eyes with her. "Francis Mueller."

Her eyes went so wide they nearly fell out of her eye sockets. "NO way!" She did a drum roll on the tabletop before adding, "Miss My-Shit-Don't-Stink? Phew! I'm so glad I'll be long gone."

"Lucky you." Tulsi laughed while Hannah nodded. "It will be interesting."

"Good luck with that!" Cortland held up her glass. "Here's a toast to Hannah Woodbridge, soon-to-be Kelly."

"Woodbridge. I'm not taking his name. Too cumbersome to have two. I'll keep my maiden name. Don't you think it's kind of barbaric that a woman is expected to change her identity just because she gets

# COURTING CHOICES

married? Times have changed, and a wife is no longer a chattel whose ownership changes from her father to her husband." She sipped her margarita. "And I won't have to change all my IDs and government records."

"Hadn't thought of it that way. I see your point," Cortland said.

"Have you seen Dawson since you've been back?" Hannah asked, locking eyes with her.

Cortland's glass froze on her lips before she set it down. "No. I haven't. I just got back yesterday." She paused. "I sent him a sympathy card when Jackson died. I was sorry I couldn't be here when it happened. It was rather sudden, and I'm sure Dawson was crushed."

"Andrew and I went to the funeral. He was crushed. But he says they did get one last good talk in before he died. He was immensely grateful for that."

"I'm glad. I know Jackson became his hero and mentor after his father died."

"Maybe he'll be more amenable to moving now?" Tulsi asked.

Cortland's gaze dropped to the table. "Not likely he'll change his mind. He doesn't want to leave Colby."

Having made her own long car journey last week from Louisiana, Tulsi nodded. "How many days were you alone together in that car?" She gave Hannah a conspiratorial wink as she loudly slurped the last of her drink.

"You guys, stop that thinking right now! There wasn't any hokey-pokey going on." Cortland felt her face flame hotter thanks to the alcohol and their insinuation.

"Uh-huh. Sure thing." Hannah tried to keep from laughing.

"Our pre-plan was for four days. But with Harris and the cats, it was much longer. We had to stop fairly frequently to give them bio time and let them stretch their legs."

"So five? Six days?" Hannah asked before cramming her mouth with a heap of nachos with guacamole.

"It took six." Cortland nodded. "What a nightmare."

"Let me adjust your veil. It's gone crooked," Cortland said to Hannah. The three of them were standing in the vestibule at the back of the church, preparing to start the ceremonial walk down the long aisle. Hannah stilled before her bridesmaids and let them set the headpiece straight and re-pin it to her chignon.

Diminishing light streaming through the stained-glass windows reflected off the white stucco walls. A soft murmur could be heard on the other side of the door, where family and friends waited.

James Woodbridge tugged at the collar of his dress shirt and bow tie as he paced the small space. His portly frame didn't fit well in his rental suit. As Cortland watched, he pulled a handkerchief out of his jacket pocket and wiped his bald head. His dark blue eyes fixed on his daughter, an expression of awe mixed with anxiety and sadness.

Toby whined at Hannah's feet, probably restless to get on with things and rid himself of the ring bearer's pillow strapped to the back of his collar. On the other end of his leash, Daniel toyed with his bow tie. He looked so cute in his little suit and patent leather shoes. He looked up at Mr. Woodbridge with a quizzical look on his face. "When are we going to start?"

Mr. Woodbridge pat Daniel's back. "Soon, young man. Hold on tight to that leash. We don't want Toby to make any mistakes."

The only peaceful one was Maggie Mae, sitting on her haunches, lightly panting. Her only job was to help Hannah's father walk her down the aisle.

Hannah's mother, Dina Woodbridge, cracked the vestibule door ajar and poked her perfectly coiffed head through the space. "They want to know if you're ready to start," she whispered.

Everyone paused. Hannah's eye's widened as she gripped her father's arm. The three friends looked at each other.

"Give us two more minutes, then start the music," Cortland said, her heart beating faster in her chest. She saw the terror in Hannah's eyes. She leaned close to Hannah's ear and whispered, "It's going to be okay. He loves you, remember?"

Tears sprang to Hannah's eyes, and she nodded her assent. She watched as her maid of honor busied herself straightening out the gown's skirt and cap sleeves before handing Hannah a bouquet of daisies from the florist's box. Tulsi busied herself checking Daniel's attire and straightening his bowtie.

The music started reverberating as they got into line; Daniel walked Toby, then Tulsi, followed by Cortland, and finally Hannah with Maggie Mae and her father. James Woodbridge stuck out his elbow, offering his only daughter his arm, while he wiped tears away with his free hand.

"Here we go, sweetheart. You look beautiful," he said as they started up the aisle in the wake of her maid of honor.

When she got to her spot at the altar, Cortland turned to watch Hannah's promenade down the aisle on her father's arm. Her A-line wedding dress flowed beautifully as she glided down the aisle, the satin under-dress shimmering through its overskirt of tulle in the candlelight. Jewels embedded in the lace appliqué twinkled as she walked toward the altar. Hannah smiled at the sea of faces on either side of her.

All except a stone-faced Bryan Plat, Andrew's brother-in-law, who still hadn't completely come to terms with losing the town veterinarian bid two years in a row. And now would be Hannah's brother-in-law.

Hannah turned away abruptly. She'd told Cortland that Bryan would not spoil her wedding day. She focused instead on a smiling Kimberly Plat holding ten-month-old Erica, both soon-to-be family by marriage.

Cortland shifted her gaze across the aisle to where Andrew stood waiting, a little back from his spot at the altar. Dawson pressed his hand into Andrew's lower back, giving him a push forward to the correct position. Her gaze went back to Hannah and caught the moment she saw Andrew waiting up ahead. Switching back to Andrew, his face lit up as his bride's had just a moment earlier.

Her eyes froze on Dawson. His classic black suit and black bow tie were striking with his tanned skin and dark brown hair. She watched as he slipped the rings from the pillow and dropped them in his breast pocket. Then he took Toby's leash from Daniel and led both dog and boy off to the right side.

"Psst." She heard Hannah trying to get her attention. Stepping forward, Cortland took her bouquet and led Maggie Mae off to the left side by the leash.

By the time she returned, Hannah's father was gone, and Andrew stood beside her. The priest droned on, barely glancing at his missal.

She felt Dawson's eyes upon her as their friends exchanged vows. As butterflies amassed in her middle, Cortland lost track of what was being said. He only broke his visual caress when he handed over the rings. His gaze returned to her as the rings were exchanged and the priest made his pronouncement. Andrew swept Hannah into his arms for their first kiss as man and wife.

The married couple walked back down the aisle. As the newlyweds cleared the first pew, Cortland and Dawson were supposed to go next. Tulsi's foot kicking the back of Cortland's ankle got her to move forward and take Dawson's arm for their walk down the aisle.

His arm pressed hers firmly to his side as though he was trying to increase their contact. Contact that was making her acutely aware of his cologne, his towering stature over her petite frame, and the electricity that zinged back and forth between them. He limped slightly, causing Cortland to match his pace. She looked down to see his foot was no longer in the cast but in a stabilizing boot.

On the front step, they were assembled and positioned by the photographer, who snapped some shots. In each, Cortland was paired with Dawson.

## COURTING CHOICES

Standing beside him for the ensemble photo, she heard him whisper, "How's Alaska?" through a frozen smile.

"White nights right now. And the salmon run is on." Cortland also clenched her teeth into a motionless smile as best she could. *Damn, he smells amazing.* "And how are you?" Cortland asked him, stepping back from her position and removing her hand from his arm immediately after the camera's click. She glanced down at his foot to clue him into her inquiry.

"Good. My ankle's better. I head back to work in a week." He also stepped back.

"That's good. I'm glad it healed well enough for you to return to work."

"Just long enough to give my notice."

She stumbled as they walked across the churchyard. She stopped. "Notice?" Her eyes met his. "You're leaving the fire service?" Had his accident been the final straw? Was he paranoid of getting hurt again or killed in the line of duty like his father? Cortland couldn't believe he'd leave Colby Fire. It was one of the excuses he had given as a reason to not join her in Alaska.

"No. Just going elsewhere."

She couldn't help the fury in her voice. "You won't leave for me, but you'll leave for some other reason? That's priceless." She turned and stomped away, moving quickly despite her high-heeled shoes. Too quickly for him to catch her arm.

"Cort!" He called after her, but she ignored him.

Andrew called out, his hands cupping his mouth, "To the reception!" He beckoned them to the limos with his hand.

The ballroom was beautifully decorated, simple, and yet elegant. Cream damask wallpaper covered the walls, and the carpeting was also a soft cream color, surrounding the wood dance area in the center of the room. The bride and groom had their sweetheart table to themselves, with a waiter caring for their food and drink needs. Eight round tables seating eight guests each were scattered beyond the dance floor. On one side, the DJ kept a low profile, playing smooth instrumental jazz music while the guests finished their dinner. The staff had already removed the hot buffet line, and pieces of wedding cake were laid out on plates for those wishing dessert.

The wedding party was split between two side-by-side tables. Dawson and Lucas Campbell sat with Andrew's assistant, Gordon Whitebush, and a few police officer friends of Andrew's. Cortland and Tulsi sat with some of the vet staff from the clinic. They left to mingle and never came back.

Dawson tapped his fork against his water glass and stood. "It's great to see everyone here to celebrate with this wonderful couple: Mr. and Mrs. Andrew Kelly."

Tulsi and Cortland smirked at each other. Dawson hadn't received the memo about the lack of name change.

A cheer went up in the large hall at the mention of the bride and groom's names.

"As best man, it's my pleasure to give this speech and toast the newlyweds. So here goes." He slipped a thick stack of index cards out of his jacket pocket. He looked at the first card, then threw it over his shoulder. "Can't tell you that one with children in earshot."

The audience chuckled lightly.

He paused, looking at the second card for a few seconds before throwing that one over his shoulder as well. "I'm sure the new missus doesn't want to hear about *that* incident."

Snorting and laughing, Hannah doubled over with tears running down her cheeks.

"You okay there, Hannah?" Dawson asked.

Hannah waved him away, grabbed her napkin, and wiped her eyes.

Dawson fanned the cards, giving them a glance before chucking all of them over his shoulder. All except the last one. The laughter from everyone was echoing around the room. "Okay, I think I'd better skip to this one. I'd like to share some words of advice for groom. Andrew. It goes something like this:

"Keep your marriage going,
with harmony unmarred,
if you're wrong, admit it
But if you're right, disregard."

The guests erupted in laughter that took several minutes to die down. When it did, he raised his champagne glass. "To the happy couple!" Then he walked over to Andrew, slapped him on the back, and kissed Hannah's cheek before sitting down.

Cortland stood up as Tulsi tapped her cocktail glass, bringing everyone's attention to her. "Thank you, Dawson, for those wise words of wisdom. I have some words of my own for Hannah.

"To keep your marriage working,
And keep his head from turning,
With a daily dose of twerking,
You can keep the flame a-burning."

Andrew jumped up, pumped his fist, and yelled, "YEAH!" Well into his alcohol, he proceeded to give a demonstration of twerking. The wedding guests laughed again while Hannah blushed cherry red and buried her face in her hands.

Cortland raised her martini glass. "To many years of happiness and love."

The reception was winding down. Nearly midnight, Tulsi and Cortland sat together at a table sipping their cocktails.

"You're really nursing that drink." Tulsi raised an eyebrow. "How come?"

Cortland stared at the martini glass. "It's pretty strong. I've arranged for an Uber, but I need to go easy on the liquor. Upsets my stomach too much."

Tulsi focused on something behind Cortland. A slow, bashful smile spread across her face, and her eyelids lowered slightly in a flirtatious manner. Cortland wheeled around in time to see Lucas Campbell returning Tulsi's smile and hurriedly hiding his crooked index finger. The one he had beckoned Tulsi with.

"Go get 'em, cowboy," Cortland whispered to her friend.

Tulsi gulped down the last of her Sea-breeze. "I'm going to get another. Do you want anything?"

Cortland shook her head, her smile stretching ear to ear.

That wasn't the entire truth; Tulsi was intuitive enough to know it though she said nothing. Tulsi had already called her on her hyper-vigilance tonight. Cortland batted her eyelashes. Tulsi had raised both her eyebrows in reply.

As she watched, Lucas and Tulsi met at the bar. In less than a minute, they were slow dancing on the dance floor. Cortland smirked. Then frowned. They made a great-looking couple; too bad she would miss seeing their relationship develop.

The last thing Cortland wanted was to get drunk and make a fool of herself in the presence of her former boss, coworkers, and Dawson. She glanced around the room, looking for the man. A minute ago, she had seen him standing at the bar placing an order. Keeping an eye on him was proving to be a full-time occupation. Over the last hour, she had physically moved eight times just to stay away from him on the opposite side of the room.

Her eyes searched, but she didn't see him anywhere. *Did he go to the bathroom? With a fresh beer?* It hardly seemed plausible, but he must have done because he was nowhere in sight.

The sight of him was something to behold. Her mouth had watered when she first saw him standing at the altar behind Andrew, and it was doing it again. The suit he wore for the wedding ceremony made him look luscious. The suit jacket accentuated his broad shoulders and chest, narrowing at the waist. The dress pants had clung to his muscular legs and the curve of his firm ass, probably more than he liked. If

## COURTING CHOICES

Cortland had read their lips correctly, he'd been hit on by every woman in the hall, including a few married women.

The DJ was playing a nice selection of dance tunes. First, a couple of fast dances to entice people to the dance floor. Then he'd played a couple of slow dances. It was a sequence he had continued over the last hour. He'd played two fast dances just now, so a slow one was sure to play next. The first chords of an oldie sounded. Well before her birth, the song had been frequently played at the Stewart household when she was young, as it was one of her parents' favorite songs. She could remember as kids, the three of them dancing in the living room as their parents either watched them or joined the merriment.

Until the day all music and all fun had become blasphemous. Cortland thought of Jessica. She would have liked to see Jessica get married, would have liked to see her father walking Jess down the church aisle. As the only daughter left, she would have to provide that opportunity for him. If she ever found a man worth marrying.

She toyed with the martini glass. One small sip remained in the bottom of the glass. If Dawson wasn't here, she could do what she wanted. Get blazingly drunk until she couldn't remember his name and let Uber drive her home.

But she had to avoid him. What little conversation they had during the photography had been tense. Not knowing what to say after his pronouncement had stymied their conversation. Her eyes swept the dance floor in front of her table and across to the other side of the room. No Dawson.

"Would you like to dance?" He stepped out from behind her like the very thought of him had conjured him up.

She turned around and looked up at him, startled by his presence behind her. Her mouth went dry. The suit jacket had disappeared. His crisp white dress shirt was unbuttoned to the middle of his chest. Wisps of his sparse dark brown chest hair peeked through the opening.

Remembering what her tongue had done to that very spot several times before sent a wave of heat through her.

He held out his hand and cocked his head toward the dance floor.

She swallowed the last of her vodka martini, laid her hand in his open palm, and rose to her feet. *Careful girl. Behave.*

On the dance floor, he held her at a comfortable distance. A stilted silence settled between them as they moved slowly to the music. What she thought of as her poker face mode. She didn't want him to suspect the things his closeness did to her body. Cortland kept her face turned away until he broke the silence with a question.

"When do you go back?" Dawson asked, glancing over her head.

"I fly back on the sixth," she said, her head turned away from his bare chest before her nose. It was entirely too tempting to look at. Her tongue wanted to reach out—

"Did you get the electrical fixed?"

Cortland drew back nearly out of his arms, but he pulled her into them again. He raised an eyebrow.

"Not yet. But it's on my to-do list." The list that grew longer every day.

"Well, you can't be putting that off. In fact, the whole house should be rewired. It doesn't have smoke detectors either."

She stepped back again, releasing him. "Would you stop already? I'll take care of it." He'd given up any say in the matter.

He gave her a blank stare and then shook his head. "I was just ... wondering."

"Well, stop," she muttered quietly, not wanting to draw attention to them.

He stood still, holding out his hands again as though prompting her to continue the dance.

She hesitated before accepting his arms again.

## COURTING CHOICES

"So where are you going?" she asked. She knew her tone was curt, but she couldn't help it. He would leave Colby for some other reason but not for her. The rejection stung her ego.

"Ohio. Assistant chief's position in the Dublin Township Fire Department."

"A step up?" When he nodded, she added, "When do you leave?"

The song ended, but they remained on the dance floor, stock still as though waiting to see if the next song was also amenable to a slow dance. "My first day is August first."

The DJ broke their silence. "Here's a song requested by Hannah for C and D." A slow song started. Cortland gently shook her head. The two of them waited to hear the lyrics. "What's the name of this song?" She didn't think she'd ever heard it before.

"Why Can't This Night Go on Forever," he whispered.

"That's the name of the song?" She listened to the lyrics. Her body tensed up with each additional phrase. How could Hannah do such a thing? The woman was trying to jerk her heartstrings and get her and Dawson back together. *Well, I won't do it.*

Cortland pulled out of his arms and stalked out of the reception.

# CHAPTER TWENTY-ONE

Cortland stayed in town for the holiday to help Tulsi at the clinic. With Hannah on her short honeymoon, Tulsi would need all the help she could get. She'd arrived a week ago and moved into Cortland's vacant apartment. Cort was staying there tonight on the couch if they ever got out of the clinic. Fervently, she hoped it was more comfortable than Hannah's couch had been.

Despite Barbra's drive to get medications into the hands of their clients before the holiday, they still dealt with at least two dozen requests. While they hadn't seen the dogs and cats, they had to review each patient's file for any incompatible diseases or medications.

Andrew's assistant had also called them several times to come medicate new guests arriving at the shelter. She had gone, leaving Tulsi to keep the clinic running, using Tulsi's car since hers was in Alaska.

Stepping outside the shelter when she was done, she stopped. The smell of smoke lingered in the air. Was it from fireworks displays? Or was there a nearby brush fire?

"Hey, Gordon," She called through the open door. "You smell that?"

He lifted his nose in the air and sniffed three times. "Yeah, I smell it too. Let me contact the dispatcher."

He went back inside, leaving Cortland alone again. As it had over the last three days, her mind returned to her dance with Dawson at the reception.

He'd looked handsome. He'd held her in his arms almost politely, as though she were made of eggshell, and he was afraid to crush her.

She should be happy he was moving on. Making a future for himself. Her chest ached, knowing he had turned down her suggestion to move to Alaska. And her nerves seethed, thinking he'd found himself another job. In Ohio, of all places. Had he even searched in Alaska for a firefighter's job?

## COURTING CHOICES

She stepped back into the shelter office.

"The dispatcher says there's a small brush fire on the high school soccer field after the fireworks display over there. The fire department is putting it out now."

A thought blossomed in her mind immediately. She could take Tulsi's car to the soccer field and get one last glimpse of Dawson before returning to Hope the following day.

She drove quickly, hoping the fire was out on the one hand. On the other hand, she hoped it was at least contained so she could see Dawson. If she remembered correctly, the high school was in Station Two's district.

The approach to the high school was impeded by a police officer directing traffic away from the school.

Cortland parked on the side of the road and crept past the man as he gave someone else directions. The front of the school loomed in shadow before her. An aura of light and the deepening smell of smoke behind the building led her to walk around to the back of the school.

A small crew of four manned two hose lines along the fire's edge. At the nozzle of the closest line stood Dawson. She'd know his stance and his silhouette anywhere. She watched for a good ten minutes until the firefighters picked up the lines and stowed them back on the rig. Dawson had retreated to the cab of the truck.

"Goodbye," Cortland whispered before she walked back to Tulsi's car, tears welling in her eyes the entire way. Back in the car, Cortland gave in to her emotions.

They had been good together. Enjoying the same things: hiking, climbing, mountain biking, and kayaking. Well, okay, she was a newbie for nearly all of it, totally inexperienced and unprepared. But she'd like doing them all, especially with Dawson. She knew he liked to snowshoe and cross-country ski in the winter. She had enjoyed both activities as a kid in the Rochester New York area where lake effect snow piled deep every winter.

A rumbling vehicle with the air brakes squealing came up beside the car. It was Dawson's fire truck. He sat in the passenger's seat, staring ahead. It was only a fleeting couple of seconds. And then the truck rumbled past.

Cortland pressed her palm against the window glass in a final goodbye wave.

• • • •

The two kittens greeted him at the door when he got home from a night out at The Irish Harp with Andrew and a few guys from the firehouse. Dawson was grateful for the vote of confidence the kittens' actions gave him because he wasn't feeling particularly cherished or desired at this minute. And it was all Cortland's fault. She'd walked off the dance floor and out of his life without a backward glance. It was probably for the best, anyway. A continent divided them, and they didn't have a future.

In the bedroom, he shucked off his clothes. In his jockey shorts, he folded down the bed sheets but paused. Thirst led him to the kitchen. Opening the refrigerator, he paused to look at the options. He reached for a Newcastle ale but withdrew his hand, changing his mind. He'd had enough at the bar. Instead, he settled for a glass of cold tap water to soothe his parched throat.

The kittens sat meowing at his feet, their big brown eyes watching his every move. He was late with their dinner. Minutes later, the food was prepared and set on the floor. He watched them greedily scarf it down before lapping up some fresh water he'd also provided. The sight of them reminded him of Cortland's two kittens. The two pairs would never see each other again. She was back in Hope by now. Where her new life was. Where he wasn't.

Refilling his glass, he took it into the living room. The remote was in his hand automatically; before he knew it, he was channel surfing. *You ought to get to bed. It's nearly midnight.* Nothing looked good

## COURTING CHOICES

on the TV anyway. He wasn't in the mood for anything except obliteration. He needed something to keep his mind off Cortland, all dressed up, looking gorgeous at the wedding and reception. Her hair silky, her perfume wafting through the air and tickling his nostrils as he held her close one last time.

Ohio. The future loomed ahead. It had happened so fast and at the worst possible time. He got the call from Dublin while he was at the hospital with Jackson. They had arranged for him to fly out for in-person interviews the following week. It ended up being the day after Jackson's funeral. He hadn't thought he had impressed them. All four interviews had gone well enough, but he had been somber. While he'd explained the reason, his countenance either didn't matter, or they had liked it because they made him an offer he couldn't refuse the following day.

Flying back to Colby, he had pondered this life-changing move. He'd already spoken to his mother, who had given him her blessing. His sister had done the same though she expressed her anxiety at being their mom's primary contact. He had assured her he would only be a two-hour flight away.

Away. In Ohio, He cursed as he strode out to the patio. It was too hot and too dry to light the firepit. The fire danger level was high. He didn't want the embarrassment of having to call the fire department. He'd never hear the end of it. Dawson was on duty again the day after tomorrow. He should rest up for a busy week putting out brush fires. Swatting at mosquitoes buzzing around his ears, he fled back inside the house.

The kittens followed him as he walked around the house in the dark, looking for a place to settle. He gave up and settled on his bed. Smokey and Sadie immediately nestled beside him. Wide awake, he replayed the dance with Cortland in his head. She was so angry he was going to Ohio. He shook his head. What was he supposed to do? Stay here alone in Colby and pine after her?

A niggling thought crept out of the back of his brain. *She asked you to move to Alaska with her, and you declined. You told her you couldn't leave Jackson and your career here in Colby.* A fierce grip clenched around his heart. He flipped onto his left side, facing the kittens. He reached out and stroked their furry spines. They purred with pleasure, their eyes closed as they stretched out.

He closed his eyes. The Ohio job was a big jump in pay and responsibility. He was old enough to realize the current chief was likely four to five years from retirement. Taking the deputy chief position now would give him skin in the game for the step up to chief. As he lay there trying to let sleep seep over his consciousness, he admitted that alluring truth.

On the other hand, staying with Cortland—was his chance to make a difference. He couldn't save his father. He couldn't save Jackson. *But I can do something to save the woman I love.*

Love. Where had that come from so quickly? He didn't know, but the strength of the emotion made him feel proud. He rolled over to open the top drawer of his nightstand. He clutched the jewelry box to his chest, his heart aching as hard for her as it had the day his father never returned home.

*She said she'd miss me.* He believed her then and now. Because he felt the same way.

He missed her. Her laugh, her corny jokes, her ornery attitude at times, her menagerie in Alaska, he loved all of it. He thought about the barn fire and what could have happened. *The homestead is too large for her to handle alone. She needs me, and she wants me.* And he needed her. Above all else, he loved her. Everything about her spoke to his heart and filled his soul with happiness. *What the hell am I doing here?*

That revelation made his heart sing. He wanted to be with her and didn't care where that was in the whole world. Ohio be damned. Without a thought, he jumped off the bed.

It was time to set some new plans into motion.

# CHAPTER TWENTY-TWO

Cortland's day followed a routine. Her life was a series of repeated tasks that kept her busy from sun up to sun still up in the summer. Or, in the case of this early winter, from sun barely up to sun down. What little light there was all in the space of six hours. If only her chores lasted six hours, she mused as she fed the horses one last meal before going in to cook her own supper.

*Was that a car door slamming?* She wasn't expecting anyone today. Certainly not at this hour of the early evening.

A knocking noise drew her attention. Dawson stood in the open barn door bathed in the kerosene lantern light.

Her heart gave a leap that subsided into suspicion. She hadn't heard from him in three months, and now he was standing in her barn? She put down the empty water bucket. "What are you doing here?" She asked, crossing her arms over her chest. "Ohio not all it was cracked up to be?"

He stepped forward a few paces and stopped again. He turned toward the stall where the fire had started. "I came to check your electrical system." Gesturing toward the lantern hanging from a nail in a beam, he said, "Isn't that a little risky in a barn?"

Cortland's ire flared even more. Who did he think he was? A building inspector? "That's none of your business, is it?"

He stepped forward a few more paces and stopped twenty feet from her. "It's my life's work, preventing fires and putting them out when necessary."

Cortland mulled over his words. Who the heck did he think he was to arrive unannounced, uninvited, and unwelcome? The last thing she needed was a man to tell her everything that was wrong with the homestead. She was acutely aware of its problems, from the barn's electrical grid to the house's leaky plumbing, the septic in need of pumping, and the field of hay bales that needed to get into the barn loft before it rained, or, more likely, snowed.

He walked closer, stopping a couple feet before her. "Nope. I quit before I even began." There was a twinkle in his eyes as he said it. "I have a different new job. I start on Monday."

Three days away? Was he insinuating he was working here in Alaska? It wasn't in Hope since their entire fire department was volunteer.

"Where?" She asked, looking him up and down. He looked great. Perhaps better than when she had last seen him at the grass fire. He'd lost weight, making him look even taller than his six-foot-one stature. The weight loss had narrowed his face though a couple days of stubble gave the impression of a wider jawline. A flame flared through her body.

He crossed his arms over his chest, mirroring her stance. "City of Whittier Fire Department. I'm their new deputy chief."

"That's like an hour from here?"

He smiled. "It is. So, I was wondering if I could bunk here. If your offer still stands." His eyes seemed to search hers. "I know it's last-minute notice, but I can pay rent." He pulled the jewelry box out of his coat pocket. "This can be my security deposit."

He could have knocked her over with a piece of hay; she was stunned by his announcement. She eyed the box. It wasn't a ring box, of that she was sure. Did he think he could just waltz in here and take up residence with a simple present? *You told him he could change his mind.* She could feel his eyes on her, unnerving her to her marrow.

She took the box and pulled the lid off to reveal a large diamond solitaire drop on a gold chain.

"You did say the offer was good anytime, right?" He stepped forward again until they were nearly toe to toe. "Or have you changed your mind about that?"

"Maybe." She fingered the gem a moment before putting the lid back on the box. Cortland cocked her head. "Depends on your motive."

Even she heard the slight tremble in her voice, the tone which asked as much a question as it made a statement.

"I decided I couldn't let you come here and live by yourself. Told Ohio I changed my mind, and then I searched for another job—one in Alaska."

She mulled over his meaning. "So, you're here to protect me?" She shook her head, her shoulders stiffening. "I don't need protection. I can handle this place on my own with a little help from the neighbors. That's what we do here in this community. Rely on each other for help."

"I'm not saying you couldn't do it alone." He sighed and dropped his chin to his chest. "I suck at this," he muttered. Then he glared at her with a fierce look in his eyes. "What I'm saying is I want to do it with you. I don't want to be without you. My motive is my love for you." He reached out and took her hand. "I love you, Cortland. I want to be where you are."

Cortland felt her defenses fall. He loved her. And she loved him. More than she could ever say. But she said it anyway because he needed, no, he deserved to hear it. "I love you too, Dawson." She nestled her body against his as his arms hugged her so tight she squealed, "Too tight!"

His arms let up just a little before his lips brushed hers, softly at first and then deeply. So deeply, her toes curled. When he came up for air, he still held her close but asked, "Any more chores left tonight?"

Her fingers lingered in his hair. "All done except our dinner and the late night check."

He grinned mischievously. "Let's skip right to dessert." He swooped her up in his arms and carried her into the house. "And if you like your present, I would love to see you wearing it. And nothing else but a smile."

# EPILOGUE

Days later, Cortland was trying to be the helpful girlfriend by making Dawson a bagged lunch. Out of leftovers, she made him lunch with a can of tuna she found in the pantry in the basement. Its use-by date indicated it was getting close to expiration, so she thought she might as well use it up. Half the can went into making Dawson's tuna fish salad. The remainder she would use to make a small tuna and macaroni salad.

The old, dusty elbow pasta box she had retrieved on the highest shelf in the cabinet waited for the pot of water to boil. Without looking, she ripped the box open and dumped the contents into the roiling water. "Holy Crap!" she exclaimed as dollar bills floated in the water along with a cup or so of pasta. And they were not just one-dollar bills, but one-hundred-dollar bills. Fishing them out with a slotted spoon, she laid them on the countertop and sponged them dry. There were twenty-one hundred-dollar bills. "Holy Crap!" She shut off the gas under the pot before heading downstairs.

Poking through the pantry goods, she noticed several boxes had been taped shut on the bottom. She took those boxes upstairs with her. One by one, she opened them and peered inside. Every box held a wad of bills. Some were hundreds, some fifties, and a lot more were twenties, tens, and fives.

She rushed back down into the pantry. She tore open everything and anything that could have been re-sealed. The oatmeal canisters held bills. The coffee tins held bills. Even the box of brown sugar held bills. She tried to keep a running total of the money in her brain, but when it got to over ten thousand dollars, she gave up for the time being. All the while, her mind tried to rationalize why there was so much hidden money.

An hour later, Cortland had filled the kitchen table with stacks of bills sorted by denomination. "Why, Aunt Faith? Why did you hide all this money?" Neither Uncle Mayer nor Aunt Faith had gone through the Great Depression, so it wasn't a habit picked up then. They might have been taught to be frugal with money by their parents, who had struggled through that era. Who would know?

Were they trying to hide their farm income from the IRS? Possibly. There wasn't a bank in Hope where they could have deposited it to keep it safe. The closest bank was in Girdwood. Or Whittier. Cortland wasn't sure which one her aunt had used.

"Hmmm." Cortland stood in from of the door to Aunt Faith's bedroom. Grasping the doorknob, she gave it a twist and stepped inside.

The smell of Aunt Faith's perfume still lingered in the air. Fainter now than when she had first moved into the house. Cortland had hoped to leave it as it was, her heart reverent for her aunt's memory and possessions. On the nightstand was the journal she had consulted after receiving the letter. Cortland had never looked at her aunt's intimate thoughts, only the last page as directed. It felt like an invasion of privacy. But maybe it held a clue as to the reason for hoarding money in odd places.

She took the book out to the living room and sank into the comfy overstuffed chair. She opened the journal to the first page. The date wasn't terribly old, February 3, 2019. Did she have more? Previous journals? Cortland would have to look later. She started reading, ignoring the rumbling in her stomach as the wall clock chimed the noon hour.

Two hours later, Cortland closed the journal and struggled to her feet. The book's last page was the same as she had last seen it. It said Pegasus Fund and held a long list of sums. Each addition adding up from the previous. There weren't any dollar signs, yet Cortland could only guess. *Could this be her aunt's running total of the cash stowed away in the basement?* None of the entries were dated. The last count said 54,693.

## DIANA ROCK

She felt giddy with laughter as she bolted for the kitchen and counted the stacks of bills. Her total was only $15,721. *Where's the rest? A whopping $38,972 was missing. Was it gone? Was it spent? Or was there more money hidden away somewhere else in the house?*

It was after midnight when Cortland called it quits. She had searched every room in the house. Every box, carton, and bag had been checked. Every article of clothing that had pockets was checked. Books and magazines were opened, and pages were fluttered. Bills fell out. Oodles of bills were found. She put them all in the sink to keep them separate from the money already counted. The lack of sleep and food made her lids droop and her energy wane. But she wanted to count one more time. She sorted the bills, laying them in stacks on the kitchen counter by denomination as she had done on the kitchen table. Then she counted, writing the total for each stack down on a scrap of paper before getting her cell phone to total the list on the calculator app.

"Another $15,269." She told Harris, who sat at her feet, his eyes looking wary. "It's okay, boy." She tried to soothe him. His soulful eyes gazed back at her accusingly. "I forgot to feed you too, didn't I? Hang tight one more minute. I have to count the grand total."

Her fingers entered the new number to the old sum. The total was $30,990. "That's $23,703 short." As she made Harris and the four cats their dinner, she mulled over the places she had looked. It seemed to her she had checked the entire house and everything in it.

A knock at the back door made her jump. Dawson's face, surrounded by the night sky, showed in the window.

Cortland hurried over to open the door. "I promise I'll get you a key tomorrow," she said, watching him silently walk past her to stare at the table and countertop.

"Sorry, I'm so late. A mutual aid fire call to Girdwood," he started to explain. Then his eyes widened. "Where the hell—?"

"All over the house. Isn't it amazing?"

## COURTING CHOICES

Cortland told him about her initial find and her extensive search. Then she showed him the journal page labeled Pegasus Fund. His eyes widened as he registered what she was saying. "Look, the total here is 54,693. But I've only found $30,990."

His eyes widened larger this time. "There's more?" His voice cracked, the incredulity evident in his tone.

"Possibly. Somewhere. Another $23,703 is missing?"

Dawson glanced back at the journal page. "Pegasus Fund. Why do you think she called it that?"

She shrugged, biting her lower lip. "I haven't a clue—" She froze. *Could it be?* She snatched up the lantern and a screwdriver. "Oh my God. I think I know. I can't believe I forgot all about it."

Following her lead, Dawson carried the lantern for her as she strode out of the house and into the barn. She went all the way down to her horse's stall. Pegasus must have heard her coming or smelled her. He stood up from his pile of straw to greet her. She slipped into his stall, patting his withers as she squeezed by him and went to the corner where his food was placed. Dropping to her knees, she waved Dawson over. "I need more light." He obliged, cautiously entering the horse's stall. Pegasus pawed at the floor and snorted. Dawson shrank back against the stall wall. "He'll be okay," Cortland said when she saw fear flicker in Dawson's eyes.

Standing over her, he held the light up, away from the hay stuffed in the bin. Cortland brushed the stray bits of hay and straw bedding away to clear the floor in that one spot. A dirty stone tile lay there. Cortland cleared the dirt from the sides with the screwdriver and her hands. Then she levered the screwdriver's tip underneath the tile and lifted it out. Underneath it was a sturdy metal box. She pulled that out also and set it beside her.

The light shifted as Dawson maneuvered to a better location to see and illuminate the find.

"This is it," Cortland said as she unclasped the lid and opened the box.

The light shone into the box, revealing two tight packs of one-hundred-dollar bills and a smaller stack of paper-clipped mixed bills. "That's another twenty thousand dollars," she said, indicating the packed bills. "I can only guess the remaining $23,703.00 is the paper-clipped stack."

"There's something else in the box," Dawson said as he peered over her shoulder.

The lantern light caused a glimmer in the bottom corner of the box. Cortland lifted the bills to reveal a sapphire brooch and an engagement ring. Aunt Faith's engagement ring, the one that had been missing when she and her father had looked for it months ago.

Dawson whispered, "I can't believe it. I've never seen so much money."

"I can. I seem to remember when I was first visiting, going to the store with my aunt. She bought a few things for Uncle Mayer with cash he had given her. As the cashier gave her change, she told me not to tell Uncle Mayer how much she had spent. I didn't think anything of it, though I thought the request was peculiar until I watched my aunt pull up this box and leave the change in it." Cortland put the tile back where it had been. Grasping the box, the couple left the stall and barn, returning to the house.

They sat at the kitchen table dumbfounded by the presence of so much cash.

Cortland reached out her hand to touch the nearest stack. "This must be the legacy my aunt's letter mentioned. She's been saving it all those years. All for me," she whispered.

"What are you going to do with all of it?" Dawson asked as he made them both mugs of hot tea.

"Fix up the place: the electrical grid in the barn, the plumbing, repaint the house," Cortland replied.

## COURTING CHOICES

They gathered the cash, stuffing it all into the metal box. Cortland started to put it away in a kitchen cabinet.

"Wait." Dawson took the box from her, set it on the table, and pawed through it. He pulled out the ring. "We might decide to use this." His eyes seemed to search hers for a reaction.

Cortland stammered, "I—I think we might." She cleared her throat. "In the future."

Dawson raised one eyebrow. "In the not-too-distant future?"

She chuckled softly and took his hand. "Yes."

# DIANA ROCK

## ACKNOWLEDGMENTS

Special thanks to Steven Long and Brian Long, who have been both volunteer and career firefighters for well over thirty years each by my estimation. And congratulations to my nephew as he embarks on his own career firefighter job! Stay safe out there guys!

Veterinarian suicide rates average 2 ½ times higher than in the rest of the population. Female veterinarians are about 3 ½ times as likely to die by suicide. Long hours, poor work-life balance, the weight of the responsibility of delivering bad news and client high expectations. Most vet schools seek out perfectionists, a personality type that is also susceptible to anxiety and depression in this demanding career choice. Add to that the meager pay scales and the mountain of school debt. Student loan debt averages about $143K with some running as high as 400K. While starting vet salaries are about 56K and the average is about 105K.

If you know a veterinarian, please give them your support.

Not One More Vet www.nomv.org[1]

---

1. http://www.nomv.org

# COURTING CHOICES

Coming Soon!

*FIRST CHRISTMAS ORNAMENT :* CHAPTER ONE

"Special order, a Rueben with a fried egg," Vanessa said, setting the order slip on the countertop before disappearing through the kitchen door at Jam Bakery.

"Oh, that sounds yum," Isabelle Becker said aloud as she started making the breakfast sandwich. The fresh, free-range egg sizzled on the small hot griddle in the corner kitchen space. Behind her, the morning baking crew was finishing up preparing the bread and pastries for the day. She threw the corned beef on the griddle for a few seconds to warm it up and dropped the swiss cheese on top, giving it a half minute to melt. The aromas made her mouth water as she assembled the stack of fried egg, corned beef, cheese, sauerkraut, and Russian dressing to the lightly toasted rye bread. Thinking she had to make one for herself tomorrow morning, she wrapped the breakfast sandwich in foil before dropping it in a paper bag.

Snatching the order slip up from the countertop, she glanced at the name. "Gilbert." She smiled as a wave of reminiscence spread through her chest. She had loved that name since first seeing the Anne *of Green Gables* miniseries as a little girl decades ago. The character, Gilbert Blythe, eventually became Anne Shirley's husband. The actor who played him soared to instant fame with teenage females for his good looks and dreamy countenance. Isabelle remembered taping his picture all over her school locker. Her mind wandered further as she threw a handful of napkins into the paper bag. Gilbert was also the name of a friend of hers in high school. *What ever happened to Gilbert Darrow?* He was also kind of dreamy looking, but they had only been friends; fellow classmates and the rest of their clique hung out between classes, during lunch, and study halls.

The swinging doors bounced open as she walked from the kitchen into the front sales and dining area. Not looking at the small crowd at the counter, she held up the bag and yelled, "Gilbert."

A man stepped forward. "Isabelle?"

Startled, she looked at the customer, her arm dropping to her side, the bag still in hand. "Gil? Gil Darrow?" And here he was, in the flesh, and boy oh boy did that flesh look mighty fine. The last time she had seen him, Gil still looked like a scrawny teenager. Here he was filled out into mouth-watering manhood.

"I thought you were in Chicago." His sparkling blue eyes peered out from under an errant wave of red-brown hair.

His sawdust-laced jeans, chambray shirt, and a two or three-day-old scruff gave him a down-home, country look that made her mouth go dry. She cleared her throat to get it working again. "Uhm, I was in Chicago for college. I've been back in Vermont for a while now."

"Hmm." His gaze roamed over her face before dropping to her hand.

"Oops, sorry. Here you go. I hope you enjoy it." She held out the paper bag. "It's great to see you again." When he took it from her, her eyes lingered on his body a moment before she turned and headed for the kitchen door.

"Isabelle, wait," he called out.

She froze in her tracks, her heart thumping faster at the sound of his voice.

When she turned back, he added, "Can you join me for a few minutes?

COURTING CHOICES

## Other books by Diana Rock
<u>Fulton River Falls Series:</u>
*Melt My Heart*
*Proof of Love*
*Bloomin' In Love*
*First Christmas Ornament*
(release date November 2022)
*Book #5-Title TBA* (releases date: 2023)

• • • •

<u>Colby County Series:</u>
*Bid to Love*
*Courting Choices*

• • • •

<u>MovieStuds Series</u>
*Hollywood Hotshot*
*Hollywood Hotdogger* (release date 2023)

• • • •

**<u>DianaRock.com</u>**

# Don't miss out!

Visit the website below and you can sign up to receive emails whenever Diana Rock publishes a new book. There's no charge and no obligation.

https://books2read.com/r/B-A-YUKN-MWFAC

Connecting independent readers to independent writers.

# About the Author

Diana lives in eastern Connecticut with her tall, dark and handsome hero and one spoiled elderly kitty. She works full time as a histotechnologist, writing in her spare time. Diana likes puttering about the yard, baking and cooking, hiking, fly-fishing, and Scottish Country Dancing. Follow her exploits on her website, in her blogs and newsletters.

Read more at DianaRock.com.

CPSIA information can be obtained
at www.ICGtesting.com
Printed in the USA
JSHW040037141022
31653JS00002B/145